VERY BAD COMPANY

Also by Emma Rosenblum

Bad Summer People

VERY
BAD
COMPANY

EMMA ROSENBLUM

FLATIRON
BOOKS
NEW YORK

VERY BAD COMPANY. Copyright © 2024 by Emma Rosenblum. All rights reserved. Printed in the United States of America. For information, address Flatiron Books, 120 Broadway, New York, NY 10271.

www.flatironbooks.com

Designed by Donna Sinisgalli Noetzel

Library of Congress Cataloging-in-Publication Data

Names: Rosenblum, Emma, author.
Title: Very bad company / Emma Rosenblum.
Description: First edition. | New York : Flatiron Books, 2024.
Identifiers: LCCN 2023055141 | ISBN 9781250906557 (hardcover) |
    ISBN 9781250360434 (international, sold outside the U.S., subject to
    rights availability) | ISBN 9781250906564 (ebook)
Subjects: LCSH: Corporate culture—Fiction. | Management retreats—
    Fiction. | Missing persons—Fiction. | LCGFT: Black humor. | Novels.
Classification: LCC PS3618.O8338 V47 2024 | DDC 813/.6—dc23/
    eng/20231208
LC record available at https://lccn.loc.gov/2023055141

Our books may be purchased in bulk for promotional, educational, or business use. Please contact your local bookseller or the Macmillan Corporate and Premium Sales Department at 1-800-221-7945, extension 5442, or by email at MacmillanSpecialMarkets@macmillan.com.

First Edition: 2024

10 9 8 7 6 5 4 3 2 1

For anyone who has ever had a crazy boss,

felt "out of the loop,"

or wanted to kill (or marry) a coworker

VERY BAD COMPANY

AURORA'S ANNUAL EXECUTIVE RETREAT!

Tuesday, April 23–Friday, April 26

Location

The 1 Hotel, Miami Beach

Attendees

John Shiller, chief executive officer
Dallas Joy, chief technology officer
Zach Wagner, chief revenue officer
Martin Ito, chief information officer
Debra Foley, chief people officer
Nikki Lane, executive vice president, engineering
Olive Green, director of communications
Caitlin Levy, head of events
Jessica Radum, head of partnerships

Organizer

Madison Bez, assistant to John Shiller

Itinerary

Tuesday, April 23

- Executive arrivals in the morning, hotel room check-ins
- Choice of facial or massage in the Bamford Wellness Spa, in the 1 Hotel
- Lunch and afternoon free, explore the hotel, beach, or pool relaxation
- 6:00 P.M.: kickoff drinks at Watr, on the 1 Hotel rooftop
- 8:00 P.M.: dinner at ZZ's, in the Design District
- After-party at LIV, in the Fontainebleau, featuring a special appearance by ANZ

Wednesday, April 24

- 9:00 A.M.: breakfast at Habitat, in the 1's lobby level
- 10:00 A.M.–noon: "State of Your Business" presentations, in the 1's business conference room on the third floor
- 1:00 P.M.: lunch at Lucali, in Sunset Harbor
- 3:00–5:00 P.M.: Jet Skiing in Lake Pancoast
- 7:00 P.M.: dinner at Carbone, on Collins Avenue, South of Fifth

Thursday, April 25

- 9:00 A.M.: breakfast at Plnthouse, in the 1's lobby level
- 10:00 A.M.–noon: the Aurora-thon! at Flamingo Park (come dressed for sports)
- Lunch at your leisure
- 3:00–5:00 P.M.: "Aurora and Beyond: Thought Starters," in the 1's business conference room on the third floor
- 7:00 P.M.: dinner at Stubborn Seed, on Washington Avenue

Friday, April 26

- Free morning
- 10:00 A.M.: parasailing at the beach
- 1:00 P.M.: farewell lunch at the Surf Club, at the Four Seasons Hotel
- Executives depart

Prologue

Never Give In

John Shiller hadn't meant for anyone to die. He'd grown up in Palo Alto, not exactly a hotbed of homicide. His dad, Erik, had been early to the tech scene, working on the periphery of legends like Bill and Paul and Steve and Steve, never quite making it into anyone's inner circle. Erik was an operations man, helped the boy geniuses streamline their businesses and did well for himself in the process—John lived in a nice house, went to a fancy private school, Menlo, and received a Jeep Grand Cherokee for his sixteenth birthday.

But his dad was haunted by the outsize success of others, the billions he'd never made. John would find Erik sitting on the grass in their groomed backyard, holding a beer but not drinking it, lost in a not-rich-enough haze. "I should have started something myself" is something John heard him say a million times during John's childhood. "Not sure why I didn't."

Early in his life, John vowed to be different from his father. He'd be one of the chosen ones. One of the Steves and Bills. Sure, he wasn't a brilliant engineer. But he understood the markets and he understood people and he understood that every company, no matter the type, was about success-fully selling itself to an audience, be it customers or investors or a board of directors. That he could do.

And now it was all coming down on top of him, piece by piece. He'd gone into this week on such a high, looking forward to being lauded in the *Wall Street Journal*, having pulled off one of the most profitable maneuvers in history. Instead, he was in an Uber, sitting next to his assistant, Madison Bez, on their way to identify a body at the Miami-Dade county medical examiner. The drawbridge to the Venetian Causeway East Bridge was up—some blowhard in a mega yacht needing to get through at midnight—giving John more time to think about how he'd gotten into this mess.

Everything he'd worked so hard for, everything he'd achieved, had nearly been ripped away from him, and by one of his own. He'd nurtured his team, he'd loved them, he'd given them so much. Money! Equity! The opportunity to work alongside John Shiller. Only to be betrayed by them, each and every one.

As his hero Winston Churchill once said, "Never give in—never, never, never, never." John wouldn't give in. John would not become his dad, filled with regret that he wasn't a titan. He would fight and win, by any means necessary. The bridge finally closed, and his car started moving. Biscayne Bay sparkled in the moonlight as John headed toward the morgue.

Aurora Adds to Its Executive Ranks

By Kaya Bircham

Aurora, the adtech startup, is adding to its executive team, *TechRadar* has exclusively learned. The tech industry darling has hired Caitlin Levy as its new head of events, poaching her from a plum role at Viacom. The move marks a strategy shift for Aurora and poses an obvious question: What could an adtech company that doesn't throw events do with a head of events?

"We're thrilled to bring Caitlin Levy on board and can't wait to see what she does in her new role," says Aurora spokesperson, Olive Green, via email.

John Shiller, Aurora's wily CEO, certainly has something up his sleeve with this one. Keep checking TechRadar.com for updates.

PART 1

Tuesday, April 23

Our Finest Hour

Caitlin Levy

———

Caitlin Levy hated turbulence. She also hated sitting in coach. But here she was, en route to Miami for her first business trip as head of events for Aurora, violently jolting up and down, her gold bangles jangling, stuck in the last row of the plane. She felt like she might be sick, but the seat belt light was on, and she was nestled between a large man with hairy forearms and a college kid who'd been snoring since the moment he sat down.

This was not the fancy executive life she'd pictured when she signed her contract with Aurora two weeks ago, but she'd been late to book the flight, and business class was already full. She'd walked past her new colleagues as she'd boarded, their headphones on, computers out, already sipping champagne. None of them had even looked in her direction, which was a relief—she'd have enough time for awkward introductory chats when they arrived at the hotel.

Caitlin was traveling to Florida for Aurora's executive retreat, an annual gathering of the company's top employees. When Caitlin had accepted her offer, via DocuSign, Aurora's eccentric CEO, John Shiller, replied with a one-liner: Just in time for Miami! (Not Congrats, not Welcome to the team, not We can't wait for you to dig in!) It was obviously an important occasion, and so Caitlin had agreed to go, even though she hadn't even officially started in her role. This was supposed to have been her time off in between jobs, which her husband, Mike, had moaned about. He was also annoyed to be left alone with the kids for four nights, so she could go "participate in bullshit team-building exercises and get drunk with her new colleagues," as Mike snarked, but Caitlin really had no sympathy. Her son, Joey, had asked if Dad was "babysitting" while Caitlin was away.

"Your father is your father, not your babysitter!" she'd snapped, loud enough for Mike to hear in the other room. Though they both had big jobs, Caitlin, like most working women she knew, took on the familial mental load. She organized all the school stuff, doctor's appointments, playdates, sports teams. She stayed home when someone was sick. She rearranged meetings when one of them needed her. Mike was an engaged dad, for sure, hands-on in a way Caitlin's father had never been. Mike changed diapers, he read books before bed. He and Caitlin earned around the same amount, but his job came first. Always.

Caitlin gripped the seat as another wave of turbulence hit. She was anxious, which was unlike her. She was forty and a success (last year, she'd made it into *Crain's* "40 Under 40" by the skin of her teeth). She'd been running events for large companies for nearly twenty years. She was very competitive. People she worked with called her "intense" behind her back. Once, an assistant mistakenly G-chatted her, "Caitlin *needs* to calm down! She's not saving the world, she's planning parties." (The assistant was immediately fired.) All Caitlin's past jobs were at known quantities: on the agency side at Edelman, then consulting for media companies like Condé Nast and Hearst, and, most recent, in-house at Viacom. They were name brands her parents and their friends would easily recognize. Aurora was not one of these, and though it had grown enormously since it launched in 2017, its newness made her jittery.

She put on her noise-canceling headphones and closed her eyes, attempting to both drown out the snoring and calm the nerves assaulting her body. Her new assistant had sent her the retreat agenda this morning. First, they'd be taken to the 1 Hotel to check in, after which everyone had been booked for a spa treatment. Caitlin had chosen an "Organic Awaken Resurfacing Facial," which she hoped would take a year or so off her face. From 3:00 to 5:00 P.M. she could go to either the pool or the beach, or relax and catch up on emails in her room. The evening's events started at

6:00 P.M., with cocktails at Watr, the 1's rooftop restaurant, followed by an 8:00 P.M. dinner at ZZ's, a private supper club in the Design District. The party continued afterward, with tables reserved at LIV, one of Miami's most exclusive clubs. A DJ named ANZ, whom Caitlin had never heard of, was playing that night. (Why was everything in Miami composed of random letters that spelled . . . nothing?) Caitlin was exhausted just thinking about it.

She and Mike hardly ever went out anymore. They were so drained from work and the kids—Joey was seven, and Lucinda had just turned nine. When they met, Mike had been a creative director at Digitas, a trendy advertising company, and Caitlin was working at Condé Nast, producing marquee events like the Met Gala and *Vanity Fair*'s Oscar Party. They were always drinking, out dancing, dressed up and ready to go. That was then. Their lives had now flattened into forty-something routines: work, homework, weekend sports, birthday parties, school fairs. Jeans. Sneakers. Pajama pants at night. Kill yourself.

They lived in Bronxville, an expensive suburb just outside the city, and Caitlin loved their house, a light-filled, four-bedroom white Colonial. She loved Mike, mostly. She loved her children, always. She loved climbing the corporate ladder, she really did. But she was deathly bored. Was this it? Had she reached her peak? She was an executive vice president at Viacom, producing all the TV networks' events, including the VMAs and the MTV Movie and TV Awards, plus the upfronts. It was a lucrative, respectable gig. She had power and money, and overall, it wasn't *that* hard. She still had time for Joey and Lucinda, time to help plan the godforsaken school fair. She hadn't been looking for a new job. But, as they say, that's the best time to get one.

John had cold emailed her one day before the holidays. Not a headhunter. Not head of Aurora's HR. The CEO himself. How he'd found her personal email, which included her married name, she didn't know—she basically used it only for school communication and spam. The subject line was Hey. She'd been sipping tea in her pristine Shaker-style kitchen, looking out at her garden, covered in a layer of early winter frost. She opened the email.

Caitlin Levy! You are a person I'd love to meet. We have a
new role here for which you'd be perfect. Events are Aurora's
future, and you can be part of that! I'm cc'ing my assistant,
Madison, to set up a meeting. It's all happening. Cheers,
John.

"Cheers"? Caitlin knew John Shiller wasn't British, so she wasn't sure
what "cheers" was all about. She'd shown the email to Mike later that
night, after the kids were in bed and they were having a glass of wine in
front of the fire. It was *Top Chef* night, and they were both looking forward
to it. Mike handed her phone back, one eyebrow raised.

"He sounds like a douchebag," he said. He leaned back on the couch
and put his feet up on the coffee table, creating smudges where his heels
rubbed against the glass. It made Caitlin crazy.

"And isn't Aurora some kind of advertising technology company?
What does that have to do with events?" Mike ran his hand through his
hair, which had thinned considerably over the past five years. There was a
bald spot at the top of his head the size of a hockey puck. Recently, Caitlin
had been having dreams in which she was cheating on Mike, always with
some faceless man. The details weren't specific—usually Caitlin was the
aggressor—and she'd wake up guilty and bothered, relieved for it to be over.

"They're not just 'some kind' of adtech company, they're *the* adtech
company," said Caitlin, bothered that Mike wasn't impressed that the
CEO of one of the hottest startups had sought her out specifically. In
truth, Caitlin had to google "adtech" after she'd received John's email. She
learned it had to do with managing internet advertisements across different channels, like search, video, and mobile, but the details were still fuzzy.

"Okay, I'll grant you that," said Mike. He was still at Digitas all this
time later, leading their media group. Unlike Caitlin, who easily got rest-
less, Mike was happy to stay in one place. "But why do they need someone
to run events?" he asked.

Caitlin didn't know. She hadn't even responded to John yet. "I'm not
sure, but I'm going to find out," she said. Mike shrugged.

"Suit yourself. I've heard through the grapevine that John Shiller is a real blowhard. That he doesn't know how to do anything but fundraise. But I suppose if he has the right people running the company, that's all he needs to do. And you'd certainly be an asset to any executive team." Mike moved over to Caitlin's side of the couch and started to rub her shoulders, redeemed.

Caitlin's eyes jolted open as the plane rocked to its side, the turbulence bad enough to awaken the sleepy teenager in the aisle seat. He pulled his baseball cap over his eyes and quickly fell back into it. Caitlin took out her phone and opened the pdf of the presentation she was set to give tomorrow. It needed work, but she didn't have enough space to open her laptop; her other seatmate's arm was nearly in her lap. The first slide said: "Events at Aurora—a New World!" on a black background. The next was an introduction to Caitlin: her headshot, bio, bullet points of her greatest accomplishments at other jobs. She'd created two additional slides, one with the header "New Events Strategy" and one with "Revenue Goals and Opportunities." But they were currently blank, and Caitlin didn't know how to fill them.

Though she'd chatted with John about the company and its amazing tech, she was still unclear as to what she'd be doing in her role. When she'd asked what he envisioned for events at Aurora, or similar examples he could point to, he went all blustery and weird, changing the topic and looking off into the distance.

This was hardly John's only tic. Before her first and only meeting with him, a few weeks after he'd sent her that email, Caitlin had done some professional reconnaissance. She'd read every interview he'd given (he was a prolific talker and spoke in full paragraphs; much of what he'd predicted for the markets had come true). But she couldn't find a single TV appearance on Bloomberg or CNBC, which must have been a purposeful choice by Aurora's PR department. "He's . . . *weird*" was something she heard repeated by people who'd met him. Also, some variation of "He's very full of himself." And most often: "He's probably on the spectrum, just like every other tech CEO."

Caitlin felt morbidly curious as she'd entered the lobby of the Free-hand Hotel for their initial interview about this mysterious job.

John's assistant, Madison Bez, had insisted they meet at a bar instead of at Aurora's office; *John wants this to be totally discreet*, she'd emailed ominously. Caitlin had found him at a corner table, already sipping a whiskey, wearing a blue Lacoste crewneck T-shirt, bright orange pants, and white Nike sneakers. She laughed to herself about Madison's note—if John wanted to hide, the pants certainly weren't helping.

He stood to greet her, and she was surprised by how short he was— five foot eight, tops, smaller than she was in her heels. He went in for a hug, which Caitlin wasn't expecting, and she instinctively recoiled, making the whole thing even more uncomfortable. It ended up as a kind of mutual back pat. John quickly sat down, motioning for Caitlin to sit next to him, making it so they were both on the same side of the small table. Caitlin was wearing a simple black sheath dress, chic but professional. Sweat was causing the wool to stick to her lower back. She hadn't been nervous like this in ages. It felt invigorating.

"Caitlin, Caitlin, Caitlin, where do we begin?" said John. It was only 6:00 P.M., but the bar was starting to fill, and Caitlin was struck by the idea that someone she knew would walk in and think she was cheating on Mike. John's face was very close to hers. He had a light brown beard and adjoining mustache, and narrow green eyes that illuminated an otherwise plain face. She realized he was waiting for her to answer. A pretty waitress put a Negroni in front of Caitlin. She gratefully took a large sip.

"How did you know I liked Negronis?" she asked.

John laughed. "I do my homework before I meet people," he said.

"So do I," she countered, feeling bold. She wondered what else he could have heard about her. She smiled at him. Was she flirting? How strange. At thirty-nine, John was a year younger than she. She knew he was unmarried and dated around, usually pictured in Getty party photos with very beautiful, very young women.

"For the most part, people gave you glowing reviews," he said. "A few former coworkers, who shall remain nameless, called you 'cutthroat' and 'overly ambitious.'" Caitlin felt herself flush. "But," said John, "to me that's a positive. I want you to be cutthroat if you're on my team! All the best generals are." Caitlin had read that John was obsessed with World War II and had spent millions on memorabilia at auction. She'd heard whispers that he owned Winston Churchill's private wartime diary and kept it locked in a safe in his house in Miami.

Before Caitlin could ask any questions about the job, John launched into a retelling of Aurora's origin story. Caitlin already knew the basics: John and his two best friends, Dallas Joy and Robbie Long, were rising stars in New York's tech scene a decade ago. They'd always wanted to start a company together, but Robbie died tragically from a drug overdose before they had the chance to. Robbie had been fascinated by adtech, so John and Dallas came up with the idea for Aurora over dinner one night in Brooklyn as a tribute to Robbie. They even gave Robbie's fiancée, Meagan Hudson, a large part of the original equity. Dallas, the engineer, developed Aurora's amazing algorithm, and John, the genius pitchman and fundraiser, got investors excited about it. Aurora grew and grew, revolutionizing the way advertising was bought and displayed online. Six years later, Aurora had over four hundred employees, office space in New York and Miami, and was valued at half a billion dollars.

"So you see, Caitlin, there isn't anyplace you'd rather be working now than Aurora," said John. His green eyes flicked back and forth across her face, never quite settling into contact with hers. "I wouldn't say this publicly, but there is no better CEO on earth than me right now." He gave a slightly deranged smile. "Not Elon, not Tim, not Sundar, and definitely not Mark, that little pussy."

"Well, you sure are good at selling yourself," said Caitlin. She knew she should feel turned off by his ego (and the word "pussy"), but his bluster was having the opposite effect. She leaned in, shifting closer to him, near enough to smell his musky aftershave.

"I can sell myself, too. But I need to know what the job is first," she said.

"All that in good time," said John. "I had a feeling you'd be the right person to complete our executive team, and I'm happy to report that—as usual—I was right." The meeting had continued in that way, with lots of banter but no substance. She'd left the Freehand convinced of John's charisma but not much else. It didn't seem like he had a baked events strategy, and Caitlin figured it was a fishing expedition rather than a real search. The feeling was confirmed when she didn't hear from him immediately afterward.

"You wouldn't have wanted to work for that guy, anyway," Mike had said (he was almost *too* happy that it seemed to have gone bust). Caitlin had settled back into her job at Viacom, filling her days with the usual putting out fires and mediating employee spats, irritated to have wasted her time. Then, three months later, she received another email from John, this one with the subject line: Offer.

Caitlin, Caitlin, Caitlin, the email read. She was sitting at her desk at work, on the thirty-first floor of One Astor Plaza, a block from Times Square. She commuted into Manhattan three days a week, happily leaving her life in the suburbs, taking the Metro-North from Bronxville and then the shuttle from Grand Central Station. She felt in control at the office in a way that she loved, even when she wasn't doing anything but staring at the downtown skyline. She liked wearing heels and putting on lipstick. She read on.

> Here I am, back to offer you the opportunity of your life-
> time. The job is head of events of Aurora. Your salary will
> be $2.5 million, with a discretionary bonus of $500k. You'll
> get 200,000 shares to start, plus more based on your suc-
> cess. And I know you'll have success! I believe in you. It
> truly amazes me how dumb most people are about their
> career choices. Please don't disappoint me by being lumped
> in with that group. You'll be hearing from Debra Foley, our
> chief people officer, shortly. She can walk you through de-
> tails. Excited to have you on board! Cheers,
> John.

Caitlin reread the email to make sure she'd seen the number correctly. Three million dollars? She thought startups only paid small salaries. Plus that much equity in the company? It must be some kind of joke. She was currently making, all in, about a million dollars a year, and that was after some serious haggling with Viacom, plus several end-of-year raises. Before she could rethink it, she'd replied, Thank you for the offer, John! But isn't that a lot? And what will I do all day?

He pinged her back not five seconds later. I pay my generals well! And . . . you'll figure it out. ☺

After a few minutes, she'd received her first email from Debra Foley, laying out the terms of the offer and attaching a DocuSign for her to return. She'd had so many questions. She still did. But, against her better judgment and without meeting anyone else at Aurora, she'd accepted the job. Mike had been begrudgingly supportive (he kind of had to be; she'd now be earning more than three times what he did). As a couple, they'd be making around four million dollars a year—more than enough to get a cute second house in Quogue or Montauk, which Caitlin had been wanting to do for years.

The plane was finally nearing Miami. Caitlin could see the blue-green ocean leading to the gridded city, white buildings rising toward the sky, the sun reflecting off the water. The forecast for the duration of the executive retreat called for clear skies and eighty-five degrees, and Caitlin was hoping to get in some beach time between team meetings and dinners.

She looked up to see a man walking down the aisle, eyeing each row as if searching for a friend. She recognized him from his corporate headshot on Aurora's "About Us" page: Zach Wagner, Aurora's chief revenue officer. She'd read in his bio that he came from the world of traditional advertising, acting as chief marketing officer of several large retail brands, including Macy's and American Eagle, before jumping to the other side and leveraging his relationships in his role at Aurora. He looked to be in his midforties, with springy black hair and a salesman's attractive, open face. He was wearing jeans and a sports coat and cool-dad New Balances. The pilot had announced landing prep, so Caitlin assumed Zach was heading to the restroom, though she wasn't sure why he'd come all the way back here. He stopped in front of her row and stared at her. She smiled tentatively, unsure if he knew who she was.

"Caitlin Levy? *The* Caitlin Levy?" Zach reached over the slumbering teen and held up his hand in front of her. Was she supposed to high-five him? She tapped his hand with her own.

"You must be Zach," she said. "I've read so much about you. That was a great interview you gave in the *Journal* the other day."

"Thanks! Nice to meet you!" said Zach. The plane was rocking a bit, and he held on to the seat to prevent himself from tumbling toward the bathroom. "I'm so happy you could make it on this trip. I'm sorry it's eating into your vacation time, but I think it's worth it. John, you'll see, *lives* for the executive retreats. And I think that he has a big announcement to make tonight that you wouldn't want to miss." Caitlin was surprised by this news; John hadn't mentioned anything imminently major during their interview.

"I'm glad I could come. It'll be great to meet everyone before I officially start," she said.

"I also know that John has huge expectations for you," said Zach, raising his eyebrows playfully. Caitlin wondered if Zach knew about her salary. A friend of a friend had told her that Zach loved to drink and was the life of any party. She'd also heard rumors that he could be hilariously off-color, a trait that served him well in the early aughts but recently had been getting him in trouble. Apparently, he'd held an all-hands meeting to motivate his team and had shown up in a Native American headdress, complete with face paint, whooping and cheering. It was a complete HR nightmare.

"And I hope to live up to those expectations," Caitlin said neutrally. She wasn't sure how candid to be. Was Zach on her side? Or had the "expectations" line been a dig about how she'd been overpaid? Caitlin usually thrived at workplace politics. She had a high EQ and could easily read what people truly wanted from her. But here she was entering foreign territory—an entire group of people she'd never met, some of whom had worked together for years. She'd have to observe their dynamics, and speak to them individually, before making any decisions about whom to align herself with.

The flight attendants announced that everyone had to sit for landing. "That's my cue," said Zach. "Can't wait to catch up later. I'm excited for LIV! Old-man-at-a-club alert!" He did a little wiggle for emphasis, and at the same time the plane veered to the left, sending him stumbling down the aisle. Caitlin swallowed a laugh.

"Sir, you need to sit down, now," a testy flight attendant, already strapped in, called to him.

"Yeah, yeah, I'm going," he grumbled, turning to Caitlin. "Everyone seems to have lost their sense of humor lately. Have you noticed that? Goodbye and good luck!" he yelled as he made his way back to business class. Caitlin wondered if perhaps he should be pacing his champagne intake. They had a long day ahead of them.

She glanced back down at her phone, yet again opening her blank presentation. She'd just have to tell John that she didn't have anything to say. She needed direction to craft a strategy, and she hoped to get face time with him to discuss it during this trip. But the empty slides left an icky feeling in the pit of her stomach, the real-life equivalent of a dream in which you arrive unprepared to a test.

They bumped into Miami International, and Caitlin fled her row as soon as possible. In yet another humiliation, she'd had to check her carry-on before she'd boarded, as the flight was packed with no overhead bins left. She didn't want her new coworkers to know; what kind of lunatic checks their bag for a four-night business trip? After exiting the plane, the Florida heat pleasantly penetrating the Jetway, she saw the Aurora group standing in a huddle by a Hudson News. Caitlin put on her Chloé sunglasses, ducked behind a large, touristy couple, and headed toward baggage claim. She'd meet them at the hotel.

During the ten-minute walk through MIA, past the Caribbean gates, past the empanada restaurants, past the retirees sipping midday glasses of wine, Caitlin formulated her game plan. She'd corner John at the cocktails before dinner and explain to him that she didn't feel prepared to give her presentation the next day. He'd have to understand, as he'd given her nothing to go on. Caitlin felt a bit queasy at the idea of disappointing her new boss so early on. She'd been an A student and, later, a top-performing employee. She knew how to manage up *and* manage down, and her events were drama-free, perfectly planned, and made money. She supposed that's why John had hired her in the first place.

Baggage claim was teeming with travelers piling suitcase after suitcase on luggage crates. Caitlin stood by her carousel, hoping she wouldn't get stuck there for much longer. She didn't want to miss her facial. Her new team should meet the best version of her, glowing skin included. She felt a tap on her back and turned to see a tall, striking redhead in a pink linen dress, her hair swept up in a messy ponytail: Jessica Radum, Aurora's head of partnerships. Caitlin knew her from around town, though they'd never actually met. Jessica had attended events that Caitlin had planned—an attractive, successful woman in technology got invited everywhere these days.

Caitlin knew that Jessica and John and Dallas all went way back. They were part of the same gang in their twenties, and Jessica still acted as John's arm candy at conferences and industry gatherings. What Caitlin didn't quite understand was Jessica's role at the company. Caitlin hadn't heard of any meaningful partnerships between Aurora and others, and she wasn't sure what Jessica actually contributed to revenue.

"Oh my god, Caitlin Levy!" said Jessica. Caitlin quickly took off her sunglasses, feeling foolish for wearing them inside. "It's great you could make it."

"Thanks, it's nice to be here," said Caitlin. Jessica was so tall that Caitlin, a not-too-shabby five foot six, had to look up to speak to her. "Just so you know, I don't usually check my bags for a business trip," Caitlin said. "They forced me to."

"I always check a bag," said Jessica. "I can never decide what clothes to bring to these things, so I just pack everything." Caitlin noticed that Jessica wasn't wearing a wedding ring. She wondered what the deal was there.

"John told me you'd be at the retreat. I'm thrilled to have another strong female executive on the team," said Jessica. "The women will now outnumber the men!" Her voice was deep and smooth, and Caitlin could see how people were drawn to her. A Barbie with brains.

Mentioning John so early in their conversation was certainly a power play. Caitlin had worked with both genders throughout her career, but women were generally more cutting and dangerous. Caitlin would have to keep an eye on her. "Debra's here, too," said Jessica, pointing toward the bathroom. Caitlin saw Debra Foley, Aurora's chief people officer, walking toward them, wheeling a black carry-on. She was in sensible khakis, Keds, and a plain blue T-shirt, her sunglasses perched on top of her blunt bob.

"Debra, look who I found!" said Jessica, tugging on Caitlin's sleeve. Debra smiled broadly, showing an attractive row of large white teeth.

"There she is! Welcome, Caitlin, welcome to Aurora," said Debra. She was shorter than Caitlin, with the sturdy build of a softball player. "I'm pleased we were able to get you in the door before the retreat. We have such a great agenda this year, and I know we're all looking forward to your presentation." Caitlin felt her stomach drop.

"Oh, it's certainly nothing to get excited about," Caitlin said. "If anything, I still really need to lock down my job description. I was hoping to do that here." The carousel heaved on, dumping bags down the side. Caitlin and Jessica looked for their suitcases, dragging them off when they appeared.

"Shall we?" said Debra, indicating the exit to ground transportation. Caitlin had been planning on a solo ride to the hotel, but she swallowed hard and followed Debra and Jessica, as odd a pair as she'd ever seen, out the door.

The hot, moist air hit Caitlin's face as they left the building, and she instantly relaxed into it, absorbing the tropical feel. They piled into a waiting taxi, Caitlin's jeans sticking to the scorching black leather seat. The driver rolled up the windows and cranked up the AC, then took off toward Miami Beach, heading over the bay on the 195 causeway. Caitlin loved that Miami was so close to New York but such a different world. She loved the palm trees and the storms and the tight outfits. She loved that everyone was so tan. She and Mike and the kids came down here at least twice a year to visit Mike's parents, who'd retired to Boca Raton. Recently, a few of Caitlin's friends had moved to Miami permanently, and every time she came, she felt the tug.

"Get ready for a crazy night," said Jessica, sitting in the middle seat, her long legs squished against Debra's. Caitlin could smell Jessica's perfume, sweet and vanilla-y. "John likes to throw a good welcome shindig."

"Sometimes a little *too* good," sniffed Debra.

Jessica laughed. "Don't worry, Caitlin, Debra's an HR meanie until you get some liquor in her, after which she's suddenly dancing on tables and buying shots for everyone," she said.

"That's not true," said Debra. "And please don't scare Caitlin, who's so new."

"You can't scare me," said Caitlin. "Remember, I plan parties for a living. I've seen it all."

They pulled up at the 1 Hotel, the entrance hidden under a massive white awning. The door to the taxi opened, and what Caitlin thought was a valet turned out to be John Shiller himself, wearing red pants, a white Lacoste T-shirt, and aggressively oversize Persol sunglasses.

"Ladies, ladies, ladies," he said, giving each of them a sweaty hug. "*Bienvenidos a Miami*, as the great Will Smith once said. You are all in for an unbelievable time. Un. Be. Lievable. This town is hot, but Aurora is hotter, especially with some of my favorite female executives in for a visit. We're going to have fun, we're going to brainstorm, we're going to emerge an even stronger company, if that's possible. Now go enjoy your spa treatments and I'll see you all tonight. I have an announcement that's going to blow your minds." With that, he turned around without saying goodbye, leaving the three women standing there together with their suitcases.

"Thanks for the help with our bags, John," Jessica shouted after him. "So typical." Debra laughed. Caitlin wasn't sure what she'd gotten herself into, but she felt ready for the ride.

Olive Green

Olive Green, Aurora's director of communications, knocked sharply on a hotel room door. No answer. She did it again, her rings pinging against the white wood.

"I'm in the room!" a voice yelled, loud enough for someone outside to hear. "Please come back later!" She continued to knock, enjoying the irritation she could sense from within.

The door finally swung open to reveal Zach Wagner in a fluffy 1 Hotel robe, his hair mussed from attempted sleep. His annoyance transformed into a sly smile when he saw Olive instead of housekeeping. She crept in, shoving Zach back toward the bed. Then she opened his robe wide enough to give him an eminently satisfying blow job.

"There, that should help you relax," Olive said in her perfect queen's English, kicking off her strappy gold sandals and plopping down on the bed beside him. She was in a long black dress that showed off her abundant cleavage. She'd worn it the other day, and Zach hadn't been able to look away from her breasts during an important executive meeting. John had caught him and winked. Olive had clocked the whole thing.

"I thought we were going to wait until tonight," said Zach. He lifted her dress and started to rub her thigh, inching up as he did.

Olive playfully slapped his hand away. "Oh, no, there'll be none of that," she said.

"That's your loss," he said, shrugging.

Zach and Olive didn't have sex. Well, not *real* sex, at least. They'd worked together for three years and had a public flirtation—Zach referred to Olive as his "Aurora wife," Olive laughed loudly at his stupid jokes. Colleagues needled them about their obvious, not-safe-for-work chemistry, and Debra Foley, Aurora's chief people officer, had once sternly told Zach to knock it off. It all culminated at last year's Miami retreat, after a particularly drunken dinner at Los Fuegos, in the Faena Hotel, where they were staying. Zach and Olive had stumbled up to Zach's room to have one last drink after everyone else had gone to bed. There, the banter led to touching, led to Olive getting on her knees and giving Zach the best blow job of his entire life. Then she'd promptly gotten up and left.

From then on, it became a pattern: on work trips and work trips only, Olive gave Zach oral sex. She'd explained to him that she wouldn't do anything else, "because that's a work line I won't cross." Zach, for his part, had a girlfriend, a bitchy ex-wife, and a moody teenage son on his hands. So their relationship was neatly contained in this box, which, for a year, had suited them both just fine.

"What's the exciting announcement that John's talking up?" Olive asked, letting her body sink into the pillow-top mattress.

"I have a few ideas, but I'm not at liberty to tell," said Zach, teasingly.

"Come on, please do," said Olive. Though Olive headed up communications, John often left her out of the loop of company happenings until the last minute, which angered her no end. For example, John told her about the Caitlin Levy hire just one day before it was set to be announced, and Olive had no time to craft a public release. She also hadn't known how to answer when reporters asked her why Aurora had hired a head of events, when they currently . . . threw no events.

"Pleeeeasssseee," she said, batting her eyes dramatically.

"I'll tell you if you have sex with me," said Zach. He crawled toward her on the bed before collapsing in a pile, and Olive laughed. At forty-three, Olive was about a decade older than Zach's girlfriend, Melissa. (Unlike Olive, Melissa was as yoga-toned as a rock.) Olive had two daughters, Poppy and Penelope, ages ten and twelve, and they lived in the top two floors of a brownstone on Twelfth Street. Olive and her ex-husband,

Henry, who worked in private equity, had bought it eight years ago after deciding, once and for all, to stay in the city.

"Have you met Caitlin Levy yet?" Olive asked Zach. "I heard she had to sit in coach on the flight. Ha. Serves her right for coming in and taking what was supposed to have been my raise!"

"You know that's not how it works," said Zach. "We had a certain amount in the budget for that role, and your compensation comes from another bucket. Don't get all competitive."

"I'm not! Why do men always think women are 'getting competitive'? It's insulting. I deserve that raise, and John told me I'd have to wait a few months, because we were keeping costs down. And then I hear Caitlin Levy, an events person"—she scoffed at "events"—"is joining our executive team. And through the grapevine, I know that she's making a *lot*." Why *had* they hired Caitlin? It didn't make any sense, unless something fishy was going on. And if that were the case, Olive had to be prepared. She was the company's front man (er, woman) and would be the first to go down should anything shady be discovered. She planned to confront John about it on this trip.

"You don't know how much she's making," said Zach with a shake of his head. But Olive did, actually. Nikki Lane, Aurora's glamorous Black executive vice president of engineering, had told Olive that Caitlin would be making nearly three million. Olive made about a million and a half. It wasn't fair. At all.

"Anyway, I did meet her," said Zach, trying to turn the conversation and Olive's mood, which he could tell was darkening. "She seemed nervous. It was endearing. I think you'll like her."

"I don't like anyone," said Olive.

"That's not true. You're friends with Debra and Nikki," he said. The three of them were a tight clique; John referred to them as the "Finger Waggers," because they liked to chide the men for their infantile behavior. "And also, it's clear that Caitlin is going to be John's new little pet, so if I were you, I'd just grin and bear it and be nice."

"I hate being nice!" said Olive.

"I know," said Zach. "Though you're nice to me!"

"Privately," she added. He leaned in to give her a kiss and she swatted him away. No one knew about Zach and Olive's arrangement. Zach wasn't technically Olive's boss—she reported directly to John, like he did—but there would be serious repercussions if word got out about them. John would lose his mind, Debra would murder them, the company's board might have to get involved.

"So, you're not going to tell me what tonight's surprise is, and you won't gossip with me about Caitlin. You're useless, Zach." She got up and slipped her sandals back on. "I'll see you at drinks! Bye!" With that, Olive opened the door, looked left and right, and then speed-walked down the hallway, taking the elevator down to the first floor, freezing in the air-conditioning. (She'd never gotten used to the American obsession with AC; she felt it was a direct attack on women, who tended to run colder than men.)

Olive didn't have to be at her facial yet so figured she'd go outside and look for someone to talk to. Debra was off napping in her room, but maybe she could find another willing target. Olive snaked around the lobby, all smooth gray marble, past the porters waiting for arrivals, and exited out back, heading toward the beach. The air was nearly wet with humidity, and her dress immediately stuck to her chest with sweat. Olive had fair, nearly translucent skin, which she'd inherited from her father, who was from North Yorkshire (her mum, from London, was the posher of the two). At the first hint of heat—or embarrassment—unwelcome red blotches snaked up her chest, crawling on her neck and to her cheeks. It was the least British thing about her, her uncontrollable flushing skin.

She wound around the first-floor pools, passing patrons reading and napping in the afternoon sun. The women were good-looking, fit and preserved, and the men were schlubby, with potbellies. The 1 wasn't a party hotel; it was too expensive for that. It mostly hosted executives like Olive, and rich families and couples on quick Miami Beach getaways. Olive also liked the Faena, where they'd stayed last year, but it was even more costly, and they'd ended up spending hundreds of thousands on the rooms alone. They were trying to be more cognizant of T&E costs this go-around. Meaning blowing $40K on tables at LIV as opposed to $80K. It was all relative.

She made her way down onto the boardwalk, the charming path that cut between the ocean and the lineup of luxury hotels. Two twenty-somethings ran past, wearing bikinis and sneakers, their large fake breasts bouncing as they went. Olive scowled at them. Girls nowadays left nothing to the imagination. She'd tried to instill some British sense of decorum in her daughters but sometimes worried that the American penchant for flesh-flesh-flesh was winning out.

Just then, Dallas Joy, Aurora's cofounder and chief technology officer, and Martin Ito, their chief information officer, jogged into view, slowing to a stop in front of Olive.

Martin, half Japanese, half white, and proudly gay, was shirtless, his defined abs glistening, reminding Olive of a steak about to be put on the grill. Dallas was dressed in 1980s running gear—short-shorts and a John McEnroe–style headband. Zach hated Dallas, and he was always complaining to Olive about him. He hated that Dallas was closer to John than Zach was. He hated that Dallas was a cofounder, and thus stood to get way richer than Zach. He hated that Dallas didn't seem to do any actual work. He hated that Dallas was free of all the life responsibilities that weighed Zach down. More accurately, Olive supposed, Zach didn't *hate* Dallas. He wanted to be him.

"When did you get in, Dallas? I didn't see you on the plane," said Olive. The thing that bothered Olive about Dallas, aside from being sober (ugh) and being a vegan (double ugh), was his tendency to speak in circles, a kind of corporate-lingo-meets-Burning-Man mystical jargon. Olive never knew what the fuck he was talking about.

"I flew in last night and spent the morning doing some A/B testing on our ad targeting, playing around with increased efficiency on our transaction automation," said Dallas, running in place, occasionally glancing at his Apple Watch. "I'm not lost, though. I'm here."

"What?" said Olive.

"You wouldn't get it, Ols," said Dallas with a knowing smile.

"I guess not," Olive muttered to herself.

Dallas traveled everywhere with his fancy Brompton folding bike. He'd given up drinking and drugs in his late twenties, right before Aurora launched, after his and John's friend Robbie fatally overdosed during a wild trip they all took to Mexico. Instead of partying, Dallas now filled his days with biking, intense exercise, and yoga retreats. This was also something Zach, a stress eater with a Micardis prescription, hated about him.

Martin was lunging deeply, alternating legs. "Gotta keep up my heart rate!" he said, though no one had asked. "Working off tonight's calories in advance!" Martin was single, a party guy, always bragging about his crazy weekends, rubbing it in that Olive was over the hill.

"You going to make it out past midnight, or do you turn into a forty-something pumpkin?" said Martin with a snide laugh.

"Oh, shove it," said Olive, rolling her eyes. "Do either of you know about this 'big announcement' that John's all hyped about?" she asked.

"Nope," said Martin with a frown. "No one tells me anything!" Martin was always complaining that he was "out of the loop." Olive generally felt the same way. Dallas also shook his head no, unconvincingly, causing a droplet of perspiration to land on Olive's bare shoulder. She shuddered.

"Okay, enjoy your run, then," she said, ending the interaction. They sped off together in the other direction.

Olive could feel herself overheating but was dreading going back into their indoor icebox. She had a few British friends who'd relocated to Miami in search of money and sun, but Olive couldn't be bothered. She loved New York. She loved the grit and speed and the competition. She'd moved to Manhattan right after she finished university, with no prospects and an empty bank account (sure, she was posh, but that didn't mean she had *money*; Americans couldn't get their head around those competing facts, which always amused Olive). She'd landed an entry-level PR job, repping low-end alcohol brands. And now here she was, leading comms at one of the hottest tech companies in America. Professionally, she was on fire. Personally, it was a different story.

Back at the hotel, Olive stepped through the large bamboo doors leading into the Bamford Wellness Spa and was hit with the pleasingly heavy scent of jasmine. She instantly felt more relaxed, the New Age soundtrack soothing her. She was ushered into a changing area, exchanging her dress for a cozy robe, and then led into a treatment room, dimly lit, warm and luxurious, with blond wooden walls and candles artfully placed throughout. Olive took a deep, restorative breath, shedding her robe and lying down on the table, covering her naked body with the provided towels. The facialist quickly got to work, rubbing oils and potions on Olive's tired, pretty, stressed face.

Olive loved working; she looked at the stay-at-home moms at school drop-off, all dressed up with nowhere to go, and pitied them. Placing stories, working angles, killing stories—she *loved* killing stories—that was her lifeblood. That's what got her through all those years after Henry stopped caring, after he'd stopped asking her how her day was, after they'd stopped having sex, like, ever. After she could sense that everything that had once charmed him about her—her outspokenness, her sense of humor, her generously proportioned body—made him want to run in the other direction.

Olive had put up with it, because what other choice did she have? They were married, they had children, they had an apartment in the West Village, for fuck's sake! She could deal with a loveless marriage, a lot of women she knew did. She had Aurora, she had her friends, she had the buzz that comes after a particularly positive story about your CEO lands in the *New York Post*. Why did your spouse have to be the be-all and end-all of your life?

But then Henry came home from the office one mild April night and said they needed to talk. Penelope and Poppy were both sleeping over at friends' houses. Henry poured himself a whiskey in their den, which she loved for its wood-burning fireplace and prewar details. His thin lips pursed over his teeth, Henry told her he was moving out. He was sorry. He wasn't leaving her for someone else (though there was someone else, men always had someone else). He just felt trapped and miserable and needed to be free. She must have known this would happen, he'd said. Of course she'd bloody known, but she'd been doing what she always did: spinning, spinning, spinning. Not to the *New York Times*, but to herself.

"At least you have your job," Henry had said. "You love your job." He'd meant to be nice, but it gutted Olive to the core.

That was the week of last year's Aurora executive retreat. She'd flown down to Miami in a daze, cracking jokes and drinking vodka tonics and giving a banger of a presentation about Aurora's communications plans. But all she kept thinking was that her life was imploding, her daughters would be devastated, and her stupid American husband was gone.

And then there was Zach. He was warm and nice and, most attractively, liked *her*. He was goofy to Henry's straitlaced banker thing, and he thought Olive was sexy and hilarious. Zach always found subtle ways to touch her; he'd playfully flick her wrist or put his hand on her shoulder to steer her into a room. She knew the rest of the team noticed—they teased her about it, called Zach her "work hubby" (Americans were so embarrassing).

So that weekend, in the wake of the worst rejection of her entire life, she'd gotten drunk, too drunk, and had allowed Zach to lead her up to his hotel room at the Faena, where she'd given him that long, laborious, surprisingly fun blow job. She hadn't given Henry one in, what, a decade? She usually hated giving blow jobs—the errant hairs, the gagging, yuck—but something had come over her, and she'd thoroughly enjoyed it. She'd gotten off on it! Olive Green!

She'd attributed this afterward, hungover and headachy in her hotel bed the next morning, to the illicit excitement of the act. They had to keep it a secret from the rest of the team. And Zach had been cheating on Melissa, whom Olive had met once at Aurora's holiday party. Melissa was young and fit but a bit of a bore. Olive hated bores.

She slowly told her coworkers about her separation, appreciating the support from Debra and Nikki, who planned numerous cheer-up drinks and listened to her whine about being newly single. Olive took calls from her divorce lawyers with her office doors shut. Henry had moved into a soulless glass condo in Midtown, near his office, and was now dating a younger, hotter, dumber version of Olive, a thirty-two-year-old named Sam who worked in ad sales in digital media.

The worst part was, Henry's lawyers had been aggressive, hoarding his earnings, which surprised and hurt Olive more than she thought it

would. Sure, she made her own money, but her savings had been deci-
mated in the split, and she was now feeling insecure about her finances.
She'd gotten the apartment, and a paltry $8,000 a month in alimony, but
her monthlies were getting tight, and she was used to a certain kind of
life. The kind of life that allowed her to shop, and eat out, and go skiing
in Telluride without so much as a thought. She was too embarrassed to
speak to her friends about it, but she did plan to talk to John about her
own compensation when she brought up the Caitlin Levy thing. Not that
he'd necessarily listen or care. John was mostly just about John.

A few months ago, Debra and Olive had burst into Zach's office together, giddy. "We've got it," Olive had said, sitting in one of the two plush
blue chairs on the other side of Zach's white Herman Miller desk. Zach's
office, which overlooked Park Avenue South, had views uptown. Olive
would often catch him standing at his window, admiring the Chrysler
Building's midcentury glint, surely thinking of the great businessmen before him who'd done the same. Astor, Rockefeller, Bloomberg. In those
moments, Olive could sense Zach's dejection. She knew he wanted to be a
CEO more than anything, but she wasn't sure he'd ever get there.

"You've got what?" asked Zach as Debra slid into the second chair.
Debra was wearing a button-down and gray slacks, and her hair was held
back by a puffy black headband—part male middle manager, part fifth-
grade girl.

"We know what John *is*," said Olive, in her favorite blue jumpsuit,
which hugged her shapely backside.

"What John is? John's a man. He's your boss. He's our CEO," said
Zach. His eyes shifted back to his computer, fed up.

"He's got narcissistic personality disorder," said Debra triumphantly.
"Olive and I looked it up, and it fits him perfectly."

Olive jumped in. "He's got an inflated sense of his own importance,
he has a need for excessive praise and admiration, and he completely lacks
empathy," she said, smiling as if she'd cracked a nuclear code rather than
stated some obvious facts about John Shiller.

"Plus," added Debra, "it's all a mask—he'll snap under the slightest
criticism."

"We're quoting from the Mayo Clinic website here!" said Olive. "That's John, exactly."

Zach shook his head dismissively.

"Yes, you don't need to be a disorder detective to know that John's a narcissist," said Zach. "Now, I have actual work to do. Mind excusing me?"

"But this is clinical, Zach!" said Debra. "I wonder if the board should be alerted."

"You're joking, right? Every successful CEO has narcissistic personality disorder. It's basically a job requirement," said Zach.

"Come on, Zach, have a bit of fun with us," said Olive. Debra giggled. Olive and Debra were one of those workplace duos who'd never be friends in the outside world. Olive was attractive and bawdy, and Debra was the opposite—mousy, buttoned-up, HR-y. But, forced to spend time together, they'd found they clicked enormously. Zach shooed them away, their laughter echoing in the hallway as they went.

Olive's facial had ended, and she was headed back to her room to get ready for dinner. She hoped the treatment helped mask her wrinkles and her anxiety. Like picking a scab, she'd often pull up her bank accounts on her phone and be shocked anew at how low her balances were. How did she have only $500,000 to show for her years of work? Fucking Henry.

"John! John!"

As Olive approached the elevators, she saw Madison Bez, John's assistant, calling out his name and rushing toward John and Zach, who were huddled together nearby. Olive stepped back behind a large potted plant, the jungle-y leaves nearly enveloping her, in order to watch the action from afar. Madison was holding a stack of papers in one hand and a comb in the other. She was in a frilly sundress, and her eyes had a wild look. Madison served as John's professional and personal assistant, even though Debra had strongly advised him against having an Aurora employee so intimately entwined in his life (that was their dynamic: Debra did a lot of advising, and John did a lot of ignoring). Madison, a southerner who'd moved to New York to "make her professional dreams come true," did everything from set John's schedule to wash his underwear.

"John, there you are!" said Madison. "I've been looking everywhere. I thought you were going to the pool."

"Madison, you could have just texted me," said John curtly. He hated when she got manic. Everything with Madison was a five-alarm emergency.

"I've got the papers for you to sign. We need to go upstairs to the conference room with the lawyers. They're all waiting. Everyone is waiting!" She was nearly shaking with stress. What were the papers for? Olive wondered.

"All in good time," said John, taking the documents from Madison and paging through them. Madison then took the comb and ran it through John's wavy brown hair, parting it all neatly to the side. John stood there like a toddler reluctantly tolerating his mother. Olive made a mental note to tell Nikki and Debra; they all still snickered about how Madison had lathered sunscreen on John's back during the snorkeling trip on the last executive retreat.

"Zach, what I've revealed is between us," said John. He'd lowered his voice, and Olive nearly toppled out of the plant in order to hear. "You are my most trusted confidant. Do you know who Anthony Eden is?" Zach, who was looking a little wan, shook his head no.

"Anthony Eden was Churchill's secretary of state for war," John said. "He backed Churchill's idea that Britain should fight on, whatever the cost, and remained forever Churchill's faithful supporter. You, Zach, are my Anthony Eden," John said, nearly smiling. There was a long-running debate among the executives as to whether John actually had teeth. None of them had ever seen them. "Then what does he chew with?" asked Martin, after he was let in on the gag. "He just sucks everything up, like a giant anteater," replied Olive.

"It's time for me to head into battle," John finished. He gave Zach a little bow, then turned and strode away, Madison trailing behind like a duckling. Olive needed a drink. Tonight was going to be something else.

Debra Foley

———

Debra Foley was feeling ill. Queasy. Tired. Bloated. Earlier, she'd told Olive she hadn't slept well last night, and so wanted to rest in her room instead of hang by the pool. Olive had been disappointed. "I can't lie there alone! I'll be a sitting duck. What if Jessica comes over and tries to talk to me? Or, even worse, John?!" But Debra had suggested she text Nikki for company and then had snuck off. She was in her suite now, draped over the couch, so exhausted she thought she might collapse. What Debra Foley was really feeling was pregnant.

She was almost four months gone and hadn't told anyone, not even her mother in Buffalo, who'd spontaneously combust with excitement and anxiety upon hearing the news. Debra could picture her mom standing in the kitchen in their split-level ranch in Buffalo, in her BEST FOURTH-GRADE TEACHER IN THE WORLD T-shirt, spitting out her instant coffee when Debra revealed that no, she didn't know who the father was, because she'd had four tequila shots that night and barely even remembered what he looked like, let alone his name.

It had been a very un-Debra thing to do, having a drunken one-night stand. When the guy, whom she'd met at her friend Lisa's fortieth birthday party, started to, you know, put it in (Debra was still imagining herself talking to her mom; she couldn't say "insert his penis" to her mom!), Debra hadn't insisted on a condom. She wasn't on birth control because it gave her migraines, but she'd been at the tail end of her period and, at thirty-nine, figured that was good enough. Spoiler: It wasn't. Four weeks later, around the time her period was due, she'd walked into Martin's office to say hi. He was eating a turkey wrap for lunch, and Debra was so shocked and violated by the smell of it, she'd nearly vomited right there.

"Martin, there's something wrong with your sandwich," she'd said, her eyes watering.

"Yeah, it's delicious, and it's mine, not yours. That's what's wrong with it." He thought she was joking.

"No, I'm serious. I think it's rotten or something," she'd said. He raised one eyebrow at her and sniffed the meat, then looked up and shook his head.

"It's totally fine. I think there's something wrong with *you*."

She'd left his office with a bad feeling and headed straight to CVS after work, picking up four home pregnancy tests (Debra ran HR; she was the kind of girl who liked to check her work). Pregnant, pregnant, pregnant, pregnant. She'd immediately called Lisa, who picked up right away.

"Why are you calling me instead of texting?" Lisa was at a work dinner. She was one of Debra's only other single friends, and they'd remained close for that reason.

"Do you remember that guy I was talking to at your birthday party?" Debra asked. She hadn't told Lisa what had happened. She didn't want people, even her close friends, to think of her as someone who went home with strange men.

"Ummmm, you mean Matt's friend from college? You said you had some work thing in common, remember?" said Lisa. Debra didn't remember. "I'm out with the Geico people at Morini, can I call you tomorrow?" Lisa worked at an advertising agency and was always entertaining clients.

"Sure, sure, I'll call you then." Afterward, Debra had done some hefty internet stalking of Lisa's friend Matt, looking through all his connections on social media to see if she could find the mystery man who'd unwittingly impregnated her. But no luck.

The following week, she'd gone to her ob-gyn, Dr. Benne, an old-school Italian woman who ran the obstetrics department at NYU. Debra had been going to Dr. Benne since she moved to the city when she was twenty-two. She *knew* Debra.

"You're pregnant," Dr. Benne had said, deadpan, as she gave Debra an abdominal sonogram, the cold jelly tickling Debra's stomach.

"I know. I don't think I want to be, though," said Debra, feeling uncharacteristically emotional.

"Why not?" said Dr. Benne, turning the lights back on and lifting the exam bed up so that Debra was at her eye level.

"I'm single, for one."

"So what? You could do this alone. You're strong. Your baby will be strong. This is a good baby," said Dr. Benne. Debra's eyes had filled with tears. She wanted to be a mom but, at this point, had thought maybe it wasn't in the cards. She'd had such bad luck dating in New York. All the women seemed to be more beautiful than she, and increasingly younger and younger. She hadn't had a boyfriend in years, and her weekends were dedicated to catching up on emails that she didn't have time to answer during the week.

"Don't worry, Debra can do it—she's married to her job," Kevin Marner, Aurora's dickish vice president of marketing, had recently remarked in the middle of a big meeting, in regard to some menial task that no one else wanted to take on. (She could have issued Kevin an HR violation for that, but she'd been too humiliated to.) But she didn't *want* to be married to work. She wanted to be married to a person. She wanted a child. So, after a week of no sleep, and some counseling from Dr. Benne, she'd decided to have the baby. She could be a mom and do her job. She could afford a nanny. She made two million dollars a year. Fuck Kevin. Fuck all of them.

At the beginning, it hadn't seemed real: it's not like a body instantly changes the minute it becomes pregnant. For the first couple of months, Debra was merely insanely tired and moody. She hadn't been puking, which made hiding her "condition," as she liked to think of it, doable at the office. She'd just been declining happy hours and going home early, blaming migraines. She couldn't bear the thought of telling her Aurora colleagues that she was knocked up, and had concocted a story about artificial insemination for the busybodies who'd ask about the father. But she was mainly worried about John's reaction. He valued her for her total commitment to the job, and she feared he'd flip at the idea of her priorities shifting (also of her taking advantage of their year-long parental leave policy, which she'd implemented to compete with Google's and Apple's).

Now she was on this executive retreat, which complicated everything. First, she'd have to fake drinking, which around this crowd, especially Olive and Nikki, would be difficult. She also didn't feel up to the hoopla of group activities—Jet Skiing, dinners, the annual game of tennis John forced them all to play. Plus, John's announcement tonight would set off a wave of drama to come crashing down on Debra, his "trusty sergeant," who cleaned up all his messes.

Debra dragged herself to the desk by the window overlooking the green ocean and took out her laptop. The document was already open on the screen: "Pending Executive Share Grants." There, next to each name, was a number, ranging from small (10,000) to medium (75,000) to large (150,000). She and John had been working on it together over the past week, and every time she looked at it her stomach hurt.

Debra's phone buzzed with a text from Nikki. Hi, can I come by? Olive said you were in your room.

Debra shut her laptop, happy for the distraction. Yes, sure, 432, she wrote back.

Five minutes later there was a quick rap on the door and in walked Nikki, dressed in a beachy sarong and a hot pink cutout one-piece. She had on cat-eye sunglasses, and her hair was cropped short and bleached blond. Debra knew that women like Olive and Nikki wouldn't have given her the time of day outside the Aurora universe. Debra's friends looked like Lisa: plain, maybe with one standout feature, like nice eyes. Debra had a lovely smile, which everyone commented on, as if avoiding the fact that everything else about her wasn't. But she also knew that Olive and Nikki truly liked and valued her, both as a colleague and a friend. Or at least she hoped they did.

Nikki sat down on the bed, facing Debra, who'd moved over to the couch.

"Where have you been all day?" said Nikki, taking off her sunglasses and eyeing Debra suspiciously.

"Here, just resting," said Debra, suddenly self-conscious of her breasts, which had grown enormously in the past month, and which she'd tried to hide behind an oversize men's button-down.

"Well, I have some news, and you're not going to like it," said Nikki. Debra steeled herself. People were continually sharing news with her that she didn't like. This was the curse of running HR. Nikki paused for dramatic effect.

"I've been offered the chief product officer role at Trade Desk, and I think I'm going to take it." Debra took a deep breath. She'd known something like this was going to happen eventually. She'd been warning John that Nikki was a flight risk for months, and Trade Desk was Aurora's main competitor. But John had ignored her, claiming that, with Nikki's level of experience, she wouldn't be offered more than she was making at Aurora anywhere else. Guess what, John? Debra was right again.

"Hold on, hold on," said Debra. "You can't just take a new job without giving us a chance to counter," she said. She'd been in this situation before and, with the right money, had managed to lure back most everyone who'd threatened to leave. This was Debra's corporate superpower: talent retention. She lived for it. Plus, after tonight's announcement, a lot would be up for grabs.

"I honestly don't think you can match, it's that high," said Nikki with a triumphant smile. "I got the official offer yesterday but wanted to wait till we were all down here to let you know. I thought it'd be sweeter to give John my 'fuck you and goodbye' speech in person."

"Let me speak to John and see what we can do. What number do you need in order to stay?" Nikki made $1.5 million, all in.

"Debra, I love you, but I'm out of here," said Nikki.

"Just give me a number. Let me work my magic," said Debra. She felt a sudden wave of fatigue, like there was a stack of books piled on top of her head.

"Three million," said Nikki. Debra's heart sank.

"Nikki, that's double your salary. Come on."

"Well, I heard through the grapevine that Caitlin Levy, who was just hired with no real job to speak of, is making that much. So I don't see why I can't make it, too."

Debra tried to hide her surprise; only she and John were privy to that information. Who was leaking? "Just give me a day or two," said Debra, in what she hoped was her most confident chief people officer voice. "John's distracted—we have a lot going on, more of which you'll hear about later tonight. I think it's going to be exciting for everyone. You might not want to leave as soon as you think."

Nikki glanced down at her phone. "I have to get dressed for drinks now," she said. "I need to know your counter by tomorrow. Trade Desk is waiting." Then she flounced out of the room, leaving Debra on the couch, miserable.

There's no way she'd be able to wrangle three million for Nikki; Nikki wasn't even in the C-suite. Debra would go to John and make the case, though: Nikki was the most senior Black executive at Aurora. She was beloved by her staff. She was a forward-facing presence, participating in "Women in Engineering" panels and appearing in *Crain's* "Executives of Color" leadership issue. It would be a huge loss for Aurora if she left and would reflect badly on the company. In particular, it would reflect badly on Debra, whose main job was to keep key employees happy, stuffing them full of money and benefits, advocating for them in front of John and the board. But who was looking out for Debra? Debra needed her own Debra. John certainly wasn't it.

She opened the Share Grants document on her laptop again, staring at the paltry number next to her name: 40,000. She hadn't even complained as John dictated it, just typed silently like the dutiful soldier she was. "I understand if this number is a bit disappointing," he'd said, his back turned to her. Debra hated when John attempted to be empathetic, like he was a bad actor reading for the role of "human."

"You know how valuable you are to me and to Aurora," he'd said. They were in his office alone. Debra was working on her laptop on a table in the corner of the large room, sitting on an uncomfortable Bauhaus-style chair. John was pacing back and forth, from his black leather sectional to Debra to the door and back again. He had a few large framed prints hanging on the wall, and he'd occasionally stop to stare at *The Roaring Lion*, Yousuf Karsh's famed 1941 photograph of Winston Churchill.

They'd waited to meet until everyone else had left for the day (besides Madison, who never left), so as not to create an unnecessary swirl. Whenever a CEO and the head of HR holed up, people assumed the worst. She hadn't replied. Let him flounder, for all she cared.

"You also know, better than anyone, all the personalities involved in this, and why we're giving everyone what they're getting," John continued. She'd nodded coldly. They'd sat there for another minute in silence, John not knowing how to move on from the conversation, and Debra not helping him. She'd worked with John at Aurora since the month after it launched, leaving her job as an HR director at Microsoft after John gave her a hard pitch about running her own department and starting something amazing with him. Mostly, he'd been right. They'd grown the company together. Her first big hires were Zach, whom she lured from Macy's, and Olive, who'd been doing comms for LVMH, followed soon after by Martin and Nikki. Jessica and Dallas were the only two employees who'd predated Debra and, she often thought with pride, the least essential on the executive team. Aurora's huge success hinged on its personnel! Why wasn't she being rewarded accordingly? She should have said something to John, but she'd chickened out. "All right." She'd finally sighed, ending the stalemate. "Who's next? Olive?"

It was now five forty-five, and Debra didn't have time to shower before drinks, even though she felt soured from the travel. Ugh, drinks. Not drinking was the worst part about being pregnant, hands down. She put on her outfit for the night, white jeans that she could barely button and a baggy blue sweater, which she thought did a decent job of camouflaging her swollen boobs. She looked in the bathroom mirror with a grimace and quickly swiped on some sheer lip gloss and a coat of mascara. Who was she kidding? No one would be looking at her, anyway. Tonight was John's big night.

She left her room in a foul mood, thinking of the fallout she'd have to deal with after John's announcement. Plus, she had to find time to speak to him about Nikki. The elevator doors opened to take Debra up to Watr, the 1's rooftop bar, and standing inside was Dallas Joy, Aurora's CTO, dressed in a muted floral top and fitted sea-green shorts. Debra smiled. Dallas was a lucky-in-life guy, blessed with good looks and smarts. He didn't cause Debra too many headaches, unlike most of the team, and for that she was grateful. She knew he annoyed Zach and Olive, but Debra didn't care.

"Hi, Dallas! How's your day been?"

"Awesome," he said. "Got in a long bike ride, went for a run, had a relaxing hour at the pool, did some dusty daydreaming. You all good? You ready for tonight?" Dallas generally leaned on Nikki to run his department, which Debra thought was a great example of delegation, even if it bothered Nikki. If there was anything that Debra hated, it was a micromanager.

"As ready as I'll ever be!" said Debra. The elevator stopped again, and there was Jessica Radum, who seemed momentarily peeved to see them before playfully sticking out her tongue and getting in.

John was close to both Dallas and Jessica, but were they close to each other? From the way Jessica fell into awkward silence, Debra had to believe the answer was no. As usual, it became Debra's job to make conversation. (Debra's mother said Debra could "talk to a wall," which was partly why Debra had found such success in HR.)

"Jessica, are you all set for your presentation tomorrow?" Debra couldn't imagine what Jessica could talk about for forty-five minutes; her job was pretty much an empty shell.

"Actually, I emailed John about it, and we agreed that I wasn't going to present during this trip," she said. She was wearing a black-and-white-striped bandage dress, which hit above her knees and clung to her very long, lean torso. Debra imagined what everyone would think if Debra arrived to Watr in the same outfit, her proto-pregnancy protruding.

"Ah, I see. He didn't tell me," said Debra, stifling a laugh at her own mental image. John was forcing everyone to slog through "state of their business" decks tomorrow and Wednesday, but it didn't surprise Debra that he'd made an exception for Jessica, who constantly got special treatment, which they all noticed and resented.

Jessica also had an irritating habit of invoking John's name during conflicts, reminding everyone that she had privileged access to the king. "I spoke to John about it earlier . . ." or "John and I were just discussing . . ." or "I know John's stance on this, and what he thinks is . . ." Jessica said it with such confidence that no one had the balls to ask if she was bluffing. Debra, then, was shocked when John had said the number to put next to Jessica's name on the Share Grants document. It was lower than anyone's.

"You're basically giving Jessica . . . nothing? *Jessica?*" Debra had asked incredulously. Perhaps he'd said it wrong. Perhaps instead of 10,000 shares, he'd meant 100,000. But John just nodded and moved on, without giving Debra an explanation. Debra stared at Jessica in the elevator. She'd always been jealous of Jessica's Amazonian aura. She thought of how Jessica would take the news when she found out John's plan.

"I'd already walked him through everything that was going on in partnerships, so we felt no need to rehash during a presentation on the trip. . . ." Jessica trailed off, knowing how it sounded. Debra thought she heard Dallas give a little snort.

"Yes, well, nice to have the time back," said Debra, thinking of all the effort she'd put into her twenty-slide presentation about head count, revenue per employee, their new dental insurance, plus Aurora's transition away from "feedback" to "feed-forward," based on employee feedback that the word "feedback" was too harsh.

The elevator reached the rooftop, and the trio exited into a small hallway that led out to the open-air restaurant, dotted with banquettes and corner couches. "Dallas, I need to speak to you," Debra heard Jessica say as they entered the space. The place was about half full, and it was still light out, the heat hitting Debra's face. She worried that her mascara, which wasn't waterproof, was going to slide down her cheeks.

They made their way over to the bar, a long wooden slab under a covered awning that mercifully blocked the sun. Olive appeared, all dolled up in a low-cut dark green dress. She grabbed Debra's arm and pulled her away from Dallas and Jessica.

"You poor dear, having to hang with those two," she said, her eyes shining with mischief. "What are we having? Shall we start with a bit of bubbly?" Debra had been dreading this—she wasn't great at hiding anything, and Olive would notice right away if she declined to drink.

"Sure," said Debra. "Is Nikki here yet? Is John?"

"No, I was the first," said Olive. "You know I'm an early bird," she said, beckoning the bartender, a curvy brunette. "Two proseccos, please," said Olive. The drinks arrived promptly. "Everyone in Miami has fake boobs and a fake butt," said Olive after the bartender was out of earshot. "Speaking of," she said, eyeing Debra's chest, "you're looking a little buxom yourself! What, are you trying to outdo me?" She laughed. Debra crossed her arms.

"No one could compete with you," said Debra, self-conscious. "I'm just a bit hormonal today."

"Aren't we all," said Olive. She drained her glass in two sips. Debra took a small gulp of her prosecco, enjoying the fizz and taste. It'd been months since she'd had any alcohol. A few drinks couldn't hurt the baby, right? Her mom had wine and smoked a pack a day throughout all three of her pregnancies. Debra and her brothers had turned out fine. Or fine-ish. That settled in her mind, she took a larger sip. At least she didn't smoke.

"Debra, I wanted to ask you something. . . ." Olive widened her eyes and sucked in her cheeks. Debra knew that look; it meant Olive was going to tell her something she wasn't supposed to. Olive was always getting in trouble for her big mouth. It's why John never told her anything, even though Olive's job depended on knowing privileged information.

"I overheard John and Zach having a discussion in the lobby. John had 'revealed' something about Aurora, and Zach looked a little shell-shocked. Do you know what they were talking about?"

Debra didn't. Zach was already looped into John's announcement, so it wouldn't be related to that. She shook her head no. What was John up to now?

Debra felt a hand on her shoulder and turned to see Nikki in a striking one-shoulder gold top. She had on bright red lipstick, and her cheeks were dotted with a glowy highlighter.

"Here are my girls," said Nikki, friendly and relaxed, as if she hadn't just threatened to leave unless Debra doubled her salary. Olive motioned to the bartender for another round.

"Is John here yet?" asked Nikki, taking in the scene. "Debra, maybe we can find you a man tonight!" she said playfully. Nikki, who was thirty-three, lived with her boyfriend, Clive. They were on the verge of getting engaged, or at least that's what Nikki kept telling everyone.

"I think not," said Debra. "Just spending time with you all is enough."

"Awww," said Olive, holding up her second glass for a toast.

"To the Finger Waggers," she said, clinking with Debra and Nikki. "The best part of Aurora's executive team. Here's to a wonderful, sun-filled executive retreat."

"To the Finger Waggers," said Nikki. "May we long be together." She gave Debra a meaningful look. Debra pretended not to see it.

"Woot! As you Americans would say," said Olive.

"Who's ready to paaaarrrttttyyyyy?" Martin had snuck up behind them and was shimmying back and forth.

"Is that supposed to be dancing?" said Zach, who'd also just arrived, rounding out the circle. "It looks like you're having a stroke." Zach had a red drink in hand and was somehow already tan. He wasn't Debra's type—she preferred men who were taller and more wholesome—but he had a pleasing face and easy smile that she knew many women found attractive. And though Zach was a total flirt with everyone, he was particularly focused on Olive. They performed their sixth-grade-crush act for the rest of the team, exchanging playful insults, finding excuses to sit next to each other. Debra didn't care if that was it. On any executive team you'll find one pair of star-crossed lovers; Debra had worked at enough companies to know that. But if she found out anything had happened between them, she'd kill them both. Mainly, she'd kill Olive, who swore to her that it was all aboveboard.

"Oh, it's dancing, my friend," said Martin. "And you're going to be seeing a lot of it tonight. Do you know John got us tables at LIV? Those are like twenty thousand bucks. And that ANZ is playing? I love her."

In terms of performance, Martin was one of the most valuable members of the executive team. His work was impeccable and delivered on time, and his ideas were both plentiful and innovative. But was he annoying? Supremely.

"How are my favorite ladies doing?" said Zach. "And I'm including you in that, Martin." Martin shot Zach a dirty look.

"Is John here yet?" asked Martin. He was in a skintight white T-shirt and fitted, cuffed jeans. His hair was slicked over his forehead. Debra liked Martin, but managing his emotions was basically her second job. He always needed reassurance about his role, or to vent about his coworkers, or to complain about John and Zach. He'd been bugging Debra lately for a raise, but it was off-cycle, and he'd just gotten one at the end of the year. He wouldn't take no for an answer. Debra was sick of discussing it.

"So what's this big to-do tonight, Debs," said Martin, stepping around her so that there was a small pod of them at the bar—Martin, Debra, Olive, Nikki, and Zach.

"Yeah, what's the mystery news," said Nikki. Debra tried to catch Zach's eye, but he was staring directly at Olive's breasts. Gross.

"Is it that John's pregnant?" asked Olive with a laugh. Debra felt herself go white.

"Zach, are you in on it?" asked Nikki. Zach winked. "Why does everyone always know things that I don't," Nikki said, frowning.

"I don't know anything either, Nikki," said Martin bitterly.

"Guys, guys, let's all calm down," said Zach. "John likes to do things his way, and we all know his way can be . . . different. But he'll be here shortly to kick things off. Then we'll all be looped in together." Zach occasionally tried hard to remind everyone that he was second in command, even though they all knew he had no real power.

Caitlin Levy came over, her curly hair pulled back in a bun. She was wearing a tasteful cotton caftan and gladiator sandals. Debra admired her mature, pulled-together style. She always felt like such a mess. They stopped talking as Caitlin sidled up, creating an uncomfortable silence.

"Hi, Caitlin, we were just discussing John and his many quirks," said

Debra in a welcoming voice. Did they *all* know how much Caitlin made? It seemed like it, based on the bad vibes emanating from Martin, Olive, and Nikki.

"It's our favorite topic," said Zach. "Can I get you a drink?"

"Sure, I'll take a white wine," said Caitlin. No one said anything for a beat. Zach handed Caitlin her wine and wandered off toward Dallas and Jessica.

"Caitlin, where were you before Aurora? Verizon?" asked Olive, faux innocently.

"Viacom," said Caitlin. "Running all events. But before that I worked at Verizon, selling iPhones on Eighty-Sixth Street." Martin laughed loudly.

"Good one, Caitlin," he said. "Now I see why John's paying you so much money. For your sense of humor!"

The air went out of the little group. Debra elbowed Martin, using her purse to shield the view. Caitlin, thankfully, didn't flinch.

"No, I think he's paying me for my charm and good looks," she said.

"Ohhhh, well done, Caitlin," said Olive, who loved all drama. "Martin, you're toast," she said, clinking her prosecco to Caitlin's wineglass.

"Ignore Martin," said Nikki. "He's just jealous." Martin glared at her and walked off, headed toward the bathrooms in the back, leaving behind Debra, Olive, Nikki, and Caitlin. They all smiled dumbly.

"Caitlin, let me be the first to welcome you to our crew," said Olive. Debra knew Olive well enough to know she was being genuine. "We are very much like a dysfunctional family at Aurora, but that's what makes it fun," she continued. "I've worked at lots of other companies, but I've never liked an executive team as much as this one," she said. "The strong, talented ladies, in particular." They all beamed.

Caitlin nodded along, absorbing it all.

"I'd like to officially induct you into the Finger Waggers," said Nikki, raising her glass.

"The Finger Waggers?" said Caitlin.

"Yes, the Finger Waggers," said Nikki. "John gave us that nickname because we're always wagging our fingers at him when he behaves badly. And we've embraced it, because why not?"

"How badly does he behave?" asked Caitlin. If this information made her nervous, it didn't show. Debra hated this part—revealing to top employees, once they'd signed and committed, how crazy their new boss really was. They were all pretty good at hiding it during the interview process.

On cue, in marched Aurora's CEO, in what appeared to be a vintage green velvet suit, with an unlit cigar dangling from his mouth. The team, who was scattered around the bar, along with the rest of the patrons at Watr, turned to look.

"Holy Christ," said Olive quietly as John made his way toward them, sporting a large grin. Debra peeked at Caitlin, who was stone-faced.

"Hello, hello," said John. On closer inspection, Debra could see that John's suit was a one-piece garment, with no separation between the top and bottom. John waited for someone to say something.

"John, you look lovely," said Olive, bravely diving in. "Is that a . . . romper?" Nikki giggled uncontrollably. Debra shot her a look.

"Funny you should ask," said John, who'd clearly prepped for this speech. "This is indeed a romper suit, so that's a very good guess," he said. "It's otherwise known as a siren suit, and it was invented and designed by none other than Winston Churchill! He worked with Turnbull & Asser to create an article of clothing he could easily slip on in the event of an air raid. This is one of three of Churchill's siren suits that's known to have survived the war, and it was documented to be his favorite of all. He liked to wear it on formal occasions, including the night he was reelected prime minister, in 1951." By this point, Martin, Zach, Dallas, and Jessica had floated over.

"I got it at auction last year at Sotheby's, had it tailored to my smaller proportions, and have been waiting for the right moment to wear it. Tonight is that night!" he said. "And the cigar is just for show. You know I don't smoke, as it makes me vomit." The group was wide-eyed, with half smiles plastered on their faces.

"Great, great outfit," said Zach, who could always be counted on to lessen the tension in a room. "But tell me, John. How do you pee?" Olive let out a honking laugh, putting her hand over her mouth to try to stop it.

"Zach, don't you worry. I had the tailor put in a button fly, with that concern in mind," said John. Debra could never tell if John was in on the joke.

"Thank god," said Zach.

"Oh, man, that's bleeding edge. Won't you be hot?" asked Dallas, shaking his head. "My body needs to breathe in this heat. My pores must be open."

"What?" said Olive.

"Indeed, I will be warm," said John. "Underneath this nifty siren suit, I'm wearing a T-shirt and pants. I'll take off the suit for dinner. Churchill really was such a genius," he said. A waitress came over to the group and handed each of them a shot of something or other, then ushered them over to a large table by the rooftop pool, away from the rest of the restaurant's guests. Debra held her shot far away from her nose—the smell of pure alcohol made her feel slightly ill.

Everyone took a seat, except John, who was standing at the head, the sun starting to lower in the Miami sky.

"Is this the big announcement?" Nikki whispered to Debra, who nodded back to her. John cleared his throat. Debra saw that his forehead was beaded in sweat, the siren suit working its magic.

"We are gathered here in Miami for a special time of strategizing and bonding. I am so lucky to have the best executive team on earth, and I'm thankful you all could find time in your busy schedules to make it down to this great city," he said. ("Uh, we were forced to come," said Olive to Debra, who kicked her under the table.)

"But before we head into our brainstorm sessions, I need to share some key information that will shift how we see Aurora's trajectory over the next few years. I'd like to preface the news by assuring you all that you're integral to the company, and this doesn't mean that anything is changing, or that your jobs are in jeopardy," he said.

"Just bloody spit it out," said Olive softly. Debra kicked her again.

"This, as my man Churchill would have said, is our finest hour. So, with no further ado . . . drumroll, please!" said John. Everyone looked at each other, unsure of what to do. Martin started banging the table lightly, and they all followed his lead.

"We are selling Aurora to Minimus for eight hundred million dollars!" said John, his green eyes shining against his green suit in the low light. Minimus, an enormous tech company, bigger than both Alphabet and Microsoft, regularly scooped up competitors, paying large sums to swallow them into its universe. "You are all going to be very rich! Now, everyone, take a shot!" John bellowed. Debra swallowed hard and gulped down the vodka. Sorry, kid. Debra needed strength.

Minimus in Talks to Buy Adtech Darling Aurora

By Kaya Bircham

Search giant Minimus is in advanced talks to acquire Aurora, the adtech startup founded by John Shiller and Dallas Joy, according to a person with direct knowledge of the discussions. Buying Aurora would get Minimus into the adtech game, put its competition for advertising in-house, and eliminate the risk of clients going outside its walls.

Terms of the deal couldn't be learned. Aurora's private premoney valuation was around $600 million at the time of its last announced funding round in 2021. Aurora was founded in 2015 and raised nearly $100 million from Red Partners, Christmas Tree Capital, and other investors to take on the difficult task of competing with adtech giant Trade Desk. Behind the scenes, Aurora is cooking up its own industry-shifting strategy: part adtech, part events, led by new hire Caitlin Levy.

There's still the possibility that Minimus, which has a market capitalization of $55 billion, will pull out of the deal, says a person with direct knowledge of the negotiations. The sale would be a life changer for Shiller and his team, who'd come into significant windfalls upon signing. Shiller, who has a reputation as a bit of a wild card (and is a known Winston Churchill fanatic), couldn't be reached for comment. Minimus's leadership is also mum. More to come on this one.

Nikki Lane

——

Nikki Lane was lying. There'd been no offer from Trade Desk, just a slew of interviews that, eventually, had led to nothing. She'd finally followed up with them last week, ten days after her last chat with Trade Desk's chief people officer, a pasty, heavyset guy named Ben Hooks.

Hi, Ben, Nikki had written. She was sitting on the couch in her charming two-bedroom in Cobble Hill, which she and Clive rented for the exorbitant amount of $7,500 a month. She knew she was throwing money away on it, but she wanted to be engaged before she and Clive bought somewhere together. He just needed to get his act together and propose; she wasn't sure what was taking so long.

> Thanks so much for chatting with me about the possibility of joining the Trade Desk team. It seems like you all have a great thing going over there, and I'd love to be part of it. Please let me know if you have any additional questions or would like me to start passing on references. Looking forward to hearing from you soon! Best,
> Nikki

She pressed send, hopeful that her message would give Ben the nudge needed to get her a real offer. She had a plan to tell Debra, John, and Dallas at the executive retreat, to have that sweet moment when she could say to

John, in person, that she was peacing out of Aurora for greener pastures, and that he was now on his own.

But since then, she'd heard nothing. Ben hadn't even had the decency to reply. It didn't make sense to Nikki. They'd been all hot on her, proactively approaching her on LinkedIn, giving her the whole song and dance about what an honor it would be to have her join their team. And then radio silence. Had she said something off in her last interview? She'd met half their senior execs, charming each one, she'd thought, with her charisma and ideas of how to take Trade Desk into the future. They'd dangled a big salary and sizable equity, allowing her to dream of that fantasy apartment in Brooklyn Heights. Imagine Nikki, raised in the Bronx, living among all the willowy, white Brooklyn Heights moms, with their old Céline and inordinately expensive, hideously ugly shoes. She couldn't wait. She could taste it. But then Ben disappeared.

She and Clive had discussed it at length before she'd flown down to Miami.

"I mean, Aurora is fine, but I should be in the C-suite, full stop. Enough with this EVP nonsense," she'd said over Thai takeout. Clive, cautious Clive, gave an annoying, Clive-y answer.

"Babe, you're an EVP at one of the best tech companies out there. You'll be in the C-suite in no time. Maybe have some patience? It always seems like the next job will be better, but you never know what you're getting into. You like your colleagues at Aurora, and John trusts you. That's worth a lot." Clive was an editor at the *New York Times*; they'd met three years ago at the Yale Club, at a Black alumni event. He was the first person Nikki had ever dated who she thought might, *might*, be smarter than she was. But she wasn't going to listen to him on this one.

"I'm going to make something happen, you'll see. I'll just tell them I got an offer. They'll come back to me with more money and a better title. I know Debra. She'll do it." Nikki wasn't afraid to bend the truth to get what she wanted. Why should she be? Maybe *this* was progress: the ability to be as shifty as her white peers. The worst that could happen was that Debra could come back with nothing, in which case Nikki would say she'd had a change of heart and had decided to stay at Aurora after all.

She'd blow her advantage and look like a fool, but it's not like they'd fire her. Then she'd wait for the next offer to come along, and do it all again.

"That's a terrible, terrible idea, babe," said Clive, shaking his head. "Sometimes you scare me." He was laughing while he said it, but Nikki sensed something real beneath the surface of the comment. Perhaps she didn't have to share everything with Clive. She changed the subject.

"I heard that our new head of events, Caitlin Levy, is making three million dollars! We don't even throw events. It's absurd," she said, putting more pad thai on her plate. Clive didn't say anything. He made about $150,000 to her $1.5 million. And while he wasn't the kind of guy to feel threatened that his girlfriend was earning more than he was, they didn't talk much about how she paid most of the rent (she'd wanted the apartment; he was fine living in some shitty place in Jersey). "I know you think we all make absurd amounts of money, but that's on another level," said Nikki. Clive nodded warily.

So, despite his disapproval, she'd pushed ahead with her plan. Soon after they'd arrived in Miami, she'd gone to Debra's hotel room, telling her about her "offer" from Trade Desk. Debra had reacted as Nikki suspected she would: terror, ass-kissing, followed by a plan to get Nikki the money she was asking for.

And then—and then!—John and his Winston Churchill romper suit had to go ahead and announce the sale of the company. She'd totally fucked up the timing. Now Debra would tell John right as he was deciding whom to dole out the incoming millions to. It certainly wouldn't ingratiate her to him when he found out she was threatening to leave.

Nikki, to calm herself, had one too many shots of tequila at Watr, and one too many glasses of wine at ZZ's during dinner, and a few too many vodka sodas once they'd arrived at LIV.

Nikki could count on one hand the number of Black people she'd seen that night, typical for when she went out with her mainly white colleagues. This wasn't her scene; she hated techno, hated the dumb way people jumped around and sweated to it. She found a seat on a red leather couch, having lost her friends at least thirty minutes ago. She knew John had bought a table—she'd seen him and Dallas sitting at it when they'd first arrived—

but she couldn't find it in the thrum. After wandering around and nearly going deaf in the process, she needed to rest for a few minutes to get her bearings.

The night had been weird. After John's announcement, the whispering started about how much each executive was set to receive, and Nikki knew the gossip would just get worse as the trip went on. She hadn't been able to corner Debra, so she didn't know whether she'd spoken to John about the Trade Desk offer yet. She hoped she hadn't. Maybe there was a way to take it all back, to tell Debra that she'd reconsidered. Clive had been right. Clive was always right.

Nikki felt drunk. She generally held her alcohol well, but even she had a limit. Where had Olive gone? She could always count on Olive to rescue her in these situations. In fact, it felt as if Olive might be avoiding her on purpose, which was strange, as they hadn't argued about anything lately. Instead, into the banquette slid Jessica Radum, in some *Real Housewives*-style bandage dress that Nikki wouldn't be caught dead in. She and Jessica had never clicked; Nikki resented the preferential treatment Jessica got from John. She also hated that, yet again, some pretty white woman was getting something for doing nothing, while Nikki worked her butt off for less. She was sure Jessica knew how she felt. Nikki wasn't good at hiding her feelings.

"Hey, Jessica, how's it going? Where is everyone?" said Nikki, speaking as crisply as possible over the surging music.

"I saw Dallas dancing, but I don't know where John is, and I haven't seen Martin in a while, either," said Jessica. Her teeth looked particularly big and white in the strobe lights, like she'd just had her dentist touch them up. "What have you been up to?"

"Nothing much, just wondering when it'd be okay to go home," said Nikki. Jessica scooched closer to her, enough that Nikki could smell her sweet perfume.

"Listen, Nikki, I know we've never been best friends," she said. "But I heard you're thinking about leaving Aurora for Trade Desk." Nikki felt her mouth get dry. So it was out. She waited for Jessica to continue, neither confirming nor denying.

"I think you're awesome, even if I've never said it," said Jessica. "And, as a fellow female tech exec, I think they'd be lucky to have you. In my opinion, you should go. There's some stuff going on with our company"—on the word "stuff" Nikki felt Jessica's warm breath in her ear—"that I don't think you want to be a part of." The beat dropped and the crowd went wild, an animal herd stomping in time, the vibrations traveling up Nikki's legs into her stomach.

"What *stuff*?" said Nikki, grabbing Jessica's arm, warm and smooth. She could feel Jessica's pulse in her hand.

"Think about my ask," said Jessica.

"What ask?" Nikki said, even more mixed-up.

But instead of answering, Jessica slipped away into the darkness of the club, leaving Nikki alone and confused.

Before she could work herself into a state, Martin took Jessica's spot. He looked shiny, and possibly on drugs. His hair, normally so perfectly coiffed, was dripping with sweat. He put his head down on the table, only lifting it when Nikki tapped him on the shoulder, hard. As the two executives of color, everyone thought they would have formed some sort of alliance. The assumption bothered them both, and, as such, they merely tolerated each other. Martin roused himself, giving Nikki a stink eye.

"I was just resting for a second, what's the deal?" he said. Nikki respected his work, but he could be such a moody prick. She didn't see what Debra liked about him. But he generally knew everyone's business, so she figured she'd give it a whirl. No one would remember much from tonight, anyway.

"Did you hear about my offer from Trade Desk?" she asked. Martin pretended to throw up.

"No, I actually didn't, but I'm not surprised that they'd want you, Miss Top Black Executive of the Year, according to *Crain's* or whatever," he said. "They've sniffed around me a few times, but nothing ever came of it." It was so like Martin to mention they'd spoken to him about a job, too. He was such a competitive shit.

"Jessica just told me I should leave Aurora and go there. She said our company has some shady stuff going on. Any thoughts as to why she'd say that?"

"You got me," he said. "I also spoke to her earlier tonight for like the first time ever," he said. "She's very . . . tall." Nikki snorted. Martin could be funny when he didn't get in his own way. "She told me she had misgivings about the sale," said Martin. "Also, what's her deal with Dallas? Do they hate each other or something?" Nikki shrugged.

"For what it's worth, I think you should stay at Aurora. We're about to get sold, and you could make some real money. I mean, *real*," he continued. "Plus, Olive's good friends with Trade Desk's chief people officer, that guy Ben, the one who looks like a large, pale toad. He went to college with her husband. She says Ben always complains about working there, and that it's a total pressure cooker."

Nikki tried hard not to show her shock. Olive was friends with Ben Hooks? Why hadn't she ever told Nikki?

"Well, I appreciate your thoughts," she said after a minute. "Please don't tell anyone about it," she said.

"I'm sure everyone already knows," he said, putting his head back down on the table. "Now, if you'll let me nap for ten minutes, I can come back to the land of the living." Nikki looked out on the dance floor. Caitlin Levy, her hair loose and springy, was out there alone, twirling with her eyes closed. Nikki pulled out her phone and ordered an Uber back to the hotel. She needed some Advil and some sleep.

Olive Green

——

Olive Green was standing at the bar of LIV, watching Caitlin Levy, the three-million-dollar woman, spin, spin, spin around, a forty-year-old executive dancing on her own. What was Caitlin doing in Miami with them, anyway? Maybe that's what John had revealed to Zach earlier in the day. If so, Olive was determined to get it out of Zach. Her blow jobs could be very convincing.

Olive was trying to flag down a bartender for a final vodka soda before she headed back to the hotel to sleep it off. The evening had been one for the books, kicked off by John's announcement of the company's sale. Olive's wheels were already turning about the best outlet to place the story. The *Wall Street Journal*, probably. Or they could do something unexpected, like announce in the digital outlet the *Information*, which would certainly create a wave. She figured she'd be looped in with Minimus's PR team to craft a joint press strategy, but she was hoping that she could take the lead.

"What's cooking, good-looking?" Zach sidled up to her, resting his damp head on her shoulder and giving it a light kiss. She pulled away, scanning the area for other Aurora execs. She'd seen John and Caitlin earlier, heads close together in conversation. She'd also spotted Nikki, wasted but still radiant, and had run in the other direction. She'd been avoiding Nikki for the past few weeks, so ashamed about what she'd done to her.

"Zach, you can't do that in public!" she said in a low voice.

"Why, who's going to arrest me? The shoulder-kissing police?" Zach put his hands on her hips and forced her to start swaying to the music. She indulged him for a minute before shrugging him off. He leaned in close to her, putting his lips to her ear.

"We're all going to get riiiiich, we're all going to get riiiich," he sang tunelessly. "Though aren't you rich already? Wasn't Henry, like, some stock-selling man? I assume you got your God- and New York State–given fifty percent out of him."

Olive ignored that part.

"Maybe *you'll* get rich," she said. "But you have a lot more equity than I do, and I think John is cold on me right now." John always had a favorite or two, and right now Olive, who'd had a falling-out with him over the Caitlin announcement, was on the outs.

"You'll do fine," said Zach. Olive was really hoping so, as she needed that money. She wanted the girls to know she wasn't just living off their daddy, who'd ditched them all and taken most of their savings with him. She had to show them she could do it on her own.

"Do you want to get out of here?" asked Zach. He wiggled his eyebrows, and she tried hard not to laugh. She nodded yes. They snaked through the dance floor, passing Caitlin, still going strong.

"Aurora's own dancing queen!" Zach said, giving her a quick bow.

"That actually makes me like her so much more," said Olive as they wound around the bar, pops of light assaulting Olive's tired eyes. "Mommy's night out! It's very cute."

"I'm going to hit the bathroom before we go; the Uber will be outside in a minute," said Zach, leaving Olive by the exit.

She stepped into the night, the humidity still hanging in the dark Florida air. Olive felt like a deflated balloon, and she was sure her hair looked frizzy and atrocious. There was a small crowd of people waiting to pick up their cars, and Olive spotted Dallas standing off to the side, staring at his phone. He looked pulled together, his floral shirt crisp, and it annoyed Olive all over again that he didn't drink or do drugs. What a snore. Apparently, Dallas was so traumatized by the experience of Robbie's death that he'd sworn off substances forever. Every American Olive knew suffered from some sort of "trauma." They all just needed to buck up.

Olive stepped back into a shadow by the building. The last thing she

needed was Dallas spreading the story that she and Zach left the club together. Just then, Jessica emerged from the club. Olive saw her walk over
to Dallas with purpose, then start speaking to him in a heated way. Jessica
was gesturing angrily, her skinny arms shaking, and Dallas was putting his
fingers to his lips, attempting to shush her.

Some of the other clubgoers glanced at them lazily, assuming a
drunken lovers' quarrel. Dallas tried to walk away, but Jessica followed
him down the sidewalk, grabbing him in order to continue their conversation. Olive pushed deeper into the nook in which she was standing.

Before she could see anything else, Zach came out of the club. As Zach
pulled her toward their Uber, an enormous, shiny Chevy Suburban, she
looked over toward where Jessica and Dallas had been. They were gone.
Olive could still hear the music coming from the club. Fuck Henry, get
your money, fuck Henry, get your money, she repeated in her head to the
pounding beat. Zach pulled her up into the car, ice-cold from the AC,
and she leaned against him in the backseat. He put his arm around her as
they sped back to the 1.

PART 2

Wednesday, April 24

Attitude Is a Little Thing That Makes a Big Difference

Madison Bez

Madison Bez had spent the past three years of her life dedicated to one thing: John Shiller. His wants and needs, his appetite, his likes and dislikes, his moods. Oh, his moods. He was up, then he was down, then he was mad, then he was elated, then he was *really* mad, then he was tired. She tracked it all obsessively, hoping to accurately predict where he was heading next. It was difficult, sometimes impossible work, but Madison loved it. She loved being involved in the day-to-day business, helping John with paperwork and meetings and emails, making sure everything in his life ran smoothly, from his schedule to his cleaning lady to his travel itineraries to his dinner dates. She oversaw it all, the master of his domain, solving his problems before they even existed. But Jessica Radum was a problem Madison couldn't yet solve. And the worst part was that it was all Madison's fault.

Madison had grown up in Alabama, the single daughter of a single mom, Sandy, who'd had Madison when she was nineteen. Sandy worked as a teacher's aide and felt her life had been cut off by her unplanned pregnancy. She loved Madison more than anything, which she told her constantly, but at the same time she framed her own journey in terms of regret. "That could have been me," Sandy would say wistfully whenever she read or watched something about a "career woman." "I always wanted to make it to New York." In truth, it pained Madison to hear her mom speak that way, but she redirected any hurt toward her own ambition.

Madison's dad, Rick, whom Sandy had dated only briefly, worked in healthcare in California. He was married and had two younger children. Madison had a half brother and half sister, neither of whom she'd met. She'd always dreamed of having a real-life father, someone to twirl her around, pay for her clothes, and take her to daddy-daughter dances. Instead, she had Rick, who called her on her birthday and sent her Barbies for Christmas, well beyond when Madison was interested in dolls. But she tried not to let it get her down.

Madison had been a good student. She was obsessively organized and diligent, though she didn't have the most creative of minds. She'd gone to the University of Alabama, with loans, and had majored in management, without a clear idea of what that was other than a launching pad to get to New York City. During college, she'd worked in retail, as a babysitter, and as a waitress at a local seafood place. Anything to earn some extra money. She'd had a few close friends, but that was it. She didn't party, she didn't date around. She was cute in an approachable way; she liked feminine dresses, makeup, and dangly earrings. She'd had one boyfriend, a mild-mannered accounting major named Matt, to whom she'd lost her virginity in the top bunk of his dorm room.

That was the first and last time she'd ever had sex. She'd broken up with Matt shortly after, uninterested in the physical part of the relationship. Sex had been messy and unpleasant, and so she'd decided to just stay away. Anyway, what if she'd gotten pregnant, like her mom had? Nothing seemed worth getting stuck in Alabama.

After graduation, she did what she and Sandy had always dreamed of: She moved to New York. Well, to Astoria, more precisely, to a room in a small apartment she shared with two other girls, strangers she'd met through Craigslist. The apartment had mice, and Madison got used to hearing their high-pitched squeaks as she lay in bed, thinking about what she was going to do with her life. She didn't have any specialized skills, and she didn't know anyone who could help her figure it out. She began searching LinkedIn for executive assistant opportunities, which seemed like the easiest place to start. After about a month, her money running out, she saw a listing for a position assisting a "tech CEO." She'd heard that "tech" was the best industry to be in right now, though if you asked her what "tech" was, she wouldn't have been able to answer. She sent in her résumé and was surprised when she got an email from the company's HR department, asking her to come in to interview for the job.

Madison researched the company, Aurora, and found it was a very impressive place, with lots of articles calling it a "hot startup" and "surprisingly profitable" and "bound for an acquisition." She forwarded them to Sandy with many excited emojis. The company's CEO, John Shiller, had been written about everywhere, and Madison stared at the smiling picture of him on the corporate website. He had a beard, a fat-ish face, and narrow eyes. She wondered if he'd be the one to save her from having to go back to Alabama. She'd said a quick prayer to God that he would.

She'd arrived at Aurora's headquarters, on Twenty-Fourth Street, overlooking Park Avenue South, an hour early for her interview. She'd worn her best floral dress from American Eagle and had curled the ends of her long hair the way her mom had taught her. Good luck, honey! You're my New York working woman! I believe in you! Sandy had texted that morning. Madison had gotten a coffee at the Starbucks across the street and then walked around the block until she had to go in, trying to burn off her nervous energy.

She then went up to the eleventh floor, to Aurora's reception, and was impressed by the sleekness of the office—its open floor plan, the cubicles occupied by good-looking people in bright outfits and cool glasses. There were conference rooms decorated with neon accents, with funny words on the doors like "Stalingrad," "Berlin," and "Okinawa." (She'd later learn that John had named each one after the location of an important World War II battle.) She'd felt insecure and intimidated; this wasn't her world, these weren't her people. It looked like something out of a TV show.

She'd been greeted by a twenty-something guy with pierced ears, wearing gently ripped jeans, and he'd led her back to a large corner office, entirely different from the rest of the space. Instead of poppy, millennial fun, this room had a dark, brooding vibe, filled with black leather furniture and framed pictures of old, strange-looking men. The guy instructed her to sit down in the uncomfortable chair at a small table on one side of the room. She perched on it anxiously as a thought crossed her mind: She was going to interview directly with John Shiller. Today. Right now.

And just then, he walked in, sticking out his hand for her to shake as he slid into the chair on the other side of the table. He was small, though not slight, and was in a white polo shirt and bright blue pants. He had striking green eyes. This was a real CEO! In tech! She couldn't wait to tell her mom about it.

"Madison Bez," he began. "Madison, Madison, Madison." He paused, looking somewhere off into the distance instead of straight at her. She didn't know what to say. She smiled.

"I was handed your résumé by my chief people officer, Debra Foley, and I was struck by a few things. First, that you worked at a seafood restaurant called Fred's Fish in Tuscaloosa. How was that experience for you?"

Madison, flustered by the question, answered honestly. "I had a boss there who used to pinch my butt every time I came into the kitchen. And I'd come home smelling like fried shrimp. So, it wasn't great. But the tips were okay," she'd said. John let out a high-pitched squeak.

"Second, I saw that you'd worked at the Gap during college," John said. "I'm very particular about how my shirts are folded. Can you show me how you'd fold my shirt?" He walked over to his massive wooden desk. Sitting next to his computer was a rumpled T-shirt, which he handed to Madison. She shook it out, releasing a slightly sour smell. Her body relaxed. This was a test she knew she could ace.

She lay the shirt out flat, drawing a middle line down the center, and pinching it in four different places. Then she lifted the shirt up—at this point it looked like a mess, and John raised an eyebrow—placing it down so that the sleeves touched the table first, symmetrically, and the rest of the fabric followed, creating a perfectly neat square. She looked at John, proud of her work.

"Madison Bez, I believe you've earned yourself a job offer," he said, extending his hand for her to shake again. "How much do you know about Winston Churchill?"

"Not much," said Madison. "But I can learn."

It had been a whirlwind since that moment. She'd started immediately, practically moving in with John, spending nearly every waking minute of the day with him. She'd take the subway from Queens to Chelsea each morning, getting to John's large bachelor pad by 9:00 A.M., sometimes rousing him out of a deep sleep, often having to shoo away a girl or two who'd been staying in his bed. She was fascinated by the women John dated, a rotating cast of plumped-up influencers and models, none of whom she thought was good enough for him. They barely said anything in the morning, just wiggled their lovely bodies into jeans and dresses, and laughed when John made a joke. She couldn't believe that they'd have sex, willy-nilly, with a guy who clearly didn't want to be their boyfriend.

Madison traveled with John on his professional trips. (She'd once asked if he'd like her to accompany him on his personal vacations, and he'd said no. Her feelings had been somewhat hurt by this, but she pretended to be relieved.) She filed his receipts and did his laundry. She dreamed of him. She woke up thinking of how she could make his life better that day. And she watched everyone and everything around him, making notes that she delivered at the end of the day, in a 6:00 P.M. email.

Thursday, May 12, she'd begin, typing on the laptop on her small desk that sat outside his office. Their headquarters on Park was over-air-conditioned, and Madison, who ran cold, kept a small cashmere throw on the back of her chair. By evening, she'd be wrapped in it tightly, her hands stiff and freezing, struggling to hit the keys. All the women at Aurora complained about the temperature, which was particularly chilly in the summer, but the building operations couldn't seem to do anything about it. Some employees even circulated a petition calling it an "environmental atrocity." (Mo, the building's super, just ignored the privileged young things who worked there.) Madison would arrive in a dress, drenched in sweat from the walk from the subway, which, upon entering, would turn to frost on her goose-pimpled arms.

Today was a good day, she'd continue, checking her notebook, in which she wrote everything down.

- Martin led a team meeting for the data crew, updating them all on the latest tracking systems, which Nikki and the engineers have started to roll out. Everyone seemed pleased.
- Olive is working on the *Times* story about our industry, trying to make sure that Aurora is in the lede paragraph and that your quotes are featured prominently.
- In the kitchen, I heard Zach tell Cynthia from finance that they were on track to beat Q2 expectations, and she was happy to hear it—she told him that he was "giving 110 percent" and that this would help with budgeting for the rest of the year.
- Debra is in a bit of a spat with Nikki because she's trying to push through some hires without going through the proper channels. Debra said to Kathy on her team, "She always fucking does this," and Kathy agreed.
- Dinner tonight is at 8:00 P.M. It's the omakase at Shuko on Twelfth Street. You have Bryan and Tyler and Jason, plus whatever girls they bring along. Remember not to eat too much salmon, as it upsets your stomach. Enjoy!
- Tomorrow you have a coffee with Jessie Malcove, the founder of that language app that specializes in translating dirty jokes, and we also have the town hall prep meeting.

And so on and so on. She was his eyes and ears, and he relied on her to make him aware (or keep him purposefully in the dark) of what was happening on every level of the company. Madison knew the other executives, particularly Debra, Olive, and Nikki, the ones who called themselves the Finger Waggers, made fun of her. They called her "John's house servant" and made jokes at her expense. In truth, it hurt her feelings, particularly that it was the women who made her feel so small. Madison had always thought that female colleagues were supposed to stick together, but in her short experience, she was learning that wasn't always the case. She was just trying to do her best! Her job was to take care of John, and so that's what she focused on.

Which was why, instead of manning the breakfast table downstairs at

Habitat, Madison was inside Jessica's hotel room (as event organizer, she had keys to every room), hoping that there weren't any security cameras capturing her movements. First, Madison pawed through Jessica's messy suitcase. Underwear, tank tops, bikinis, summery dresses. Nothing out of the ordinary.

She went into the suite bathroom, with its long, wide sink and gray marble shower, and saw Jessica's toiletry case, her creams and potions peeking out. She inspected its floral-scented contents. Face wash. Blush. Makeup brushes. Foundation. Melatonin. She'd noticed a small side pocket on the outside edge, unzipping it to reveal a few plastic bags filled with pills and powders. Madison pocketed them. Maybe they'd be useful somehow. Then she tiptoed out the door, racing to the elevator and heading down to the lobby. John would be hungry, and someone needed to be there to order his eggs.

Caitlin Levy

Caitlin Levy wanted to die. Dying would be preferable to the horrendous, debilitating pain she was in. She could barely open her eyes. She could barely walk. Her head felt like it was being continually hit with a large rock. She was on the verge of throwing up. She was green. She was gray. She hadn't been this hungover in years. Nowadays, it was a big night if she had three glasses of wine. Any more than that, and she'd pay for it. Well, she was certainly paying now.

It was 8:55 A.M., and she was on her way to breakfast at Habitat, the Mexican restaurant on the 1's lobby level. The team was set to eat there at 9:00 A.M. sharp, according to Caitlin's agenda, and she didn't want to be late. The rest of the day was filled with planned activities: presentations from ten to noon in a conference room on the third floor, lunch out at Lucali in Sunset Harbor, Jet Skiing in Lake Pancoast in the afternoon, followed by drinks (sigh) and dinner at Carbone. Caitlin wasn't sure how she'd manage to get through it all. Bile kept rising in her throat. The idea of bumping through waves on a Jet Ski made her want to curl up and disappear.

She could barely even remember the end of the night; after they arrived at LIV, it all became a blur. Had she been dancing? Her feet hurt, which led her to believe she had been. How had she gotten home? She'd miraculously woken up in her hotel room at 7:00 A.M., dry mouthed and groggy, and dizzily checked her phone for evidence of her movements. She'd sent Mike a text around midnight that read All good, looooove you xoxoxo, but that was it. She hadn't mentioned anything about John's announcement, or about how she'd possibly be receiving a bulk payment on top of her new, large salary. She was still processing it all herself, and she didn't know how Mike would take the news.

She entered the restaurant, spare and wooden, with large vegetation hanging from the walls, and looked for her group. All she saw was a long empty table in the back, with a small sign in the middle that read WELCOME, AURORA EXECS! Had she gotten the time wrong? Caitlin wondered as she sat down in one of the nine free chairs. She pulled up the agenda again on her phone—no, she'd been right, breakfast called for 9:00 A.M. It was now 9:05. Still no sign of anyone. She ordered coffee, hoping that it would make her feel more human, though she worried it might have the opposite effect and make her vomit.

Bits and pieces of the night were coming back to her. She'd had a long conversation at dinner with Dallas, who seemed like a nice enough guy, if a ponderous conversationalist, in which they'd discussed his folding bike, at length, his role at the company, and his vegan diet. (Why did vegans enjoy talking about veganism so much?) She'd gone to the bathroom after the main course and had passed Jessica Radum, who was emerging suspiciously from the men's room. Jessica was rubbing her nose, and Caitlin had wondered who'd provided the cocaine. Martin was her best guess. On Caitlin's way out, she'd seen John by the inside bar, checking his phone. His face was anxiously pinched but instantly smoothed into a Cheshire cat grin upon seeing Caitlin.

"Caitlin Levy! How are you? Are you having fun?" She'd not spoken to him alone since their first meeting, and immediately felt the same odd attraction she'd experienced at the Freehand Hotel.

"Yes, very much," she said, stepping closer to him. It was as if there were an invisible string between them that he kept tugging toward himself. She'd felt the wine at that point, but it was still hours away from LIV. She was loose but not untethered.

"Wonderful," said John. They were eye to eye; Caitlin was in flat sandals, so she didn't tower over him. She noticed that his chest was defined under his polo, and then was grossed out that she'd even given it a thought. He was both alluring and repulsive in equal measure. It was unsettling, and she was rarely unsettled.

"I wanted to talk to you about my presentation," said Caitlin. She was wary of having a drink-soaked conversation with her new boss, but she also didn't know when she'd get another chance to talk to him. "As in: I don't really have anything to present," she said, not letting him interrupt. "You still haven't told me what my day-to-day will look like, nor do I have a clear sense of how events fit into Aurora's strategy. I'm feeling a bit nervous about it all, which isn't how I normally am heading into a new job," she said, regretting the last sentence before it was even out of her mouth.

"Caitlin, Caitlin, Caitlin," said John. Was John's name-repetition thing just another tic? It had a kind of hypnotizing effect on Caitlin, which was maybe the point. He put his hand on her shoulder, and she liked the weight of it there. "Tonight, I just want you to enjoy the evening and meet your new colleagues. Aurora has a special executive team, which you'll see as the week goes on. Please don't worry about your presentation. I'm sure it'll all come to you when you get up in front of the room. I have faith." Caitlin nodded, realizing he was saying nothing with a lot of words. "And now I must go back and join the fun, and so must you." He escorted her out the door, placing his hand on the small of her back as he did, causing her to feel a pleasurable but unwelcome buzz.

Sipping her coffee at the lonely table, Caitlin thought about what Mike would make of John. They'd certainly meet eventually, at some holiday party or corporate gathering. Caitlin preemptively dreaded that day. She checked her phone. Nine fifteen. Where was everyone? She picked at a piece of toast. No appetite yet.

She saw Debra Foley enter the restaurant, dressed in a billowing black tent dress that was about three sizes too big. Caitlin and Debra had chatted last night, Debra giving her an "I'm sorry that everyone is being rude to you" spiel after Martin made that comment about how much money Caitlin was making. Debra had apologized profusely, clearly embarrassed that she was captaining a leaky ship. Caitlin had waved it off, though she'd been rattled—even more people she'd have to prove her worth to.

Now Caitlin, battling one of the worst hangovers of her life, was the one who was embarrassed.

"How are you this morning?" said Debra, sitting down next to her.

"Late night for me! I never go out anymore, I'm such a lightweight." She worried Debra could smell the booze on her. She'd showered but could still feel it brewing inside.

"I'm not feeling too great," said Debra. Caitlin was relieved to hear it. "Looks like everyone else also had too much fun—it's nearly nine thirty, and we're the only ones here!"

"Madison's agenda said nine A.M. sharp, so I've been here since then," said Caitlin.

"Yes, we all just ignore Madison during these trips," said Debra. Caitlin could see Debra had tried to apply brow liner, but one eyebrow was filled in more than the other—a Mrs. Potato Head with missing pieces. "I'm sorry, I should have told you that. Things seem to be escaping my mind lately," said Debra. "I must need a vacation." Caitlin gently smiled. Debra was one of those sad HR ladies, thanklessly working all hours, unmarried, no kids, doing the glory-less behind-the-scenes tasks that kept the company running. Everywhere Caitlin had worked had at least one of them. A Debra. Or a Karen. Or an Ann.

Zach plopped down next to Debra and lowered his head onto the table. He was in a rumpled T-shirt, his eyes red, his face covered in salt-and-pepper stubble.

"Here are my dancing queens," he said, lifting his head up for a second.

"Nope, not me," said Debra. "I did one lap at LIV and then went back to the hotel. It was the best decision of my life."

Caitlin felt her cheeks get hot. He must have been referring to her. She ignored the comment.

"I must say, that was the wildest first night of an executive retreat we've had yet," said Zach, sitting up and motioning to the waitress for coffee. "Did anyone see John leave LIV? I headed out without catching him."

"No, I never even saw him there," said Debra. Caitlin shook her head no. She had no idea if she'd seen him or not.

In walked Martin and Nikki, both in sunglasses, followed by Olive, wearing bright red lipstick. They were all in variations of a Miami theme, the women in bright prints, and Martin in a breezy linen shirt and fancy men's sandals. Everyone sat down. It was now nine forty-five.

"Olive, you look fine," said Zach. "Why do all the rest of us look like shit?"

"It's called putting lipstick on a pig," she said, laughing. "I am truly shattered, but I've put on makeup to cover it up."

"I tried that, too," said Debra with a sigh. "Clearly it didn't work as well on me."

"Debra, you look fresh as a daisy," said Zach. "I can't say the same for old Martin over here. . . ."

"Zach, shut up," said Martin. "Look who's talking. You look like a guy on a bender, with all that scruff."

Caitlin was getting a sense of the dynamics among Aurora's executives; it felt like a group of trash-talking college friends rather than coworkers.

"I feel like I was hit by a truck," said Nikki, sipping an iced latte. "I used to be able to hold my liquor, but last night kicked my butt," she said. Caitlin was feeling better, both physically—the nausea was subsiding, the headache wasn't quite so brutal—and mentally. They were all in as bad shape as she was. Dallas arrived, walking in with a skip in his step. She'd put her foot in her mouth last night when she'd given him a hard time about not ordering a drink at dinner. He'd explained to her nicely that he'd been sober for years. But she'd still felt like an idiot.

"Hey, all you hungover nerds," he said, scanning the menu. Caitlin stared at him in the daylight, admiring his rugged good looks. It occurred to her that he probably thought she was way too old for him, even though they were basically the same age.

John finally entered the restaurant, wearing his gigantic Persols, a cream T-shirt, and electric blue pants.

"Hello to my amazing executive team!" said John, sliding into a seat at the head of the table.

"You sound perky," said Zach. "We're all suffering here. What gives?"

"What gives is that before bed I took a new antihangover pill that my friend Gregg Massa gave me. He's a founder, too. He launched a granola bar brand for gluten-free dogs that sold to Kellogg's last year for a fortune. He got the pills from this special doctor he sees who'll only take on new patients if they have a net worth of over fifty mill," said John, taking off his sunglasses at last.

"Do the pills work?" asked Zach. "If so, can I have one?"

"They do indeed work. I feel like I went to bed at nine and didn't drink a thing. And no, you can't have one. I have only a limited supply, and I need the sale to Minimus to go through so that I can potentially get in to see this doctor." Zach laughed but John didn't. He surveyed the table, his eyes landing on Caitlin, who looked down to avoid his gaze.

"Caitlin Levy! Did you have fun last night?" The entire table quieted, everyone waiting to hear her answer. A spike of shame ran through Caitlin at the thought of them all seeing her so wasted.

"I did!" she said enthusiastically. Might as well own it. "I haven't been that drunk in ages. It was marvelous. I don't even know how I got home."

"Caitlin wins the award!" said Olive, her coffee mug raised. "Caitlin, every retreat, we give out an honorary medal to the executive who parties the hardest. You are the woman of the hour."

Caitlin felt herself blush.

"To Caitlin, the best dancer at Aurora," said Zach, clinking his water glass to Olive's mug.

"To Caitlin!" echoed John. "Hear, hear!" They all took sips of their drinks, and Caitlin relaxed into her seat, relieved to have gotten that over with. The table broke into separate conversations as they ate. Caitlin ordered buttermilk pancakes, which she devoured in minutes. She wondered how her kids were doing. Mike hadn't answered her text from last night, likely annoyed that she was out having fun while he was on childcare duty.

"Does anyone know where Jessica is?" John asked midbite of an omelet, a tiny piece of egg hanging unappealingly from his chin. No one answered. Zach shrugged.

"Still sleeping?" Zach said.

"Maybe she's working out?" said Martin.

"Swimming laps in the pool?" offered Dallas.

"The spa?" said Olive.

"It doesn't open until eleven," said Madison, who'd crept up behind them without anyone noticing. She was carrying a clipboard and was in a white baseball cap, as if ready to coach a lacrosse game.

"Maybe she ran away from us all," said Nikki, rolling her eyes.

"Maybe she's dead," said Zach.

"That's not funny," said Debra. "I'll text her." They waited a few minutes, everyone looking at their respective phones.

"Anything?" asked John. Debra shook her head no.

"Jessica always answers texts right away. It's weird that she hasn't responded," said Debra, her forehead wrinkles flexed.

Caitlin wasn't concerned. She'd seen Jessica coming out of the bathroom at ZZ's and knew she was most likely still sleeping off the drugs. But Caitlin wasn't about to volunteer that information to the larger group.

"After breakfast, we must find Jessica," declared John. "We need everyone accounted for before we start the presentations. I won't leave any of my generals behind!"

"But, John, we need to stick to the agenda," said Madison, worry spreading over her young face. "Today is Jet Skiing day!"

"The agenda is now: Find Jessica Radum. Write that down, Madison." She dutifully did. "No presentations. No lunch. We can go Jet Skiing after we find her."

If this executive scavenger hunt meant that Caitlin didn't have to give her PowerPoint, she was all for it.

"Let's break into teams," said John, taking another large bite of his omelet. They all groaned in sync.

"John, she's probably just recovering. Let's get on with the day," said Dallas. "This is a waste of time. Time is money, efficiency is life." ("WTF?" Olive said loudly.) Caitlin noticed that Dallas spoke to John in a way the other executives didn't: directly, harshly, as if they were peers, which Caitlin supposed they were.

"Dallas, you're with Nikki and Olive," said John, ignoring him. "You go look for her in the lobby restaurant. Maybe she got confused about the venue." Dallas shook his head and stayed put.

"Debra, Zach, Martin, you head up to her room and give the door a strong knock—Madison, what number is it?"

"Eight three four," said Madison on demand.

"Caitlin, you're with me," said John. "We'll go to the beach! I have some additional business to discuss with you as we go." Caitlin saw Nikki stick her tongue out at Debra. Were they all talking about her behind her back?

John stood up. Everyone else just sat there.

"Troops! One of our own is missing! Saving Private Radum time, people." John waved his finger in the air. No one moved.

"The fact that I have to even say this leads me to believe that you don't have your eyes on the prize," John continued, frustrated. "We're about to undergo some heavy due diligence for our sale, and Minimus and the press are going to be all over us." Caitlin noticed Olive perking up at the word "press."

"We cannot be seen—by anyone—to be in any sort of disarray. One of our executives hasn't shown at breakfast. If she's sick, if she's sleeping, if she's just relaxing at the pool, we must know. Do you hear me? Do you want the team at Minimus to catch wind of this? Do you want to potentially derail our sale? *Not* get your money?" Caitlin watched as each of the executives stood up and gathered into their assigned groups.

"I'll start a text thread so we can stay in touch," said Debra with a sigh. "I think this is silly, but I'm sure we'll find her soon, and then we can get on with the day."

"It's Jet Skiing day," whimpered Madison.

Without a goodbye, which Caitlin was realizing was his "thing," John turned and walked out of the restaurant, fast. Caitlin struggled to keep up as he hurried out the front entrance of the hotel.

"We could have gone through the back," said Caitlin breathlessly as she lightly jogged at his pace. The sun was strong and it was already midsummer-ish hot.

"I like to cover as much ground as possible, as a general rule," said John, checking his Apple Watch. "So far today I've done five thousand steps. I took a walk this morning down the beach before breakfast." As they crossed the boardwalk, they encountered an enormous iguana, green and mottled, with a hanging orange beard, scurrying in the other direction. Caitlin, unused to seeing small dinosaurs in the wild, gasped.

"Ah, yes, the iguanas have taken over Miami," said John as they walked onto the beach, dotted with lounge chairs and umbrellas. "They originated as pets from Mexico and have now become a full-on invasive species in South Florida. They're real pests and very sneaky, to boot. They eat my plants and leave poop all over my pool deck. People kill them with traps and pellet guns."

There were a few sunbathers out, early birds getting in a tan before lunch. Caitlin and John wove in and out of the setups, checking each chair for Jessica, but she wasn't among the small crowd. Caitlin's head throbbed in the heat.

John sat down on the edge of an empty chair, facing the ocean, calm and colorful, and patted the seat next to him for Caitlin. She hovered but didn't accept the invitation. She didn't have her sunglasses, and her eyes were burning in the bright light. They watched a motorboat speed by, pulling a pair of parasailers high in the air, their legs dangling. Caitlin couldn't make out their faces.

"Jessica could be anywhere," Caitlin said. "This feels like a waste of our time, going out looking for her. She'd answer her phone if she wanted to be found. Has she done anything like this before?" What would Mike think if she told him she'd spent the day looking for a missing team member? He'd most likely tell her to renege on her contract before she started, and to look for a new job. That's why she'd already decided to keep all of this from him.

Caitlin, exhausted, finally took a seat next to John, which he didn't seem to mind, shifting a few inches to the left to accommodate her on his chair. She was wearing flouncy cotton shorts, and her exposed knee pushed into John's blue pants. She hadn't done it purposefully, but she also didn't move it away.

John looked around the beach—the chairs surrounding them were empty—and then surprised Caitlin by leaning into her conspiratorially. She looked at his lips and wasn't repulsed. "Caitlin, I need you to keep what we spoke about last night to yourself," said John softly, causing her to reflexively shiver.

Right then, Debra, Martin, and Zach came marching up to them, looking defeated. Caitlin willed her face to look neutral and moved her body away from John's.

"Not in her room. Or, at least, not answering her door," said Martin.

"I know I said this was dumb, but now I'm starting to get worried," said Debra.

"Let's give it until lunch. If we still haven't heard from her, we can start to panic," said Zach.

"Let's head back to the hotel and check in with the other platoon," said John.

Caitlin walked along the beach with her colleagues, her feet still aching from last night's escapades. She had a flash from LIV. Had she spoken to Jessica? She could picture her black-and-white dress under the club's lights, looking up at her face, half-hidden in the darkness. And what did John mean—she should keep what they'd talked about to herself? Caitlin felt sick at the thought that she couldn't remember any of it.

"They haven't found her in the other restaurant," said Debra, holding her phone. "We're going to meet everyone in the lobby."

As they entered the hotel Caitlin scoured the depths of her brain for any shred of memory. But nothing came.

Dallas, Nikki, and Olive were standing near the boutique in the lobby, a small shop that sold overpriced women's bathing suits and cover-ups. Madison was pacing next to them.

"Jessica's not here," said Olive. "And we've all texted and called her. Nothing." John scrunched up his face. Caitlin was desperate to know what else he had been going to say to her on the beach.

"Oh. My. God," said Olive in a loud whisper. They closed in around her. She put her finger to her lips. "Don't look, don't look, don't look, but over there, sitting on the leather couch by the door, is Kaya Bircham, from *TechRadar*." *TechRadar* was an influential online publication that regularly broke juicy industry news. Kaya Bircham was their star reporter, and, right now, her beat was entirely Aurora-slash-Minimus. Someone had leaked info to her last night about the sale, and the story she'd written was the number one most shared article on TechRadar.com.

"This is *not* good," said Olive. "She must have gotten wind of our executive retreat and is now trying to dig. Let me handle this. No one say anything to her. You all go somewhere else, please."

Olive sauntered over to where Kaya was sitting.

"Do you know where we can go?" said Madison with a sweet smile.

"Back to bed?" said Nikki.

"Jet Skiing!" said Madison. Zach booed.

"Yes, let's do that," said John, eyeing Olive and Kaya warily.

"Yay!" said Madison. "Please go up to your rooms and change into your bathing suits. I'll call Ubers for everyone in fifteen minutes. See you all downstairs in a bit!"

Caitlin needed another coffee. She'd felt okay at the beach, but her hangover was still clinging like a small child. She went to the lobby café near the check-in desk, and was perusing the muffins when she felt a tap on her shoulder. It was Martin.

"I feel like we got off on the wrong foot," he said. He was mischievously handsome, with brown eyes set in an angular face. "I shouldn't have made that comment last night about how much John was paying you," he said. "I'm just going through some stuff. It's me, not you, as they say."

Caitlin waited a beat before answering, making him squirm. She knew his type—dramatic, demanding, good but never quite as amazing as they think they are. She'd forgive him, but he had to know she wasn't a pushover.

"Yes, it was inappropriate," she said, staring straight at him. "And I'm sorry if you think you're undervalued, but that's not my problem."

"No," said Martin, his cheeks red. "It's not your problem." Caitlin figured she'd push her luck with him. If it had a chance of solving the where-is-Jessica problem, why not?

"Well, I'm off to change into my Speedo," he said, backing down.

"Before you do, I have a quick question for you," said Caitlin. The color drained from his creamy skin. "I saw Jessica coming out of the bathroom last night. The men's bathroom. Do you know anything about that? I haven't told anyone yet, but I thought I'd ask you first."

For a second, Caitlin thought Martin might turn and run away. Instead, he pulled her sleeve and gestured toward the elevator. "Room four seven two," he whispered, then walked off quickly. Caitlin bought an iced latte before following him up a few minutes later.

Martin's room was pristine. He'd unpacked meticulously, with toiletries lined up neatly in the bathroom and clothing hanging from the open closet, color coordinated. The suite smelled like him, a delicious, musky cologne hanging in the air.

He sat down on the mini couch next to the kitchenette, crossing his legs. Caitlin stood nearby, her latte bringing her back to life.

"I haven't told this to anyone," said Martin, "and I'd appreciate it if you don't, either." Caitlin nodded, though she wasn't sure what she was agreeing to.

"Last night, at ZZ's, I shared some cocaine with Jessica," he said, the words tumbling out. "I'd gotten it from a dealer that Dallas knows, a guy named TJ. He'd delivered it to the room earlier in the afternoon." Martin got up and started walking in circles. It made Caitlin uncomfortable.

"We only did one line each in the men's bathroom. It was just a little! I felt fine, it barely even did anything," he said. "If there was something wrong with the drugs, wouldn't I have been affected as well?" His eyes were wide with anxiety.

"I'm not an expert on drugs, Martin," said Caitlin. "I'm a forty-year-old mom with two kids." She was beginning to feel bad for him and was annoyed with herself for it. He'd gotten himself into this mess by bringing drugs to a company party.

"Do you think I killed her? Was it laced or something?" Martin finally sat back down. His voice had gone shaky. He was clearly about to lose it.

"I don't think people die from one line of cocaine," Caitlin said in the tone she used to calm down her children.

"Oh, thank god," he said. Tears spilled from Martin's eyes. Caitlin reached over to the bedside table and grabbed him a tissue.

"Do you think we have to tell Debra? It'll end up being a whole HR thing if we do. . . ." said Martin pleadingly.

"We don't have to tell her yet," said Caitlin. "Hopefully Jessica turns up soon. My thought is that she partied too hard, and she's still passed out in bed."

"Listen, I don't like Jessica," said Martin, dabbing his eyes. "But I don't want her dead. There are only two people in my life I'd murder—my ex Wes and my ex Archie, and they're both alive and well and married to each other, with a baby on the way."

Caitlin laughed.

"Was there anything about her that seemed off?" asked Caitlin. She saw Martin flinch.

"Well, I don't talk to Jessica that much, so I wouldn't know what was normal for her," he said. "But she did mention to me that she had reservations about the sale, which I thought was odd. She said Minimus should be wary of what John was selling." Caitlin took this in.

"I also briefly spotted her and Dallas arguing outside the club later—I was smoking a cigarette, I know, gross. Then I saw her again in LIV at some point, but it was kind of a blur," he said. "She had on that black-and-white dress, the bandage kind that was cool in like 2005. Jessica has a terrible sense of style."

Caitlin was amused by his bitchiness. She looked at her phone and saw they were late for Jet Skiing.

"I have to change. This will stay between us. Thanks for the apology."

Martin nodded gratefully. Caitlin left his room, but not before she could feel the musk settling into her skin.

Nikki Lane

———

Sometimes, Nikki Lane thought about having sex with Aurora's chief technology officer, Dallas Joy. Dominating him. Making him squeal. She loved Clive, but that didn't mean she couldn't be attracted to other men. And there were things about Dallas—his engineering swagger, his handsome, white-boy charisma, even the way he was constantly speaking corporate gibberish—that Nikki couldn't get enough of (despite him, in theory, annoying the shit out of her).

Sometimes, when they were both working late, she'd loiter by his office and watch him disappear into his computer, figuring out puzzles and making everything look beautiful. He'd zone out, reach flow, and come to hours later, with no sense of time having passed. Nikki would bring him a coffee and he'd smile at her sleepily, then he'd take her through what he'd accomplished. Coding, he'd told her once, was when he felt most alive. Ketamine, he'd confessed, used to be a close second.

Nikki resented how easily everything came to Dallas. She hated that he dumped his work on her and then left to go ride his precious bike. She hated that everyone deferred to him, even though *she* was the one running the place. But she still couldn't resist him. Dallas had grown up in Los Angeles, and he had that bratty LA attitude. His dad was a successful lawyer, working with entertainment companies, and his mom stayed home and played lots of tennis. They were an impressive family. Nikki had met his parents when they'd visited the New York office, Dallas's dad in Gucci loafers, his mom with her perfect blowout.

Nikki had never even *thought* to bring her mom and dad into the office. Not that they were embarrassing—they were kind and attentive; her mom was a home nurse, and her dad was a retired bus driver. But why would she invite them to work? To see the piles of paper on her desk and the fancy craft beer kegerator in the kitchen that no one ever used?

Nikki, an only child, had grown up in a nice area in the Bronx, solidly middle class. Her mom had been savvy enough to get her bright girl a scholarship, and Nikki had gone to Sacred Heart, in Manhattan, from kindergarten to twelfth grade. It was thirty minutes and a world away on the 6 train, Nikki getting off at Ninety-Sixth Street, stepping out into the sunshine-y wealth of the Upper East Side.

It turned out that Nikki was genuinely brilliant with numbers. This both pleased her—it was fun to be talented at something, particularly something she enjoyed—and pissed her off. Everyone at school was so happy that she was remarkable, as if that justified having her there among the elite. She decided at a young age that she would eventually make as much as her friends' dads did. Herself. A young Black woman keeping up with the Park Avenue Joneses. Then her kids could attend the best schools without feeling like they had to *be* the best in order to do so. She wanted to have mediocre, privileged children. Wasn't that the real American dream?

Nikki was sitting on a smooth stone bench outside the hotel lobby, waiting for the rest of the team to arrive. Dallas came and plopped down beside her. He reminded Nikki of the boys she'd known growing up, the ones from St. Bernard's and Trinity, born with confidence in their own abilities.

"What's up? You going Jet Skiing?" Nikki said. His smell, reminiscent of orange bitters, was familiar to her. They'd spent so many nights huddled together at a desk, working on Aurora's CMS, or dealing with a Google algorithm change, or attempting to improve their tech.

Nikki had gone to Yale, but Dallas had gone to Harvard, which he never let anyone forget. Afterward, he'd landed at Facebook, becoming one of the young company's stars, palling around with Mark when he visited Menlo Park, staying in New York to lead the East Coast team. There he fell in with a group of tech bros, led by an engineer named Robbie Long, a legend in their circles. Robbie, according to lore, was a charismatic, creative, funny guy who was generous with his money and time. He liked connecting people—it was through Robbie that Dallas had met Jessica Radum and John Shiller—and always had great advice for young grads trying to break in. Robbie had been engaged to his college sweetheart, Meagan Hudson. Nikki knew that Meagan owned a piece of Aurora. Meagan was about to become rich, too.

"I suppose I have to. John is insisting," said Dallas. His arm, tan and warm, touched hers, and she shifted away from him. She wanted to tell him about Trade Desk; she wanted to confess everything. Dallas would be pissed she'd used a fake offer for leverage, but he'd never rat her out. She was too valuable to him for that.

Instead, since he surely knew the ins and outs of the Minimus deal, she decided to push on that front. "About *my* equity . . ." she said, waiting for Dallas to jump in. But he didn't. "You know you can't run the engineering team alone, and I hope my share grant reflects that," she continued. Dallas didn't say anything. A souped-up Jeep went speeding past, and a thumping bass hit the air, reminding her of last night at LIV, suffering through the pulsing beat. Dallas and John had secured the tables when they'd arrived, checking in with the manager at the door as the rest of the team wandered away to take in the scene. Nikki had a mental image of John and Dallas huddled together in the darkness, punctuated by flashes and deafening music. There was a bucket of vodka sitting in front of them, but neither had poured a drink.

"Dallas? Dallas?" Nikki noticed he was in his own world, not paying attention to her question. "Dallas, Jessica said something to me last night. . . ." She saw him stiffen, his face go blank. "She said there was stuff going on. What stuff? You know I won't tell anyone," said Nikki. "You know I'm loyal to you—"

"Listen," he said, cutting her off. "This sale should be good for you. I'm going to take my payout and skedaddle, head off into the sunset, maybe start raising some goats. And you're going to get everything you want."

She frowned. Why was he being so weird?

Nikki missed Clive. She missed her real friends, a group of successful, like-minded Black women whom she'd met in college. They were the only ones who could truly relate to her, unlike Olive and Debra and Caitlin, who thought that because they were all women in the workplace, they were the same. Well, newsflash: They weren't. They didn't know how it felt to be spoken down to, discounted, mistaken for the maintenance staff or worse.

It had happened to Nikki, at her first job out of college, when she was working as an entry-level engineer at AOL. She'd dressed differently then, more casually, in jeans and tees, trying to fit in, even though she knew it was impossible. She'd been entering a team meeting when some guy walked by and said, "Thanks for tidying up last night; I know I left my desk a mess." Then he'd skipped off, pleased as pie that he'd remembered to thank "the help." Nikki had seethed, her whole body shaking with humiliation, but had gone into her meeting anyway, pretending she was fine, ready to discuss operations.

She'd vowed then that no one would ever mistake her for a cleaning woman again. She'd buzzed her hair, dyed it blond, started spending all her money on designer clothes. Luckily, her trajectory up helped cover those costs, and now here she was, with the opportunity to become Aurora's CTO in reach. At this point, she'd kill to keep her job.

Then Dallas abruptly patted Nikki's arm and headed inside, leaving her alone on the bench, sweating and confused.

She pulled out her phone and texted Debra.

Where are you? I need to speak to you.

I'm in Jessica's room! Come meet me here, Debra responded.

Nikki's heart sped up. What was Debra doing in Jessica's hotel room? Intrigued, Nikki headed back into the lobby. She passed Martin on the way to the elevators.

"Where are you going?" he asked suspiciously.

"Just back up upstairs. I forgot my wallet," she said, panicking a little.

"Why do you need your wallet to go Jet Skiing?" said Martin. Nikki shook her head dismissively and walked past him to the elevators, which she took up to the eighth floor. Debra let her into the room after a light knock.

Debra was in her Jet Skiing outfit—boys' board shorts and a long-sleeve rash guard. Her Oakley sunglasses were perched at the top of her bob, and she was radiating a nervous energy.

Nikki looked around to see Jessica's room filled with Jessica's stuff—her suitcase on the floor, toiletries in the bathroom.

"So she didn't pack," said Nikki. "How did you get in here?"

"I keep everyone's second key, in case someone loses theirs," said Debra. "It's an HR thing."

"Ew, that's so unnecessary. So you can come into my room while I'm sleeping? I bet Madison has the keys, too. You guys can come murder me together."

Debra ignored her, scurrying to and fro, lifting up the bedsheets, looking under the couch.

"Have you found anything?" asked Nikki, opening Jessica's dresser drawers and rifling through some clothes in her suitcase.

"No, not yet," said Debra. "It all looks normal to me. I told you to come because . . . look. . . ." Debra pointed to Jessica's messy bed. On top of it was Jessica's Aurora company laptop, closed.

Nikki sighed.

"I thought you might be able to . . ." said Debra.

"Wouldn't it be an HR violation to break into someone's work computer?" said Nikki with a grin.

Debra didn't return the smile.

"I don't know what's going on, but I do know that it's not good. For us, for John, for Aurora." Debra was starting to get worked up, something she did when she felt out of control. "I get that you have your foot out the door," Debra continued. "But I need to find a missing employee. It's my job as chief people officer, and I need your help."

Nikki picked up the laptop with a groan. Then she laughed, even though she knew it would piss Debra off. It did.

"Sorry, sorry, but in what actual world is it your job to find a missing person?" said Nikki. "We work in tech. We sit behind computers all day and drink expensive kombucha teas. You're not NYPD."

They heard a rap on the door, and both froze. Nikki looked at Debra, her eyes wide. The banging came again. Then they heard someone tapping a key card on the lock.

Debra roughly grabbed Nikki's arm, and pulled her toward the door to the mini balcony off the bedroom. They slipped outside, huddling off to the side so they were hidden by the floor-to-ceiling curtains inside the room. Nikki had a quick second of appreciation for the view—the cloudless sky melting into the blue ocean, the white sand, sunbathers dotting the shore. From here, the seediness of the place was hidden: the women in cheap thong bikinis, the loud peddlers of soda and water, the homeless people sleeping, spreading their unwashed scent. It all looked pristine from the eighth floor of their luxury hotel, the dirt concealed underneath the surface.

Nikki peeked into the room through the tiny area not blocked by the curtain. She saw Dallas standing near the entrance, taking in his surroundings. Then he started going through drawers. Debra dug her nails into Nikki's palm. Nikki felt the cold metal of Jessica's laptop in her other hand.

She watched as Dallas raided Jessica's room for a few minutes, disappearing into the bathroom, opening closets, eventually shaking his head, as if to signal to himself that he'd found nothing. Then he left, the door clicking behind him with a thud. Debra and Nikki stayed out on the balcony for another five minutes.

Eventually, Debra motioned to Nikki to head back inside. They did so, in silence. What was Dallas looking for? Maybe he was searching for clues and was just as innocent as Nikki and Debra. But maybe it was something more sinister. Nikki put the laptop in her Vuitton tote. She'd hide it in her room before they left for Jet Skiing. Jessica was probably too smart to put anything incriminating on her Aurora-provided MacBook, but Nikki would check anyway. She owed that to Debra.

The hallway was empty. They rushed back to the elevators, Nikki's bag heavy with stolen evidence. Jet Skiing awaited.

12:00 P.M., Tuesday, April 24

Aurora Team in Miami; Minimus Talks Ongoing

By Kaya Bircham

A quick update to yesterday's breaking news about search giant Minimus's potential acquisition of adtech biggie Aurora.

It seems the Aurora team is enjoying a swanky "corporate retreat" at the 1 Hotel in Miami Beach. Shiller relocated to Miami during the pandemic and hosts an annual getaway there for his top brass, which include his cofounder and CTO, Dallas Joy; his CRO, Zach Wagner; Aurora's new head of events, Caitlin Levy; and their communications director, Olive Green, among other company leaders.

According to a source with direct knowledge, Shiller hopes to complete the deal in the next couple of days, which would give the Aurora team much to celebrate during their trip. Minimus, for its part, wouldn't comment on the deal, but insiders say there are a few naysayers in its midst. Concerns around the deal center on Aurora's new events strategy, the details of which are still under wraps. Check back for more updates.

Olive Green

———

Olive Green felt fabulous. Well, more like fabulous with a sprinkling of stress. She was bouncing over the waves in Lake Pancoast, first in command on a Jet Ski, driving recklessly, having a grand old time. Zach was grabbing on to her waist, the water spraying their faces at every sharp turn. Occasionally, when they were far enough away from the rest of the team, Zach's hands would travel up to Olive's breasts, peeking out from her life jacket like taut balloons.

They'd set out earlier from one of John's tech buddy's homes, a large, blocky house, right on the water. His friend, Stewart Holden, was the CEO of a company called Cardeo, which sent out digital birthday messages from long-lost relatives. Though he was a single forty-two-year-old, Stewart owned five Jet Skis, which he'd lent to John for the occasion (John owned only one Jet Ski, which was currently being serviced). "Let's gooooo!" Zach kept yelling, urging Olive to speed faster over the waves, racing alongside the others. She did as he commanded, feeling better than she had in ages. Caitlin and Nikki were also on a Jet Ski together, Debra and Martin on another, and Dallas and John were both riding solo, one-upping each other with twists.

Zach had finally convinced Olive to have sex with him last night, real sex, and it had been amazing. Olive couldn't remember the last time she'd enjoyed sleeping with someone so much. Maybe when she'd first gotten together with Henry? Maybe at university? They'd gone back to the hotel together after LIV, traveling to Zach's room in separate elevators on the off chance someone from Aurora was going up at the same time. Olive arrived a few minutes after Zach, her dark blond hair frizzing out of its careful knot, her mascara smudged attractively.

She'd pushed him toward the bed and started to get down on her knees, initiating their usual routine, but Zach lifted her up next to him. She'd given him an opening that day. She'd even let him cuddle her in the back of the Uber, which was a first.

"Now, Olive, you know how much I enjoy what we've been doing," Zach had said, rubbing her back up and down as he spoke. She closed her eyes. "But, to me, even though the word 'job' is in blow job, oral sex is as much of a work violation as penetration. I bet it would make Debra *pretty* mad if she knew you've been sucking my dick."

She'd nodded, her eyes still closed.

"So, what I'm saying is . . ."

She opened her eyes and looked at him.

"I know what you're saying," she'd said, and Zach knew he'd won. He'd asked her to stay afterward, but she'd refused, sneaking out at about 4:00 A.M. to go back to her room. She'd then had a dreamless, peaceful rest, not waking until 8:30 A.M., feeling like a new woman. Her hair still smelled like his cologne.

The Jessica thing, the Kaya thing . . . Both annoyances she hadn't seen coming, but Olive was trying to put them out of her mind. She was enjoying Jet Skiing. She'd been worried she wouldn't make it, but Olive had dispatched Kaya Bircham quickly, giving her a few nuggets with which to write a short, harmless item about their executive retreat, and dangling a carrot of an exclusive John Shiller profile if Kaya agreed to leave them alone for the time being. Kaya had been excited by the idea and had promised to go back to New York. So here Olive was, on the open water, erotically bumping up and down. Life was good, and she was about to get rich.

Olive swerved to a stop in the middle of the bay, pulling up alongside John, who was signaling for them all to gather. John was in neon-green swim trunks and was shirtless under his undone life jacket, his chest pale and hairless (the rest of the men—even Martin—were in T-shirts).

The group idled together, the small waves bobbing them around as John spoke.

"Team, team, team, it's lovely to see you all enjoying the water on this gorgeous Miami day," he said. Olive wondered if John was purposefully flexing his pecs, as they seemed permanently hardened.

"We're down an executive, but the fun continues anyway. If you thought you were going to get out of Florida without racing a Jet Ski, you thought wrong!" he said.

"Are you fucking kidding me?" Olive said into Zach's ear. "He's going to get us all killed."

"Uh, John," interjected Debra. She was sitting in the driver's seat, her hair pulled back into a small ponytail, a smear of zinc down her nose. Martin was nestled behind her, holding up his phone in order to get a flattering selfie.

"I don't think we should race," said Debra. "Someone could get hurt. We haven't signed waivers for any of this. Aurora would be liable."

John scoffed.

"Debra, relax. We are with the A-list here, no one's suing anyone. Isn't that right?" They all nodded reluctantly.

"This is how it's going to work: Everyone will line up here, next to me. I'm going to say one, two, three, go! And when I do, you'll take off toward the canal, about a five-minute drive away. Madison's waiting there at the entrance to see who arrives first."

"What does the winner get?" asked Nikki, fashionable in an orange bikini. Caitlin was clinging to her and looking a bit green.

"This is the best part!" said John excitedly. "The winners get five thousand extra shares each."

A murmur went through the group. Zach pinched Olive's butt. "Go get 'em, Olive," he said into her hair.

Olive would happily take an additional 5,000 shares on top of whatever else John was doling out. She was hoping for another grant of around 100,000, which would equal a couple of million after the sale. That would be enough to make her feel secure, to stick it to Henry, as she dreamed of doing. She was the director of communications, after all, and had crafted

Aurora's image, landing John on magazine covers and strategically keeping him away from TV (the no-eye-contact thing didn't go over well on-screen). And, most important, she'd protected John from negative stories.

Last year, she'd managed to kill a potential piece in *Jezaroo*, a feminist news website, in which a few women had accused John of being rough during sex. The reporter had unearthed a mini community of scorned girls after she'd heard a rumor that John was into S&M (true). They'd slept with John and subsequently been ditched by him, and were threatening to go on the record about John's predilection for whipping and chains. Olive had to track each down, meeting individually with these beautiful, pathetic creatures, and convince them it wasn't in their best interest to publicly accuse a powerful CEO of doing something that, frankly, was perfectly legal. "This will be your top Google result for the rest of your life," Olive said to them, putting her hand on their shoulders for emphasis. "I'm a mother; I would tell my daughters the same thing. So you slept with a playboy. We've all been there. Did he force you to have sex with him?" They'd sadly shake their heads no.

John didn't force them to have sex! John was rich, John was successful, John was famous. They'd thrown themselves at him and then been disappointed when he hadn't called them the next day. One by one, they agreed to recant.

Olive considered this while she and Zach drifted on the Pancoast, waiting for their CEO to start the race. The main competition, Olive thought, was Debra and Martin. Dallas would probably win if he tried, but he'd think it was lame to put effort into one of John's games. Debra had grown up in Upstate New York, vacationing on the Finger Lakes. She was a Jet Ski queen.

"One," John called out. Olive revved the engine in preparation. "Two!" he continued. Olive looked to her left to see Debra and Martin lined up next to them, Debra's body coiled and ready, Martin holding on to her with a death grip. "Three!!" Olive took off, pushing the throttle at full tilt, sending them shooting forward, salt water spraying Zach's face. She could see Debra and Martin in her peripheral vision, sending small waves in their direction, causing their Jet Ski to keel from side to side.

Olive spotted Madison standing at the entrance to the canal in her bright white hat, the metal of her clipboard glinting in the sun.

The bay was light on boat traffic, it being late morning, midweek. So Olive was surprised when, as they barreled toward the finish line, toward Madison and the bonus shares, a large motorboat came from behind and sped loudly in front, engulfing them in its wake. Olive, determined to win, didn't let go of the throttle, and the Jet Ski soared over a swell, sending them flying up in the air, twisting in the wind, and then crashing down on the water, tipping precariously. For a moment, Olive thought they might be okay, that they could right themselves. But instead the Jet Ski fell to its side, sending Zach and Olive sliding into the bay. Olive was thrust underwater by the force of the fall, her life jacket finally bringing her back to the surface to see the Jet Ski fifty yards away, floating like a dead body. Where was Zach?

Debra and Martin zoomed over, stopping a few feet from Olive.

"Are you okay?!" Debra hollered. By that point, John and Dallas had also come to check on her. Olive was still trying to get her bearings, wondering if Zach was hurt. The water was warm. She realized she'd lost her sunglasses in the fall, so as she squinted over to where Nikki and Caitlin were circling, she was relieved to see Zach's head poking out of the bay.

"I think I'm fine," said Olive. "Miraculously."

"Here, get on my Jet Ski with me," said John, inching toward Olive. She hoisted herself, with difficulty, onto the vehicle, sitting behind John, who then circled around toward Zach. Dallas followed, and they stopped in a line formation in front of him.

"For the love of god, someone get me out of the water," said Zach loudly. Relief flooded Olive's soaked body.

"I'll help you," said Dallas. Zach paddled over to him, and Dallas leaned over and lifted him, settling him into the second seat.

"Light as a feather," Dallas said, half-jokingly, and Zach punched him in the back.

"I cannot believe we survived that," said Olive. They'd shut off their engines and were in a semicircle. In the distance, Olive saw a brown pelican crashing down into the water, only to emerge a second later with an unlucky fish in its beak.

"I'm not going to say 'I told you so' about the race, or having everyone sign waivers, but, well, I told you so," said Debra, shaking her head. Debra was also the queen of "I told you sos." "As head of HR, I hold myself responsible. I'll never be so flippant again."

"I've called Rodrigo to come get Stewart's abandoned Jet Ski!" Madison yelled over to them with a wave. John gave her a thumbs-up.

Olive was ready for bed, and it wasn't even lunchtime. She'd started to feel a crick in her neck from the crash, and her head was pounding. She heard John clear his throat, likely preparing for a motivational speech. Olive wasn't sure she could take it.

"Team, team, team," said John. The waves were starting to build, and for a moment Olive had the impulse to grab John's waist to steady herself. She resisted. She'd rather fall back in the water.

"While that wasn't the race we'd planned, it was one that we'll all remember," John said.

"Yes, my whiplash will be a nice reminder," said Olive.

"Now, Olive, we're all happy you're safe and sound. I don't think you were close to death. But what you were close to was winning those five thousand shares," said John. "So, for your trouble, and so you don't sue me and Aurora"—he paused for laughter, but no one made a sound—"you and Zach will be awarded the extra shares. Congratulations to you both. May you enjoy your equity in good health." Everyone clapped. Olive was happy that she'd get a token for what was turning quickly into a very sore neck.

"All right, let's wrap up Jet Skiing, folks," said Debra. "It was fun while it lasted."

The speed limit in the canal was low, and so the executives slowly wound their way back to Stewart's house through the narrow inlet, passing the enormous homes that lined each side, half modern monstrosities, half faux-Mediterranean mansions. People in South Beach had no taste, but they sure had a whole lot of money. Olive thought again of her potential equity in the sale, and what it would mean for her lifestyle.

She could stop worrying so much about the long-term and try to enjoy her newly single life. She'd go on a shopping spree with the girls, get them all-new wardrobes. Maybe she'd buy herself a nice piece of jewelry, something as a reminder that she could be her own breadwinner. That had been the idea behind joining Aurora, a startup, and that's how John had pitched it to her. "Olive, you strike me as someone who should be in charge of your own destiny but isn't," John had said to her during their first meeting, over burgers at Minetta Tavern. "And I'm going to be the one to fix that."

Olive wondered what Zach would buy with his winnings. A Miami condo? A small yacht, perhaps? Zach would most likely get a year contract from Minimus for transition's sake, and then, Olive knew, he'd try for a plum CEO role in either retail or noncompeting tech.

"I know I'd be a great CEO, I just know it," Zach had said to Olive recently. They were lingering together in a conference room after a meeting, not wanting to part company yet. They often did this. "I have good instincts. I know how to rally a team! I'm great with investors!" he said, slightly unconvincingly. Zach resented that, at this stage in his life, he was still answering to someone else, not to mention someone like John, who was seven years his junior.

Olive stared at the back of John's head as they bumped along the inlet.

"John, can I speak to you about something?" said Olive. John didn't answer.

"John?" Nothing.

"JOHN," Olive said louder.

"Olive, I can hear you," said John, his voice even. "I'm just choosing not to engage." Olive had a sinking feeling.

"John, I want to talk to you about Caitlin Levy."

"Olive, now's not the time," said John, snapping at her. Then he sighed, relenting. "Have you ever heard of hiring to fire?"

"I think so," said Olive. "It's like at Amazon, when they hire people they know they're going to fire within a year in order to make turnover targets."

"Very good," said John. "Caitlin Levy was hired to be fired. But I can't go into more details yet. You'll know when you need to."

Now it was Olive's turn to sigh. The sun was drying her off, though her neck was still aching. She looked to her left to see Zach and Dallas floating by, Zach jokingly resting his head on Dallas's shoulder. Nikki and Caitlin overtook them, an intense look on Nikki's face behind her designer sunglasses.

Olive's stomach twisted. She'd been distracted by everything else going on, but now she was reminded of what she had done to Nikki, and it pained her anew.

A couple of weeks ago, Ben Hooks, the chief people officer at Trade Desk, had emailed Olive for a quick chat. She knew Ben through Henry—they'd gone to Dartmouth together. She and Ben kept in touch, mainly through social media, where they liked each other's career updates on LinkedIn and posted empty "Happy Birthday" messages on Facebook every year.

In truth, Olive thought Ben was emailing her to speak about a potential job at Trade Desk. Over the years, he'd hinted that she'd be a great fit at the company and had said that their CEO, Simon Horn, knew of her and was a fan of her work. An offer from Trade Desk was an appealing thought—lately, John seemed to think everything she did was wrong, and she wasn't sure how much longer she could take feeling rejected, first by her husband, then by her boss.

She hadn't even really meant to do it. She wasn't a vindictive type, or particularly jealous of people. She was confident in her own abilities and didn't feel slighted by others' successes, especially those of her female friends. Yes, she'd wanted a job offer of her own. She'd wanted to hold it over John's head and make him feel like he should have valued her more when he'd had the chance. So, she'd called Ben, feeling some excitement at the thought of being wanted, professionally, at least.

She was in her office, door closed, scanning her glass doors to make sure no one entered unexpectedly. John had a habit of popping by when he was bored, between calls and meetings. He'd pace back and forth in front of her, talking about the date he'd gone on last night, or a theory he'd arrived at about the differences between genders, or his latest Churchill purchase at auction. Olive would sit and nod and ask questions, both happy that he'd chosen her to chat with, and wishing he'd go away and let her do her work.

"Hi, Olive," Ben said, his voice cutting in and out. "Sorry for my bad reception. We're skiing this week in Telluride, and the cell service in the mountains is atrocious." Olive involuntarily winced at the news of Ben's family vacation. She and Henry had always liked each other most when they were away with Poppy and Penelope. Now she had no one to travel with.

"How's everything with you?" he asked tentatively. Ben knew about the divorce.

"All good over here," she'd said breezily. "The girls are great, work's a treat, Aurora is thriving. What would you like to speak about?" Maybe their chief communications officer was leaving, Olive thought, and Simon told Ben to personally reach out to her about the job. Maybe they were thinking about creating an entirely new role for Olive, something that combined PR and marketing. She'd been hoping to expand her purview at Aurora. She felt she was ready. But she hadn't yet found the right time to speak to John about it.

"I'd love to chat with you about Nikki Lane," said Ben, the phone dropping the signal at "Lane." Olive, stung and disappointed, felt her eyes wet with tears, which took her by surprise. She *never* cried at work. She barely cried at home—with notable exceptions, including at certain Adele songs and videos of soldiers returning home to surprise their children. She hadn't even cried when Henry told her he was leaving. Why was she crying now?

"She's a top candidate for our chief product officer role, and I'm reaching out to people who've worked with her. This is highly confidential, and I wouldn't have contacted anyone at Aurora other than you. I know you're close with her so figured you wouldn't go tattling to John about it. . . ." Olive swallowed hard. Nikki? Nikki was too young for a C-suite role like that—Olive was forty-three and still gunning for chief communications officer. The role didn't exist at Aurora, but Olive had been lobbying for a title change for years.

"Can you describe the job to me?" asked Olive, stalling. "How many people will she oversee?"

"That department handles everything product related for Trade Desk and has around a hundred people, total," said Ben. "The position reports directly to the CEO." Olive knew Nikki would love that. She hated reporting to Dallas and would love to have a bigger team at her disposal. How lucky was Nikki? Young, in love with a great guy who loved her back, no baggage, cool job, big salary. She was beautiful and stylish, and though she did occasionally lose her shit unnecessarily, she was kind to her allies and cared about her friends.

As Ben spoke, Olive looked at her reflection in the small desk mirror she used to reapply lipstick. Her jawline looked a little soft. There was one deep, straight line running across her forehead, reminding her that she was divorced and over the hill. Would anyone love her again? Had she topped out in her career? Over the years, she'd watched as her older female mentors had, one by one, been pushed out for men or younger women. There seemed to be a fifty-year-old cliff for women in her industry, and Olive was deathly afraid of the inevitable plunge.

"I don't know, Ben," she said, the words tumbling out. "This is between us, but Nikki has a temper problem that might be an issue for you. She screams at her staff and has an HR file that's longer than a Harry Potter book. I wouldn't tell you this if you weren't my friend, but if you vouch for her, it might come back to bite you." There was a pause on the other end of the line. Olive immediately wanted to take it all back, but she was silent.

"This isn't great news," said Ben eventually. "I've heard this—in a more modified form—from others, and your feedback is the nail in the coffin. Particularly because Simon prides himself on a respectful workplace, unlike that joker you work for, John Shiller, who acts like a giant six-year-old." Olive felt panic rise in her chest. Did she just ruin Nikki's chances of a huge new job? 'Cause she'd seen one wrinkle in her forehead? She cursed herself.

"John's all right once you get to know him," she replied. "He means well, he just has, um, maturity issues."

"And ego issues," added Ben. "And fashion issues."

"Okay, okay, you don't have to be mean," said Olive, suddenly defensive of her boss, who only a few minutes ago she'd wanted to ditch forever.

"Anyway, thanks for chatting, and please let me know if you think of other candidates for our CPO," said Ben. The phone then cut out, leaving Olive to her own guilty thoughts.

But then she'd heard from Martin this morning that Nikki had gotten the offer after all. Had Ben ignored Olive's comments? She couldn't imagine he'd go forward with the hire after hearing that Nikki was an HR risk. So was Nikki lying? Olive felt slightly nauseated about all the duplicity surrounding her, including her own.

John and Olive were now nearing Stewart's dock, John awkwardly maneuvering the Jet Ski into a parking slot. He cut the engine, and the two of them struggled to get off the seats. Olive's inner thighs were killing her from the ride (and from the sex the night before), and she had a hard time hoisting one leg over the side, getting entangled with John, who was doing the same thing. They both stumbled onto the dock, the rest of the team already standing there, watching and giggling.

"All right, laugh it up," said Olive. "I hope everyone remembers that I just endured a maritime crash, and I could have drowned. Who among you would be capable of taking my place as director of communications, or Zach's place as CRO?"

Debra, Olive, Martin, Nikki, and Dallas all raised their hands, laughing. John, life jacket off, was standing with Madison, who was drying him with a towel.

Olive heard a loud gasp come from Debra and Nikki. She turned to see them facing the back door. Stewart Holden ambled out of the back entrance of his house, accompanied by a woman. He was, for an entrepreneur, strikingly handsome, with olive skin, black hair, and wide blue eyes. Olive often saw him photographed with models, and she knew John was jealous of Stewart's looks and bank account. Before Cardeo, Stewart had created a different app, one that provided photo filters based on your astrological sign. It had been bought by Google for $50 million. In the tech world hierarchy, Stewart was a few rungs above John, and Olive knew that killed him.

Who was Stewart with? Was it Jessica? Olive hoped so. As they came into focus, she recognized Kaya Bircham. She was small and plain, with long brown hair and wire-rimmed glasses, and was overdressed for the Florida heat in jeans and a black blazer. Stewart walked her to where John and Zach and Olive were standing, an apologetic look on his face. What the hell was Kaya doing there?

"Kaya," Olive said loudly. "I thought you were headed back to New York." Kaya shook her head no.

"I decided to stay after I got a little tip. And Stewart here owes me a favor, so he kindly let me in." Stewart's tan skin turned pink.

"What tip?" asked Olive, standing in front of John like a PR bodyguard.

"I heard that one of your team members has disappeared. And I'm going to write a little piece on that. Unless you have something bigger you can give me. . . ." How did she know about Jessica? Olive wondered. John's lips twisted together, his hands clenched into fists.

"First," John said, clearing his throat, "we've crashed one of your Jet Skis, Stewart. Apologies." Stewart shrugged, embarrassed by the entire situation. "Second, Kaya Bircham," said John, flashing a fake smile, "let's talk."

Debra Foley

———

Debra Foley wanted to know where Jessica Radum was. Jessica Fucking Radum, more like. Debra didn't have time for this. They were eating dinner outside at Carbone, grazing on prosciutto, mozzarella, and calamari at a big table for nine, though only eight seats were taken. They'd spent the afternoon recuperating from the Jet Skiing disaster, canceling the presentations entirely, Debra lying prostrate on the couch in her suite, thinking of all the time she'd wasted on her never-to-be-seen PowerPoint. Dallas and Martin had continued to search for Jessica—around the hotel, at the beach, the pool, walking through South Beach, all the way from the 1 Hotel on Collins to Joe's Stone Crab on Washington Avenue and back again. No sign of her. Debra was still waiting for Nikki to give her a report on what she'd found on Jessica's laptop, but she didn't know how long that would take.

Goddamn Jessica. Where *could* she be? At some point, Debra would have to alert Jessica's family, but she had no idea who to call; there was no emergency contact listed in her file. Jessica's parents were both dead. Her dad had passed away when Jessica was just a baby, and her mother died when Jessica was in college at Princeton. Jessica was an only child. Debra didn't know much about her pre-Aurora, other than that she'd held an entry-level job at Apple and had hung around with John and Dallas, playing the role of the pretty girl who helped get them into clubs.

Debra imagined her own mother, Chrissy, receiving the news that Debra was missing. Debra was sure that Chrissy would immediately fly down to Miami, scouring the city block by block until she found her. Then she'd hug Debra tightly and smack her arm. "You scared the shit out of me," she'd say. Debra smiled thinking about it.

Debra had grown up the youngest girl in her family; her older brothers, Don and Jeremy, still lived near her parents in Buffalo. Debra had been the smartest of the three, an honors student who graduated top of her class at SUNY Buffalo. She'd moved to New York right after college and had gotten a gig in HR at AOL, working her way up for the next ten years until she was overseeing a team of forty. Microsoft had come calling next, and she'd jumped for the higher salary and greater responsibility. (Debra wasn't really motivated by money, though it satisfied her to be paid well for her work. She thrived on doing things perfectly, on getting *results*, on running a smooth ship.) She'd been a director at Microsoft, and she'd loved it.

She still loved it, though Aurora was an entirely different beast, a startup at which she'd had to set up every process and work scrappily across all departments. In the beginning, when the company was tiny, they'd rented a coworking space in Prospect Heights, in Brooklyn, everyone piled into two rooms, mapping out the future. Debra was in recruiting mode then, which was one of her favorite parts of the job, and she'd scroll through LinkedIn for hours, searching for the perfect fits for their open roles. Each time she hired someone great, she'd take herself out for a celebratory glass of champagne at a small wine bar nearby. She had a recurring fantasy that some cute guy would walk in and ask her what she was doing alone. She'd launch into an explanation of her job, and he'd be so wowed by her ambition and brains, so impressed by her dedication to her company, that he'd pull up a chair and order a drink, just to hear more about it.

It never happened. Instead, here she was, sitting at a work dinner, single, pretending to drink vodka. (En route to the bathroom, she'd told the bartender to make her cocktails without alcohol—she'd capped last night at three champagnes and a shot and was still feeling guilty about it.) She was secretly knocked up by who knows who and was about to incur the wrath of her executive team by telling them, one by one, how much money they were about to make in the sale of their company. Plus, Aurora's head of partnerships was still MIA, and if *TechRadar* ran with the story, they'd be totally screwed. Minimus would likely put a hold on the sale, as even a whiff of bad PR, let alone a missing persons case, would freak out their board. Then everything she'd worked toward for years would crumble. So, there was that.

She'd also had an awful conversation with John on the ride to the restaurant. They'd taken a car together from the 1, just the two of them, at her request, as she hadn't yet had the chance to speak to him about Nikki. She knew he'd be annoyed to have to deal with it, particularly with everything else going on, but she hoped she could at least get him to agree to a sizable salary bump. Nikki was already set to get 80,000 additional shares, which Debra could use in the negotiation.

They were headed down Collins Avenue, stuck in traffic next to a bouncing Ford Ranger blasting Dua Lipa.

"She's threatening to leave?" John was facing away from Debra, looking out the window. He had a hard time making eye contact generally, let alone during a conversation of any importance.

"Well," said Debra, trying to think of the best way to position it in Nikki's favor. "She knows her value, and it's more than we're giving her. I think if we can get her up to two million, she'd stay. And I think she's worth it."

John was stewing. Debra knew him so well—like a baby, she recognized his every grunt and gurgle. But he could be unpredictable, and he valued loyalty above all else. He also hated Simon Horn, Trade Desk's CEO, with a passion.

"Not happening," he said with finality. "She's out."

"But, John, we can't lose her. She's our only Black executive. Kaya Bircham and co. will go wild with the story."

"Kaya is taken care of," he said. "We're going to give her the exclusive of the sale, let her break it in *TechRadar* right after we sign. No one can ever know we were the ones to leak it. Minimus would have our heads." Debra added this to her trove of Aurora secrets. John trusted her completely, which was a blessing and a curse. If he went down, she was going down, too.

"Nikki's not getting one more penny from me." He was becoming angrier as he went on. "I've already given her so much. She's lucky to be here. If she wants to join those assholes at Trade Desk, let her." Debra knew the best way to handle John in these situations was to disengage. Anything she said would rile him up more. So she shifted gears.

"Do you think we should call the police about Jessica? Or local hospitals?" She said it lightly, probing to see his reaction.

"Uh, yes, probably, soon," said John, clearing his throat. "But I don't want to cause any alarm when we're not sure if that's necessary. This city is crawling with press informants, and I don't want anyone getting wind of the situation. The fact that Kaya Bircham knows is problem enough." They rode the rest of the way in silence, and Debra made sure to sit far away from him at dinner.

Martin took Jessica's empty chair next to Debra, pushing it closer until his face was directly in front of hers. He'd gotten darker in the course of two days, his skin nearly the color of his brown eyes.

"Nice tan, Martin," Debra offered. She knew he'd come over to talk about something or other, but she didn't feel like giving him the opening. Olive and Zach were on the other side of the table, sharing a tomato and burrata salad. Caitlin and Nikki were next to them, drinking red wine, clearly recovered from their hangovers. Nikki kept shooting Debra searching looks, which Debra was avoiding. And John and Dallas were at the heads of the table, at opposite ends, both on their phones. The dinner certainly didn't have the festive air of the previous night. John, in a white polo and purple pants, had retired the siren suit, no Churchill cigar in sight. Everyone seemed tense, shoulders raised.

"When are we going to find out about our equity?" said Martin. He was in a jungle print T-shirt and was freshly shaved, his face smooth and bony.

"Soon. Very soon. Can we talk about something else, please?" Debra pictured the cozy king-size bed in her hotel room, thinking longingly of snuggling up under the covers.

"What are we going to do about Jessica?" Martin said anxiously. "If we don't find her, can I have her extra equity?"

"Don't be a dick," said Debra.

"But you know that I deserve it, way more than she does. Or Nikki. Or Olive, for that matter. This place would fall apart without me!"

"Can you please just shut up for one second?" said Debra. It came out louder than she'd meant it to. Martin, taken aback, frowned. They were interrupted by John, who banged his wineglass with his knife, calling for attention. They quieted and looked at him, sitting there in front of a large plate of lobster ravioli. He took a bite and chewed slowly, making a "mmmm" sound as everyone watched. Debra saw Olive do a retching motion. She tried not to laugh. He cleared his throat.

"Comrades: We are under siege, but we are fighting," he said. Debra looked around the restaurant to make sure no one else was listening in. The surrounding tables were filled with trendy Miami patrons, the men in shirts unbuttoned to midchest, the women in minidresses and heels. Unsurprisingly, no one was paying attention to Aurora's boring table of middle-aged executives.

"We are still down a man, or, rather, a woman, and haven't made the progress in finding her that I hoped we would. We've also been infiltrated by the enemy—the press—and that's an ongoing situation that I'm dealing with," he said. Olive pointed to herself, and mouthed, "He means *I'm* dealing with."

"But the sale to Minimus is still on, and we're going to proceed accordingly. Tonight, I'd planned on sharing how much equity you'll be getting, and our lawyers are bringing the documents for you to sign. Right here and right now. Yes, we could have done this digitally, but I thought it'd be fun to do it the old-school way. Adds a little glamour to the process."

Right then, two men in slacks and crisp button-downs walked in from the sidewalk, past the maître d', toward the table, nodding at the waitress as they passed. These weren't the lawyers Debra had met with previously about the deal; they must be new. Debra's heart lurched into her throat as she got a clearer view of the guy on the right. He had neat brown hair parted on the side, expressive brown eyes, and brown shoes that were maybe a bit too square. He stared at her at the same time, and she quickly looked down at her plate of pasta, worried she might throw up in front of her entire team.

Marc. She remembered his name as soon as she saw him. It was Marc. He was Matt's friend from college. He was a lawyer whose firm did work with Aurora; *that's* what they'd talked about at Lisa's party. And he was the father of her unborn child.

John Shiller

——

John Shiller wasn't who he said he was. But no one was, were they? Think of his dad, Erik, sitting alone in an assisted living facility outside of San Francisco. He was no longer the same person who raised John, the warm, quick-witted man who was maybe too nice for his own good. Instead, early dementia had rendered him a kind of ghost, stuck in the past, present, and future, angry, confused, and depressed. Was that the real Erik Shiller? People had different selves based on audience, based on needs, based on environment, based on age and health.

Right then, every version of John Shiller was in a total panic. He could feel that his time was running out, the ticking bomb about to go boom. People could only get away with scams for so long, and John's number was up. Was this how Elizabeth Holmes felt when she'd wheeled out a fake blood-testing machine? What Adam Neumann experienced as the extent of WeWork's losses was publicly revealed?

John was lying on a lounge chair at the pool on the rooftop of the 1, next to Watr. People were milling about, drinking and chatting, no one taking notice of the small man in purple pants biting his nails. It was around 11:00 P.M., and he didn't know what to do or whom to speak to. He couldn't go back to his room. He couldn't be alone. At least there were other humans here to distract him, even if he didn't know any of them.

The dinner at Carbone had been a disaster. After the lawyers had arrived, John had seated the two of them, himself, and Debra at a separate table, on which Madison had placed a sign that read CONGRATS ON

YOUR SHARES! (John knew that Madison bothered the other executives, but he didn't care. She was *his* assistant, she was loyal, and she made his life better.) One by one, he'd had each employee come over, handing them an intricate piece of origami created by a pupil of Akira Yoshizawa, the original grandmaster in Japan. He'd instructed them to unfold their colorful creation—a bull for Zach, a cat for Olive, a horse for Debra, a monkey for Martin, a fish for Caitlin, an elephant for Nikki. Jessica's giraffe stayed in Madison's bag. Inside, a number written in calligraphy revealed the amount of equity they'd get before the sale.

Debra had warned him against doing it that way—"Are you insane?" is how she'd put it—but he'd brushed her off, calling her a "fun sponge." She'd also chastised him for spending $5,000 per origami creature, which she argued would have been better put toward, say, a small bonus for someone at the VP level. And she'd been right. Martin had gotten pissed. ("A monkey? Is that some kind of racist joke?") Olive had scowled. Zach had grumbled. ("Is the bull impotent?") Dallas had left before the ceremony was over; he'd been in a pissy mood all day, and John had a pretty good idea why. The dinner was just another in a recent line of John's miscalculations, and it scared him that he'd bungled something else.

It wasn't like John to have a crisis of confidence, at least outwardly, and especially at this point in his life. He'd been an awkward, overweight kid, bright but weird—he had a party trick of reciting the cabinet members of every president, which didn't go over well with other fifth-grade boys. He'd always felt most at home sitting at a computer, creating fantasy worlds. In high school, he'd found a community in Dungeons & Dragons, and had gotten involved in the early world of AOL chat groups, connecting with other World War II fanboys. The Churchill obsession was real; John felt a kinship to this squat, funny-looking man who'd managed to manipulate and motivate millions of people into doing his will.

The first time John felt normal was at college, at Stanford, where he'd met a group of similarly nerdy guys who also had goals of tech world domination. After graduation, John joined his friend Adam Gaston's new company, Cheapen, a low-rent coupon app that had a burst of popularity during a quick economic downturn. There, John had learned the startup ropes and had made an easy $5 million when it sold. Adam, who John viewed as less intelligent than he and less deserving of wealth, had made $30 million, and John vowed that next time he'd be in the driver's seat, getting the big payout as his employees took the scraps.

Soon after, he moved from San Francisco to Brooklyn. He figured if he was ever going to live in New York, that was the time; he had no ties, but he had millions to burn. That was when he met Robbie Long. Robbie took John under his wing, introducing him to a crowd that also included Jessica, who worked in partnerships at Apple, and Dallas, who was on the rise at Facebook. Robbie was engaged to his college girlfriend, Meagan, who worked at PayPal, and the five of them became a close unit, attending Burning Man, traveling together, hosting wild parties at each other's apartments.

That was probably the best time in John's life. Everything big was on the horizon, and he didn't yet have the pressure of running a real business. With the help of trainers and a tiny bit of plastic surgery, John even managed to become marginally attractive. He lost weight. He began sporting a beard to contour his doughy face. He paid a scrubbing service hundreds of thousands of dollars to remove pictures of him on the internet in which he looked chubby. A few, though, still existed, and to this day, the press trotted them out whenever they could. (A regular part of Olive's job was to call and complain when outlets used fat pictures, which he hated.)

John loved hanging out with his new friends, particularly Robbie, whom he viewed as a kindred spirit. He and Robbie would sit and talk for hours about life, about technology and entertainment, about their dreams for the future. He'd never had a buddy like that before, someone who accepted him for who he was, and seemed to like him unconditionally. He still missed Robbie every day.

John looked up at the Miami sky, dotted with just a few visible stars. A helicopter flew overhead, likely searching for a shooting suspect. Mayhem was rampant in the city—crime, drugs, fraud—but John liked it anyway. His peers had descended here a few years ago, when Florida became a refuge from the pandemic, an "open for business" state in which wearing masks was for losers. Founders and investors flocked from California and New York, forming a wealthy, connected pod, trying to one-up each other with waterfront homes and the hottest, youngest girlfriends. John now spent exactly 181 days in Florida, for tax purposes, though he still lived part-time in Manhattan, where he owned a four-million-dollar bachelor pad in Chelsea, from which he could walk to Aurora's offices. John loved walking. He walked everywhere, tracking his steps, his anxiety abating as the number ticked up, up, up.

In Miami, he was planning to gut renovate a house he'd bought recently for the bargain price of $3.5 million, and he had the right connections to do it—he was friendly with a guy on the Miami Beach zoning board, and he'd contributed enough to the mayor's office for them to ignore any construction violations. But he needed his windfall from Minimus to do it right. He was banking on that money.

The real estate market in Miami was insane, and John had been smart to get in when he did. He'd always had a talent with investments. He'd gotten in and out of crypto at just the right time. He had a collection of Rolexes that had doubled in value. He'd done well in the markets and contributed to early rounds of now-household-name companies.

John was also supremely talented at raising funds. Walking into a room of potential investors, explaining his vision, that was when John truly came to life, shedding all quirks, a snake oil salesman hawking magical algorithms. He told the same old story about Aurora to anyone who asked: the press, employees, their families. After Robbie died, John and Dallas had wanted to honor him, to make sure his legacy endured. That's why they'd called the company Aurora—Robbie was the bright light shining down on them. As these things sometimes did, it all worked out as they'd planned. That was all true. That was what everyone needed to know.

What everyone didn't need to know was precisely what John was trying to hide. Aurora had never made a dollar, and they never would. The algorithm worked, sure, but they'd been spending more on staff and expenses than they could ever bring in. Dallas knew, of course. Jessica knew, as well, which is why John was lying on a pool lounge chair, paralyzed with fear. She knew everything.

Jessica had been with John and Dallas all those years ago, the night they'd formalized the pitch for Aurora, at dinner at Pomodoro, a small pasta place near John's apartment. They'd ordered pizza and salad to share, and Jessica and John had already gone through one bottle of red wine, with another on the way. Robbie had been dead for over a month.

"I've been noodling on this for a while. Robbie had been interested in the industry, which is what got me going," Dallas had said, his facial hair shaved into a neat goatee. "If a company implements the code, they'll be able to bypass Google and Facebook. The proceeds from every purchased product will go directly to them, with us taking a small cut. It's going to blow minds," said Dallas, smiling, his lips parted attractively. John had stared at him for a moment too long. "We're going to take on the big guys, and win."

"How long have you been working on this?" John asked.

Dallas didn't say anything. Jessica cocked her head quizzically.

"Dude, it's brilliant. You can sell it. We can do it together," Dallas went on. "We're going to be billionaires. All of us. Think of it. You'll be the next Steve Jobs. The next Bill Gates. All hail John Shiller!"

John grinned at that, his small, square teeth briefly on full display.

"Let's do it for Robbie," Dallas said, smiling back at him. They'd toasted to that.

Dallas had hired a small team of engineers to perfect the tech, John had immediately started fundraising, and Jessica worked in every capacity needed, as John's assistant, as early HR, as the person whom John or Dallas called when they needed paper in the printer, or a breakfast reservation for an important meeting, or introductions to bankers and lawyers and the best VCs. Jessica knew everyone in those days, and she used her many connections to help Aurora succeed.

John raised a few million to begin with, and then they were off to the races. They moved out of John's apartment into a coworking space in Prospect Heights. Debra came on board. Then Zach. Then Olive and Martin and Nikki. They'd eventually set up in a fancy office building on

Park Avenue South, filled with colorful modern furniture, and a staff of overworked, overcaffeinated millennials. John started framing Aurora not just as a company but also as a mentality. "Like Churchill, we want to make the world a better place," he'd end all his town halls, to roaring cheers.

Early on, John had given Jessica the title head of partnerships, even though she'd complained it felt amorphous, and Aurora basically had no partnerships to speak of. "You're a doer, Jessica, you do everything. That was your area at Apple, and I think partnerships is a good place for Aurora to expand into," John had said. They were still working out of Brooklyn at that point, and Jessica had mainly been tasked with keeping the books.

"I should be a cofounder," she'd told him angrily. They were alone in the office, late, standing near the window, the Manhattan skyline lit up in the distance. "I was there when we started all of this! You couldn't have done it without me. Even Meagan has more equity than I do." They'd given Meagan a large number of shares when Aurora launched. It was the least they could do, John had explained to Jessica at the time, given how they'd let Robbie down.

"Look at me, John," Jessica had said. He did, with a smirk.

"Now, Jessica, let's not get out of sorts here. Dallas and I are the co-founders of Aurora, but that doesn't mean you aren't integral to the place," he'd said, placing a hand on her shoulder. She pushed him off. "I'm sorry to say, but men have an easier time giving money to other men. VCs balk if a woman walks into the room to ask for funding. Let's stick with head of partnerships for now, and see how everything evolves in the next year," John continued, not leaving any room for her to object. "I know this might seem far off, but someday the company will be sold for a billion dollars. And, for your work and loyalty, you will be rewarded handsomely."

"How are we going to sell the company if we can't even make a profit?" Jessica had asked, stepping closer to him, her nose nearly touching his. He'd grimaced.

"We're going to figure it out," he'd said, leaning back. "You don't have to be profitable to sell, as you well know. We just have to grow, and that's what we're going to do."

And that's what they did. Over the years, Jessica became increasingly estranged from the inner circle. She didn't vibe with the other executives. She found them to be catty, always tussling over compensation, gossiping about who was in John's favor and who was out. She'd list her complaints to John: Martin was a drama queen, Nikki had outbursts, Zach never stood up for himself, Olive had a big mouth, and Debra indulged their bad traits.

"John? John? What are you doing here?" John snapped out of the memories. Caitlin was standing next to him, still in her outfit from dinner, a silk camisole and printed silk pants. He was happy to see her. John took pains to separate his private and professional lives, and generally it was easy to do so. He hired women he wasn't attracted to: smart, driven, never his type. People joked that he and Jessica must be a secret item, as they spent so much time together socially, but that wasn't the case. They'd never even kissed. There was a masculine energy about Jessica that allowed him to be close to her without worrying about sex or love. She didn't have "feelings" the way other women did.

"Are you okay?" Caitlin sat down and put her hand on his forehead, as if checking for a fever.

He'd been surprised by their chemistry the first time they met, when he'd pitched Caitlin the job (he knew she'd end up taking it; she didn't have a choice). She was the best in the business, and her reputation would be a boon to Aurora. He'd heard she was tough and clever, which weren't qualities he looked for in women he dated. He preferred gorgeous, docile, disposable girls, who admired him and didn't add much conversationally. He thought of them as puppies. He'd feed and take care of them—and slap them around during sex, consensually—and they'd provide him with affection and status.

The women he worked with were a different species, purposefully. So, he'd had a moment of doubt when hiring Caitlin. He'd known she was the right candidate, but their connection worried him, and he'd spent an extra month on the search, speaking with people who were subpar. Only when it became clear that he needed her to get the deal done did he pull the trigger on her $2.5 million.

"Caitlin Levy!" he said, sitting up, her soft hand still on his skin. She looked nothing like the women he normally had sex with. She was older, her features more defined. She had lines at the sides of her eyes. Her lips weren't injected with filler.

"What are you doing up here?" he asked. Her cheeks looked sun-kissed from the day, and John had the urge to touch them. A warm breeze passed.

"I couldn't sleep," she said. "I took a long nap this afternoon after Jet Skiing, and so I'm not tired yet. How about you?"

"Same, same," said John, which was a lie. He'd spent the afternoon hours holed up in a room with Olive and Kaya Bircham, doing damage control.

"How did the rest of the dinner go for you? It seemed like people were pretty upset afterward," said Caitlin. In fact, everyone *but* Caitlin had ended the evening in a grump. She'd gotten a small equity grant of 15,000, and he'd been worried that she'd ask for more. Instead, she'd taken apart her origami fish, read the number, and smiled. "Thanks, John. You didn't have to give me anything. I haven't even started." Though Debra and the lawyers were looking on, John had felt like he and Caitlin were the only two people in Carbone.

"Ah, well, you know how people are," he said. "No one's ever satisfied with what they have. Think about Hitler." She didn't answer. He knew she was married to some guy who worked at Digitas, a creative type. She should have found someone more in John's league—super-successful, a CEO, not some creative director wuss.

"Would you like to get a drink?" she said. She went to take her hand off his head, but he grabbed it back, caressing her smooth fingers, feeling the shape of her engagement ring. He shouldn't be touching her like this, but he felt out of control. She didn't pull away. He allowed himself to look her in the eyes. She stared right back, daring him to do something more. He leaned in and so did she, their faces less than an inch apart.

They heard a commotion at the long bar at Watr, a crash followed by someone shouting, "I'm totally fine!" John and Caitlin quickly separated and stood to see Martin wobbling toward them, followed by Debra, looking aggrieved.

John braced himself. Martin had been disappointed about his equity, even though, as John and Debra had explained to him, his grant, at 75,000, was one of the biggest. John did value Martin. He was a data wizard and took on more work than anyone else at the company. But he could be such an insolent pain in the ass.

Martin stumbled up to them, tipsy.

"John! Caitlin! Fancy seeing you here, together," said Martin, a bit slurry.

"We were just heading to our rooms to go to bed," said Debra, running interference. She grabbed Martin's shirtsleeve and pulled him back toward the entrance, but he resisted.

"Debra, I told you, I'm fine, stop treating me like a child," said Martin. They all stood there, no one knowing what to say or how to end the interaction.

"What are you and Caitlin talking about?" said Martin, eyeing them warily.

"First, it's none of your business. And second, it's none of your business," said John. He knew it was mostly his fault that his top employees felt comfortable speaking to him so casually. He encouraged the rowdy air among the team, and shared things—anecdotes about his dating life, gossip about other tech execs—that he shouldn't. He admittedly viewed his team as built-in friends, talented people he paid to both work at his company *and* keep him company.

"Caitlin, have you told John anything?" said Martin. She shook her head no.

"Told me what?" John asked.

"Nothing," said Martin.

Olive, Zach, Nikki, and Dallas appeared, walking over from the bar carrying drinks.

"The gang's all here!" said Zach. He was in a fine mood, which John took as a sign that he'd gotten over his initial grousing and was satisfied with his 125,000 shares ("I thought maybe I'd get a hundred and fifty" was his tepid response). He certainly should be thrilled, as it would equal an extra $5 million once the deal went through. John needed to keep Zach's spirits up; he performed best when he was happy, and John knew he'd been riding him hard. Aurora's numbers must be strong going into the sale, to fit with the story John had crafted for Minimus, and Zach had to hit his targets for them to have a prayer.

Nikki was standing glumly next to Olive, sipping a pink drink. John truly felt betrayed by her, and it was bothering him immensely. To go behind his back and solicit an offer from Trade Desk, of all places, to work for that asshole Simon Horn! John and Simon had known each other for years, ever since Aurora came on the scene as a competitor. They'd been at conferences together, on panels, at the same industry events. Simon was slightly older than John, in his midforties, with slicked-back black hair, a fondness for red ties, and a stodgy, corporate vibe. He ran his company with a steady hand and looked askance at John's outfits, his outsize personality, and the looser way John conducted himself with his staff. Simon would never dream of hosting a wild executive retreat in Miami, and here John was, revealing share grants in some elaborate setup, with one team member mysteriously missing after a drunken night out.

John could tell that Nikki had been nervous as she sat down at the table at Carbone, smoothing out her red dress underneath her. John appreciated Nikki's style. He liked when people cared about their appearance, as that was something he'd always struggled with. For a moment, he'd questioned himself. Perhaps he should just let it go. She would likely stay, now that Aurora was in the process of being sold, and the team at Minimus *would* be pissed to hear that they'd lost their top Black executive so soon before the sale. But then he'd pictured Simon Horn sneering at him in one of his stupid red ties. Simon worked in tech! No one in tech wore ties!

"I hear you have something to speak to me about," John had said to Nikki. Debra looked away, wanting to avoid confrontation. The restaurant was bustling with hot Miami energy, loud laughter and squealing coming from neighboring tables. He knew this wasn't the place to address Nikki's offer, but he couldn't help himself. His feelings were hurt. And he hated when his feelings were hurt. It meant someone had power over him.

"Well . . ." Nikki started. "After much thought, I've decided to tell Trade Desk I won't be accepting the offer. I'd love to stay here and continue my mission at Aurora, er, Aurora 2.0, or whatever it will be under Minimus. This is the right place for me. No need to counter." Debra gave a little gasp of relief.

"Oh, I think I'll be the one to decide if you're staying," said John. He handed her the origami elephant, which opened to reveal a message instead of a number. It read: "Traitors get zero." He could see Nikki getting worked up, her lips pursed unhappily. Debra had spoken to Nikki about her temper at every performance review, and she'd ignored her every time. Nikki threw the unraveled elephant on the floor next to the table.

"You know how much value and hard work I bring to this company. And you know your senior diversity numbers would plummet without me," Nikki said sharply. John felt Debra kick Nikki under the table. "I've had this EVP title forever, and I haven't complained! I do everything for that department," she said, the color of her face beginning to mirror the scarlet of her dress.

"I wouldn't say you haven't complained," said John. "I've heard about it, from you, from Debra, from everyone on the team, about a million times."

Nikki grumbled under her breath.

"Listen," she began again, her voice lower. "I don't want to leave. I made a mistake. But it's up to you." John had a disturbing thought. If Trade Desk was offering her so much, why would she stay and take his abuse? What if she'd informed them about the sale, and they were paying her to be a corporate spy? He tried to shake it off, but his mind wouldn't stop spiraling.

He cringed, thinking about how much Jessica knew, how many skeletons she could unearth. He should have just given her the goddamn equity that she'd asked for in the first place, but he knew Minimus would have scratched beneath the surface of her job to find . . . nothing. And then they would have started asking questions. Real questions. It had been a no-win situation for him. But he'd made the wrong choice. He'd been doing that too often lately. He felt woozy with worry.

"Nikki, Nikki, Nikki," he'd said, trying to slow his heartbeat. "As Winston Churchill said, 'Attitude is a little thing that makes a big difference.' And if you're going to stay, I need to see a big shift in your attitude." She looked at Debra and back again at John, motioning them to come closer. John scooched his chair toward her, knocking over the CONGRATS ON YOUR SHARES! sign as he did. Madison scurried over, a darting mouse in a floral dress, and placed it back on the table in a flash.

"I hear you on attitude," said Nikki, her voice a loud whisper. "So I'm going to tell you what really happened last night with Jessica," she said. "Somehow she'd heard about the job at Trade Desk." Debra swallowed her water a little too loudly. "She came up to me at LIV to talk about it. She never speaks to me, so I thought it was strange that she did. And then she said I should take the offer. She said there was 'stuff' going on at the company that I didn't want to be a part of."

John's hands went clammy. He needed to sort it all out in his mind, but he couldn't think with everyone surrounding him. He cleared his throat loudly. Debra looked at him with concern. "I appreciate your honesty, Nikki, even though it's coming a little late. I'll take this into consideration when deciding your fate at Aurora...."

Debra had interjected. "We'll get you an answer by tomorrow. John and I will discuss." He thought he saw Debra flash Nikki a quick thumbs-up. Fucking Debra. Always letting people off easy.

He looked hard at Debra now, standing behind Martin at Watr, in some unflattering button-down and khakis combo, her arms crossed over her stomach. Martin was giving him the stink eye. Even Caitlin had moved away from him, frowning in his direction. Why didn't they love him? He was trying his best to make everyone rich, lying and scheming in order to do so, and no one seemed to care. John's chest started to ache, a dull throbbing that radiated down both of his arms, sending tingles into his fingers. What was happening to him?

His body constricted, and the ache turned into a sharp pain. His breathing came fast, and he felt like his throat was closing all at once. Churchill had suffered a minor heart attack during a visit to the White House in 1941—is that what was happening to him? Was he having a heart attack?

"John, are you all right?" asked Zach. Olive took a step closer, as if she wanted to comfort him. John couldn't answer. His tongue was glued to the bottom of his mouth and searing hot flashes were rushing through his limbs. He shook his head no. He went to sit down on the lounge chair but stumbled as he did, catching himself right before hitting the ground. He didn't want anyone to see him like this. He didn't want Caitlin to see him like this. Debra rushed to his side and lifted him into the chair.

"Should I call nine-one-one?" asked Martin, crouching nervously. John couldn't go to the hospital! He was in the midst of a billion-dollar deal, he couldn't die right now. Everyone knew what had happened to Apple's stock when Steve's cancer returned. He shook his head no, trying desperately to get his voice to emerge.

"John, don't be a nob, if you're feeling ill, let's get you to a doctor," said Olive.

"Here, let me show you what to do," said Nikki, taking control as the rest of the crew floundered.

"First, put one hand on your stomach and one on your chest," Nikki instructed, sitting across from him and demonstrating.

"Take a deep breath in through your nose, and exhale from your mouth," she said slowly, taking him through the exercise. "In and out." She paused. "In and out." They did that for what felt like an eternity, and John eventually felt the pain begin to subside and his breathing regulate.

"Close your eyes and picture yourself in a beautiful field," said Nikki in a soothing voice.

"I have hay fever," said John. Nikki laughed.

"I think you're going to be okay," she said. "You were having a panic attack. I used to get them in college during exams. You need to focus on your breathing. It takes practice."

John continued to breathe in and out as his team made a little circle around him, everyone checking their phones, sipping their drinks. The mood had calmed, and John was thrilled to have avoided death. He had so much left to accomplish. He had to make sure Minimus went through with the sale. He felt motivated and happy. He loved his team. And maybe they *did* love him back. His phone buzzed next to him, and the number was "unavailable." He sent it to voicemail; it was probably just spam.

He looked at Caitlin, sitting off to the side alone, her hair up, her lovely neck exposed. He stood on the lounge chair, wiping his sweaty hands on his purple pants. "Drinks on Aurora!" he roared to the entirety of Watr, and everyone clapped and cheered. As Churchill once said, "Nothing in life is so exhilarating as to be shot at without result." John Shiller would come out on top. He had to. "We want to make the world a better place!" he bellowed again to applause, then jumped down and did a little twirl.

He saw that he had one new voicemail. He pressed the phone to his ear—if it had something to do with the sale, he'd need to know.

"This is a message for John Shiller," a deep voice said. There was a pause. "Your employee Jessica Radum is dead. She was found in the bathroom at LIV. An overdose. We're thinking she snorted a bad batch of cocaine, likely laced with fentanyl. We are still trying to locate her next of kin but don't have that info yet. As such, you'll need to come to the morgue to identify her. Please call us back at this number." A jolt of orgasmic relief shot through John's body, causing his penis to instantly harden. He observed his team, chatting over drinks, looking forward to their millions. Then he snapped his fingers, beckoning them to come closer.

PART 3

Thursday, April 25

Now This Is Not the End.

It Is Not Even the Beginning of the End.

But It Is, Perhaps, the End of the Beginning.

Olive Green

———

Olive Green was in quite a state. Jessica Radum was dead. She couldn't believe it. Well, she supposed she *could* believe it. Jessica was a recreational drug user, a habit that Olive had always thought was unladylike. And this time, Jessica had gone too far. Probably served her right, Olive thought a little guiltily. You shouldn't be doing drugs in your thirties! These tech executives and their arrested development: Elon and his ketamine, Sergey and his mushrooms. Get over it, people. Grow up. Jessica must have gone back into the club after Olive had seen her fighting with Dallas. Why?

Olive considered whether she should be feeling sadder. But no, Jessica wasn't her friend. They barely spoke at all, Jessica wandering the halls alone, cozying up to John, refusing to engage in their banter.

This presented an enormous work challenge for Olive, but nothing she couldn't handle. John, upon telling them all the news, already had a clear, John Shiller–ish plan in place. They'd keep Jessica's death under wraps until the deal with Minimus closed, only then revealing that their head of partnerships had overdosed on their executive retreat. This was no one's fault; Jessica had a problem, it wasn't a company issue, yadda, yadda, yadda. Jessica's family needed to know, surely, but it would take time to figure out her next of kin. And they wouldn't tell Minimus until the proper relatives had been alerted. Thank god Jessica's parents were already gone. What a nightmare, otherwise.

Now Olive's main job was to keep the news out of the press. Unfortunately, Kaya Bircham was following the lot of them in Miami, sniffing around the sale, and so Olive was possibly screwed.

Also, she'd just *been* screwed. It was 1:00 A.M., and Olive was lying next to Zach in his hotel room bed, naked, the sheets tangled between her legs. She felt sore from the Jet Ski crash and drained from all the drama. Zach was passed out, breathing deeply, and she wanted so badly to join in, to let herself fade away from this long, tiring day. Jessica was dead. Jessica was dead. She was dead! This wasn't the normal workplace antics Olive was used to. Lying, cheating, stealing, all that she'd handled before. But this was beyond the pale. How far would she go to protect Aurora? Especially as it seemed like John barely valued her at all.

A couple of weeks ago, Olive, upset about how John had been treating her, had convened a meeting of the Finger Waggers in Debra's office. It was 5:00 P.M. on a Friday, and most everyone else had cleared out for the weekend. Cubicles sat empty, lonely papers scattered on desks, half-empty bags of pretzels littered about. Nikki sat on Debra's mauve couch, eating a bag of SmartPop! from the pantry, Debra was behind her desk, sipping a cold brew, and Olive perched on a side chair, on her fourth cup of tea of the day. She appreciated that they'd both stayed to hear her vent. She hadn't yet betrayed Nikki, so their camaraderie still felt natural.

"He's just so difficult, I don't think I can take it anymore," Olive had said to sympathetic nods. "He doesn't tell me anything, and the whole Caitlin Levy surprise really threw me. There's nothing I hate more than being caught flat-footed with a reporter."

"I know," said Nikki. "If it makes you feel any better, the other day, when John was strutting around in those hideous neon-green pants, his fly was completely unzipped." They all laughed.

"You should have had Madison come zip it up for him; isn't that in her job description?" said Olive. They continued to giggle.

"Don't take it personally," counseled Debra. "You know John loves you. He's in a mood. There's some other stressful stuff going on, and he's probably just taking it out on you."

"What other stuff? See, this is what makes me go mad," said Olive. "I can't do my job if he doesn't tell me what's happening!"

It made Olive feel better to complain to her work friends about John, the man she spent her life protecting from bad press. Without Henry around, she had no one to help her endlessly dissect John's foibles (not that Henry was listening when she spoke, but he was polite enough to occasionally pretend to). She did feel loyal to John. He'd hired her, promoted her twice, given her raises, and allowed her to mainly run her own department without interference. But Olive was continually annoyed that he withheld information. Yes, she liked to gossip, she admitted that. But not when it counted. She could keep a secret. No one knew about Zach. And she'd never tell anyone about how she'd torpedoed Nikki's offer from Trade Desk out of jealousy.

She closed her eyes and tried to will herself to sleep. No luck. Instead, she picked up her phone. Maybe scrolling through old photos of Poppy and Penelope would calm her. She had one unopened text message that had arrived at 12:30 A.M. It was from Kaya Bircham. Shit. They'd spent hours with her that afternoon, finally convincing her that an exclusive on Aurora's sale to Minimus was better than a gossipy item about a potentially missing executive. And now that executive was dead. It had taken all of Olive's PR prowess to sell the trade. Kaya was tough, which annoyed Olive, but which she respected. Olive opened the message.

Deal's off. I got something even better. Let me know when you can talk. Olive felt a thrill run through her. Nothing excited her more than a potential crisis.

Can you meet me now? Olive texted back.

Yes, I'll see you in the lobby in ten.

Olive blindly searched for her clothing, piling it in her arms, and then changed in the bathroom. She looked a bit of a mess, but Kaya wouldn't know she was doing a middle-of-the-night walk of shame. She crept out of the room, shutting the door lightly so as not to wake Zach. She'd see him tomorrow. This whole thing—the sex, the inkling that Zach was seriously interested in her (and perhaps she him)—was something to be figured out, but right now she had more pressing concerns.

Olive briskly navigated the hallway, checking her phone to see if she'd gotten any emails that might prepare her better for the meeting with Kaya. Without looking up, she bumped, hard, into someone walking the other way. In front of her was Madison, in pink pajama pants and an over-size T-shirt that read SLEEPING BEAUTY, carrying a bucket of ice. They stood there for a second, Madison rubbing her shoulder where Olive had crashed into her. Olive could see she was wearing a night guard from the strange way her lips were bulging.

"What are you doing here? Your room is on the seventh floor," said Madison, lisping a bit as she spoke.

Madison was young, maybe twenty-five or twenty-six, and from one of those states that blurred together in Olive's British mind—Oklahoma? South Dakota? Alabama? She had long dirty-blond hair and wide blue eyes, adorned by those cheesy eyelash extensions that all the young women favored. And she spoke with a twang that Olive had a hard time deciphering—"Aww-live" instead of "Oh-liv"—and that, as a semiposh person, hurt Olive physically to hear.

Olive knew she was being a snot, but she couldn't help it. She didn't like Madison, and Madison could tell. She didn't like the way Madison buzzed around John, tending to his every infantile need (though in her more gen-erous moments, Olive knew she was being unfair to Madison, as "tending to John's needs" was basically the entirety of Madison's job description).

"The only people on this floor are me and Zach," said Madison. "Are you lost?" Olive seethed. Any other assistant would have said hello and run in the other direction.

"Just having a bit of a night wander," said Olive, making to move past her toward the elevator. "Thinking about Jessica, and what she meant to the team." Kaya was waiting, and Olive was desperate to know what she had on them.

"So you weren't coming from Zach's room?" asked Madison. Olive was shocked at her audacity. Who did this little bumpkin think she was? Olive was an executive at the company, rungs and rungs and rungs above Madison. Olive was sick of being disrespected by everyone. Her husband, her boss, this pathetic ant.

"How *dare* you ask me that?" Olive boomed, harsher than antici-pated. She felt her skin begin to redden, the telltale spots climbing up her neck. "Where I'm coming from is none of your business, so I suggest you take your ice and go back to your room, without a word about this to anyone."

"I . . . I . . . I was just asking. I'm sorry. . . ." said Madison shakily. "I was just at the morgue with John!" Madison choked back a sob, surprising Olive with her genuine distress. Olive was stung with regret that she'd yelled at a guileless girl who was closer to her daughters' ages than her own. Madison paled, turned around, and walked away, her pink pajama pants swinging.

Olive, feeling a bit queasy about her own behavior, hopped on the elevator down to the lobby. It was practically empty, save for some staff milling about. Just one amorous couple perched on a sofa, making out, his hands underneath her tiny skirt. Olive bristled with disgust. PDA was so uncouth. She spotted Kaya sitting on a leather love seat, checking her phone. She was still in her black blazer from earlier in the day, looking even more rumpled than when Olive had last seen her. Olive shivered in the cranked-up AC, missing the warmth of Zach's large bed.

She'd stayed at Watr for another hour after they'd found out about Jessica—everyone was oddly calm for learning that a teammate had died, but perhaps they were just in shock. Olive was British; she wasn't going to lose her shit. Even Dallas, who'd known Jessica forever, didn't seem distraught. A little rattled, maybe. They all sat together on lounge chairs as John promised that he'd take care of the communication with Jessica's family. He'd take care of everything, he said. Their job was just to keep it quiet until the deal was done.

"Are you okay?" Olive had whispered to Debra at one point.

"I don't know," Debra said. "There are . . . things . . . that don't seem right about this." Olive winked at Debra, their signal that they'd speak about it all later.

Afterward, Olive had snuck down to meet Zach. It was the fourth time they'd had sex that day. Once in the morning before breakfast, once after Jet Skiing, and then again after the dinner at Carbone, where Olive had found out she was getting 60,000 additional shares before the sale to Minimus. It was a good amount—enough to have her own Henry-less nest egg for the girls. Zach wouldn't tell her what he'd gotten, but she assumed it must be more than she did.

"Is it wrong that we just fucked?" Zach had asked. They were lying in his bed. She was snuggled in the crook of his arm, enjoying the sensation of his chest hair tickling her skin.

"An executive is dead," said Zach.

"I know," said Olive. "It's horrible. This is so strange. John is acting bizarrely, as usual. Why do we work here, again?"

"Money? Lots and lots of money," said Zach with a resigned laugh. She thought to ask him about what she'd overheard near the elevators but stopped herself before she did. It was becoming clear that no one at Aurora could be trusted, perhaps even Zach.

Olive wound around the couches toward Kaya, then plopped down next to her.

"I thought we'd already been through this," said Olive. She always liked to start conversations with reporters, never letting them immediately take the lead. This was her zone; she'd already forgotten about running into that pest Madison. "So, what's the new info you've gotten?"

Kaya cleared her throat nervously. She was on the rise (and knew it), but she was still young for the game, in her early thirties, and Olive could be purposefully intimidating.

"I know we agreed to the exclusive of the sale to Minimus, and in exchange I was going to ignore the tip about Jessica Radum going 'missing' from your executive retreat." Olive nodded.

"But I think I've got something even juicier." Olive's body tightened. Had Kaya heard about Jessica somehow? Olive wasn't used to reporters having the upper hand.

"And what's that?" Olive asked, her mouth feeling dry.

"My source says John is misleading Minimus about Aurora's numbers," said Kaya. "That he's inflating revenue somehow. That your EBITDA is fake, and that you've changed your depreciation schedules to inflate your profit projections."

Olive felt both relief—at least Kaya didn't know about Jessica—and dread. Why wasn't she in the fucking loop?! Also, she'd better get up to speed on her financial language, stat. She had no idea what Kaya was talking about.

"What are you going to do with that information?" said Olive. If Kaya wrote that item, or anything about Jessica, they were ruined. The sale wouldn't go through. Olive's nest egg would disappear. She couldn't let it happen. She wouldn't.

"Nothing, for now. But I'm sticking around Miami while I figure it out. I wanted to give you the courtesy of that heads-up. I have a feeling that whatever I uncover will be far more interesting than a glorified press release," she scoffed.

"You don't have to be rude," said Olive. "And if you're staying in Florida, I suggest you buy some proper clothes. You must be hot in your little blazer." Kaya flushed, embarrassed. Olive knew she shouldn't have said it; she was trying to control Kaya, not make her an enemy. But she was unnerved. And when she was unnerved, she said stupid things. Her girls had told her to see a therapist in the wake of the divorce, and she'd rolled her eyes at them, emotive American Gen Zers that they were. But maybe they were on to something. She decided to make nice.

"I must say, it was an impressive move to show up at Stewart's today. What do you have on him? Tell me, pretty please." Olive smiled charmingly and Kaya's eyes glittered. Journalists couldn't help themselves. They were as ego-driven as anyone else, if not more so.

"This is between us," said Kaya, leaning closer to Olive, "but Stewart is a furry. Do you know what that is?"

"Isn't that someone who dresses up like an animal?" said Olive. Kaya nodded yes.

"A few months ago, I got an anonymous tip directing me to a furry party on the Lower East Side. Stewart was there in a life-size mouse costume, socializing with cats and dogs and one enormous elephant." Kaya giggled. "He gave me a whole spiel about how it wasn't sexual, and that he was just a 'furson' who identified as a mouse, and how it didn't affect his work at Cardeo whatsoever. But you *know* how that board would react if they found out their CEO was a furry freak. They'd oust him in a minute."

"They certainly would," said Olive, for once feeling thankful that John dressed up as Winston Churchill and not a rodent.

"I told him I wouldn't write about it so long as he acted as a source for other stories," said Kaya proudly. "And he's been very helpful to me since!"

"Well done, you," said Olive. "I'm off to bed now, but we will be in touch. I know you won't publish anything without consulting me first." Olive said it firmly enough that Kaya knew she meant business.

Kaya got up and walked out the front entrance. She was staying at the Marriott Courtyard nearby; *TechRadar* was a media company, and media companies didn't put reporters up at hotels like the 1. She watched Kaya shuffle out, and then pulled up John's contact in her phone. She braced herself.

"Olive, Olive, Olive, is this a booty call? Why are you phoning me at 1:37 in the morning? I've just gotten back from the morgue, believe it or not. The body was indeed Jessica Radum's. She looked . . . strange. In that dress still. Her red hair still alive. But dead. She was dead. Olive, do you know that's the second time in my life that a friend of mine has died of an overdose? Was it something I said?" He chuckled menacingly and sounded slightly drunk.

"I've just had a conversation with Kaya Bircham," Olive said, not sure of the best way to deliver the news.

"Our friend Kaya? What does she want now? I thought we'd made the deal, and she was getting out of our hair. I must say," he said, slurring somewhat, "even with everything going on, my hair is looking pretty great tonight. I'm so happy I still have my hair, I really am. So many men my age don't have hair, and while I have other things working against me—my height, my tendency to gain weight in my stomach—my hair is a reliable plus." When John drank, which wasn't that often, he went on tangential rants. It became difficult to steer him back into any normal conversation. But Olive had to.

"Kaya says she's dropping the deal. Thankfully, she doesn't seem to know anything about Jessica yet." She could hear John breathing.

"Did she tell you why?" he asked, the goofiness from a minute ago completely gone from his voice.

"She said she heard there was something fishy with the sale. She said we've been fudging numbers."

John was silent for a moment. "This is not good," he finally said. Olive suddenly felt dead tired. She'd fucked Zach countless times today, she'd fallen off a Jet Ski, she thought she'd killed a story that she hadn't really killed, her boss was losing his mind and was possibly committing fraud, and Jessica Radum was dead. It was all a bit much.

"We'll help you," she said. Why did she feel the constant need to protect this odd little man? "I've never covered up a death before, but there's a first time for everything!" John laughed softly. She wanted to hate him but couldn't quite bring herself to. There was something about him that hooked you in.

"Olive," he said, a spark back in his voice. "Do you know who Joan Bright Astley is?"

"I'm afraid not."

"Joan Bright Astley was a remarkable woman. Like you, she was a Brit! She oversaw the Special Information Centre for Winston Churchill during World War II, handling all the secret documents with care, and being the guardian of classified reports throughout the war. Also like you, she was a brilliant lady who knew how to get and give information, one who was savvy and helpful and always put people at ease." Though Olive knew it was pathetic, she felt a warm glow at the compliments from her boss. Maybe he really did value her. Sixty thousand shares wasn't nothing. Sixty-five, if you counted the Jet Ski winnings.

"You are my Joan Bright Astley!" he nearly shouted into the phone. "As my director of communications, you are the keeper of my secrets and the person I trust the most. As always, I appreciate you fighting on my behalf. Let's convene in the morning and strategize. Now I'm off to take my hangover pill. Get some rest!"

Olive arrived back at her room in a daze, quickly washing her face and brushing her teeth. She settled into bed, happy to be sleeping alone, even though it had been nice to have someone to snuggle with for a day.

She turned off the lamp next to her bed and slipped her eye mask on. Visions of Madison outing her and Zach floated through her mind. She rubbed her hip, still tender from the crash. She would call Poppy and Penelope first thing in the morning. Hearing their voices would cheer her up. She lay there for a moment, her mind still whirring. Sleep seemed impossible. She took off her mask and picked up her phone. She'd look at pictures of her girls when they were young; that always made her happy.

But first, she'd check her email. Nothing new. Then she went into her spam folder, which she occasionally did, just to make sure she hadn't missed anything. There, she saw an unread email from yesterday afternoon. It was from JRadum@gmail.com. Jessica's personal address. With a shaky hand, Olive clicked on it.

Listen to Ladies of Tech. That was it. No signature. No Best, Jessica. No Talk Soon! Olive knew that *Ladies of Tech* was a popular industry podcast, one that featured up-and-coming female tech executives and engineers. She'd been pitching them Nikki for months. Why was Jessica telling her to listen to it? Olive put on her headphones and settled into the bed. She pressed play on the latest episode, an interview with Meta's CFO, Susan Li. Then Olive promptly fell asleep.

Debra Foley

———

It was 11:00 A.M., and Debra Foley was standing on a pickleball court, next to Martin Ito, nearly melting from the heat. They were at the annual Aurora-thon, John's version of a corporate "sports day." It was held at Flamingo Park, a large outdoor sports complex about a ten-minute Uber from the hotel, and the agenda included a tennis match, followed by a relay race, capped by three rounds of tug-of-war. Debra was in Umbros and an oversize AURORA-THON T-shirt, which Madison had distributed earlier and insisted they all wear. Martin, as usual, hadn't listened. "I don't do polyester," he'd sniffed. Instead, he was wearing a bright pink shirt and crisp white shorts, all Nike, inspired by an outfit he'd seen on Rafael Nadal. Martin certainly looked sporty, but unlike Debra, steady and coordinated, Martin had the gait of a baby deer, his legs all slippery-slide-y, his feet pointing in the wrong direction.

John had sprung the pickleball surprise on them when they arrived at Flamingo Park, leading them to a formerly grassy lawn that had been paved over into six small courts. ("Aurora is a cutting-edge company, even when it comes to recreational sports," John had responded when everyone complained about the switch.) None of them knew how to play pickleball, and so Madison had been tasked with googling the rules, then barking out orders as they broke into groups of four. "I'd rather be at the pool, sipping a cocktail and reading a trash novel, instead of cooking in this outdoor oven," whined Martin, standing next to her.

Debra felt the same way. She was weary and irritable, and had been hoping they'd cancel the events in light of Jessica being, you know, dead. But no, John had insisted they go forward. "As Winston Churchill put it, 'I never worry about action, but only about inaction,'" John had said during breakfast at Plnthouse, a casual restaurant in the lobby of the 1. "That means: the Aurora-thon is ON," he'd proclaimed. Madison, standing behind him, had raised her arms above her head triumphantly.

So that was that, and now Debra was swatting around a little racket in 89 percent humidity. The pop-pop of the ball was already giving her a headache.

She and Martin were playing against Zach and Nikki; the court next to them was a matchup of Caitlin and John versus Dallas and Olive. (The surrounding courts were filled with people who could actually play pickleball, and Debra was embarrassed to be part of this unathletic group.) John had also ordered the two lawyers working on the Minimus deal, Marc and Chase, to accompany them to Flamingo Park and act as line judges. Madison demanded that they, too, wear AURORA-THON T-shirts, and they looked miserable on the sidelines, surely wondering how their professional lives had come to this.

Debra couldn't bring herself to look at Marc. She'd been thinking about him nonstop since she saw him last night, obsessing about the man who'd impregnated her being on her executive retreat. She'd been turning it all over in her mind, the better to distract herself from the real HR disaster at hand: an accidental lethal overdose of an employee on a work trip. Were they liable? Would Jessica's extended family, whoever they were, sue the company into oblivion? Debra noticed the other lawyer, Chase, was making eyes at Martin. Chase was out of his business-casual look and in tight athletic shorts. Martin was a goner.

Zach served, Marc called "In!" and Martin shanked a shot into the net, distracted by Chase's flirty gaze. Debra turned around, annoyed.

"Just get the ball over," she said. Debra played tennis growing up, as well as lacrosse, field hockey, and every other sport available to a girl in Upstate New York. She was quickly figuring out pickleball—it was like tennis, but wrist-ier, with more dinking and donking and less running.

"You know I don't play racket sports!" Martin huffed. Zach and Nikki gave each other a high five, purposefully gloating to annoy him. "Why do we have to participate in athletics together?" Martin asked, sticking out his tongue. "How does playing shitty pickleball boost morale?" Debra shrugged. As an HR professional, she did think there was value in bonding with coworkers in ways other than Slack and Microsoft Teams. On the other hand, Debra didn't necessarily need to see Zach's hairy arms, or Olive's breasts bouncing around in her sports bra, or the growing line of sweat down the middle of John's shirt.

"I'm retiring," said Martin. "I hate humiliating myself."

"You can't retire," Debra said, frowning. "You can't retire, because then we can't play. We have eight people, enough for two games. Our one sub, if you recall, is up in tech company heaven." Debra was surprised by her own macabre sense of humor. A team member was dead. A life had been lost. What was wrong with all of them, playing pickleball as if nothing had happened?

"Fine, then, that lawyer can play." Martin pointed at Marc, who was checking his phone, pretending to be busy. Debra quickly shook her head no, but Martin wasn't having it.

"Hey! Hey!" he called out, walking over to Marc and handing him his racket, which Marc limply accepted. "You know Debra; she's our chief people officer and is a fabulous player. You can be her partner." Marc nodded, fear in his eyes. "I do have to warn you: Debra might scream at you. She's a yeller." Debra, who'd walked up behind them, smacked Martin on the arm, hard. "Ouch!" Martin yelled. "See? She's a total wacko."

Debra smiled shyly at Marc, who trotted out onto the court with athletic ease. She didn't know how to act or what to say: "Hi, remember me? The girl you had unprotected sex with?" She supposed she'd just play pickleball and ignore it all. The other game was paused midmatch. Caitlin and John were whispering to each other at the back of the court, while Olive and Dallas had stopped for a water break. Debra saw John giving Caitlin a quick shoulder squeeze. She'd have to speak to him about that later. For all his out-of-office womanizing, John had never crossed a line with any female employee, much to Debra's relief. Now would be the worst time to change that.

Debra and Marc quickly took control of their game, running Nikki and Zach around the court and hitting volleys directly into their bodies. After a particularly great shot, Marc sweetly patted Debra's arm, and she felt herself blushing against her will. They ran away with it quickly ("Unfair! You brought in a ringer!" Zach groused), and everyone turned to watch the other match wrap up.

"Game!" Dallas yelled, trotting over to Olive and giving her a big hug. John and Caitlin walked dejectedly to the net, John offering his hand for the opponents to shake.

"Good match," said John, sweat dripping from his forehead and disappearing under his Persol sunglasses. "As Churchill said, 'You do your worst, and we will do our best.' You two certainly did your best today."

"Thanks, John," said Olive. "I just want to thank you again for putting this on. It's a fantastic day, and we all appreciate you hosting us here." It was very unlike Olive to brownnose, and Debra didn't know what her end game was.

"Nice one, guys," said Dallas, smiling. "That's what I call quick-win synergy." ("What is he talking about?" Olive said softly.) They all walked off the court together, Debra finding shade under the awning of the white Tennis Center building.

She looked up to see John approaching, carrying his little racket, his hair wild in the humidity. He had a serious look on his face. Debra imagined herself running in the other direction, all the way to the airport, disappearing into the comfort of her little Upper West Side apartment, alone.

"Debra, you have a second?"

Debra nodded.

"We just got a call from the team at Minimus that's running due diligence," said John. Debra had the sudden sinking feeling that her afternoon wasn't going to be so relaxing after all. Had they gotten wind of Jessica?

"There's a woman there, Chief Information Officer Monica Wu, do you know her?"

"I know her," said Debra. "She and Martin worked together at Google. She has a reputation as a hard-ass, and I've heard some other rumors about her. I know she and Martin didn't get along. Why?"

"She's saying she's found something in the due diligence documents that she'd like to discuss with us."

Debra looked over at Martin, who was fanning himself with his hand, frowning.

"Martin!" Debra yelled. He walked over slowly.

"Yeeesss?" he said when he arrived. "What? Am I fired 'cause I hate pickleball? I'll sue for discrimination."

"Monica Wu from Minimus is saying there's something she discovered that she wants to address with you and John," said Debra, turning on her HR voice. Martin's body language immediately shifted; he crossed his arms defensively.

"I'm not sure what she's talking about, but I do know that she always hated me. We were vying for the same role at Google, and I ended up getting it. So I'm not surprised she found something 'wrong'"—Martin did air quotes—"with my work."

"Well, we know how women are," John said. "Very competitive, very emotional. I'm sure this is nothing." Martin nodded gamely. Though Martin was gay, John often spoke to him in the way Debra imagined straight men spoke to each other.

An enormous crack of thunder interrupted their conversation, and Debra was grateful for it. If Martin had done something shady, she really didn't want to know. The sky opened, releasing a tropical deluge, steam rising off the grass nearby. The team, soaked, ran to take cover next to Martin, John, and Debra. They huddled together, watching the storm move through.

"I suppose this means no relay race or tug-of-war!" said Olive happily, her wet AURORA-THON T-shirt clinging tightly to her body. Debra noticed that Zach couldn't stop looking at her.

"Wrong, wrong, wrong," said John. "This will last five minutes, then we will continue with our itinerary. It's an important bonding day for us, and neither a Miami thunderstorm nor an accidental death will ruin it." Madison cheered, and everyone else moaned. Debra found herself standing next to Marc, and she could feel the heat from his body. He turned to her and smiled, a real smile. Dallas was to their left, running in place, readying for the relay race. Nikki was some yards away, staring at her phone. Debra smiled back at Marc. She would lean into this distraction. Why not? Everything else was a total mess.

Nikki Lane

———

Nikki Lane was running, slowly, on the damp green track at Flamingo sports complex, her teammates, Olive, Dallas, Chase the lawyer, and her boss, John Shiller, cheering her on. Well, more like screaming at her to run faster. But she wasn't fast. And she didn't care at all about this race. She hated forced group activities with a passion, she always had. During her previous job, at Instagram, she'd had to attend a weeklong retreat in Maine. They called it, uncreatively, "Summer Camp," and Nikki had slept in a log cabin, in a bunk bed (a bunk bed!), gone sailing and swimming in a slimy lake, and made s'mores with some of her least favorite coworkers. They'd listened to hokey, inspirational speeches from the company's leadership and had never-ending brainstorming sessions in between crafting and soccer games. The long days finished with evening "socials," at which a DJ played 1990s pop and colleagues snuck into the woods to hook up like teenagers. The crazy part was how much everyone else, besides Nikki, seemed to enjoy it.

Nikki worked to *work*. And she was smart enough to know that a company wasn't your friend (nor should it be part of your identity). Anyone could get fired at any time, and the CEO was only loyal to his own bank account. It continually shocked her how few of her millennial cohort understood that. But then most of them hadn't grown up in the Bronx.

"Run, Nikki, run!" bellowed John. She continued at her leisurely pace, ignoring their cries to speed up. She needed time to process the DM she'd received from Jessica Radum.

When they'd taken cover from the storm, Nikki had logged into Instagram, which she barely ever checked—ironic, as a former employee, but Nikki viewed social media with an eye toward the addictive algorithms she'd helped to develop. She knew the evils firsthand; she'd coded them into existence. But she'd suddenly had the thought to check Jessica's account. There was nothing suspicious on it—the last picture posted was from before the retreat, a selfie of Jessica running in Central Park, with the caption "I run harder than you party." Nikki had rolled her eyes. What a nerd. Nikki then went into her DMs, deleting the junk, but noticed she'd received one from none other than Jessica herself, on Tuesday, the day they'd all arrived in Miami. The day Jessica died.

Didn't want to use work email, the message started. Nikki had walked farther away from the group, covering her phone with her hand so no one could see what she was reading.

> I was hoping you could send some information about our engineering systems, including our original algorithm. You know better than anyone how this company runs. I understand that this is a big ask, but I trust you not to tell anyone. Can we talk?

"Goooo, Nikki!" cheered Olive. Nikki was trailing the competition, Martin, the other slowest runner in the group, by about a hundred yards. It was oppressively hot, and she could feel sweat dripping down her yellow Tory Burch tennis dress. Why was she running in a race? She wasn't a child. This was ridiculous. Nikki wondered what kind of information Jessica had been after. This must have been the "ask" Jessica had referred to at LIV, but why hadn't Jessica spoken to Dallas about it? She thought back to Dallas in Jessica's room, looking for *something*. He was the one who'd invented the tech in the first place. Nikki had been slowly combing through Jessica's laptop, but nothing suspicious had yet emerged. She'd get back to it as soon as this goddamn race was over.

Nikki's two times around the enormous track were finally coming to an end. She saw Chase ahead of her, hand outstretched for the custom-made baton, which Madison had made sure was the exact blue shade of the Aurora logo. Martin had finished long ago, and Debra was huffing along in front, looking particularly winded, which was odd. Debra usually sprinted the entire way. Nikki did the handoff, and Chase took off like a shot, his gym-toned legs pumping madly until he'd overtaken Debra and was comfortably in the lead.

Nikki wandered away from the track, sitting down in the grass in the shadow of the bleachers, wiping herself off with her Aurora hand towel. Peace, at last. For a minute. Because then John came over and sat down next to her, his skinny legs delicately folded under, as if riding sidesaddle on a horse. If you'd told Nikki, fresh off her summa cum laude graduation from Yale, that in ten years she'd be working for this batshit character, she wouldn't have believed you. But this was the world they lived in, ruled by weak white dudes with "ideas" who could get funding for them from their white dude friends.

Nikki had always wanted to start her own company. She had a plan, based on an algorithm she'd been working on, for a service that combed through secondhand retailers to deliver versions of the items customers were looking for. It had been difficult to nail—there were so many different sites, and each one used varying keywords and sizing for their clothing—but she was nearing something real. She even had a name: Thrifteez. But she wasn't sure she'd ever have the courage to go for it. She'd just read an article in Bloomberg that said only 2 percent of venture capital went to women, and of that, she had to imagine the amount that went to women of color was even more minuscule.

"Nice run, Nikki. Way to stick with it," John said halfheartedly. Nikki snorted.

"Please, we all know I'm slow. Yet it continually surprises everyone that I'm not, like, Flo-Jo or something. Black people can be slow, too!"

"Indeed, we are having such a nice day," John said, doing his usual pivot whenever Nikki brought up being Black. Nikki imagined Debra had warned him off discussing race with his employees, but it always left

Nikki feeling slightly deranged, like he wasn't even hearing what she was saying.

"I wanted to thank you again for the calming words during my, um, episode yesterday," said John, averting his eyes. "I'm slightly more stressed than normal—I'm not sure if you can tell"—here Nikki snorted again—"but on top of everything else, including the sale and Jessica's inconvenient death, the idea that you'd leave me for Simon Horn was quite distressing. We need you here, Nikki. We love you very much."

This was the thing about John: He could be awful and unpredictable and demanding and childlike, and then he'd say something like that, luring you back into his company of brilliant delinquents. Nikki thought John was crazy, but she'd worked for a string of crazy white guys her entire career.

"I assume this means I get to keep my job," said Nikki, resigned.

"You absolutely do," said John. "We're all in this together! Particularly now, with a dead body on our hands." Nikki cringed. "And I might even give you some extra shares before the sale, if you're lucky. Or learn how to run faster." Nikki couldn't stop herself from giggling.

"And now I must go and do my part for the team. I see Chase is chugging along, and I'm next up. I'm glad we had this chat, Flo-Jo." He got up and tiptoed toward the finish line, his tiny calves flexing as he went.

Nikki spotted Debra and Olive standing together, heads bent toward each other. She'd been feeling distant from both for the past couple of days. Debra was clearly upset with her about the Trade Desk thing, and Olive had been avoiding her, too. She felt the urge to reconnect with her friends. She walked over to them, smiling. The race was on its last lap. It was Dallas against Marc, one of the lawyers, and Dallas had the slight edge, his arms going, his sweatband soaked through. She thought about what he'd said to her yesterday—"You're going to get everything you want." She'd nearly lost it all.

"Hi, guys, what's shaking? How are everyone's legs holding up?" Nikki said.

"I'm beat," said Debra. She looked a little white.

"You and Marc played really well together," said Nikki, pointing to him as he ran by, his brown hair flopping. "Is he single? I sensed some pickleball chemistry there." Debra shrugged.

"I think he's single."

"Ohhh, yes," said Olive, coming to life. "Debra, he's *perfect* for you. A lawyer hottie, knows all about our industry, loves sports, nice face, good smile. What's not to like?"

"We should invite him to our dinner tonight at Stubborn Seed," said Nikki. Olive nodded enthusiastically.

"I don't know. It's hard for me to get excited about a guy when I'm in the middle of an HR mess, dealing with a death, the sale, and all you angry birds about your equity," said Debra. She looked dejected and tense. Nikki wanted to help her. She'd lied to her face. She'd been a bad friend. She knew it was a risk, but she thought: fuck it. These were her people. The Finger Waggers. She'd been through the corporate trenches with them. She loved them. Caitlin ambled over, red-faced from the race, hair in a tight ponytail. Nikki felt for her. She didn't know any of them and was trying hard to fit in.

"Anyone else feeling like total shit?" said Caitlin, panting slightly. They all raised their hands at once, then simultaneously burst out laughing.

"This is my second day of a terrible hangover, and I haven't spoken to my husband at all. He's returning my texts with one word: 'yes' or 'no.' I have no idea if my children are even alive. I don't know why he's so pissed at me—this is my job, I *had* to go," said Caitlin. "It's work!" They nodded sympathetically. It's something they all understood: men, even the most enlightened of them, resenting when their wives or girlfriends were dedicated to their careers. Nikki decided to dive in. Everyone was in a sharing mood.

"Guys, please come a bit closer to me," she said. They all did, their eyes shining.

"Before she died, Jessica asked me for . . . info," said Nikki ominously, enjoying the reveal.

"*Drama*," said Olive loudly.

"Be quiet, Olive!" said Debra, slapping her on the back with a whack. Nikki kept going.

"She sent me a strange DM on Instagram. She wanted information on the tech side of Aurora. She didn't tell me why. And obviously now we can't ask her." Nikki felt better already. Lighter.

Olive looked like she wanted to say more, but she paused, her mouth shut.

"Come on, Olive," said Debra. "We all know when you have a secret to share."

"I really can't . . ." said Olive.

"I just told you mine!" said Nikki. Olive looked at Nikki, then looked down at the ground.

"All right, all right," said Olive. "You know we're dealing with this potential article by Kaya Bircham." They all nodded.

"But I thought you'd quashed that," said Debra. "Given her something else in return."

"Well, we did, but then she came back to me late last night, saying that someone gave her a tip that John was cooking our numbers." Nikki whistled ominously. "And then . . ." continued Olive.

"There's an 'and then . . .' to this story? I'm not sure I can take it," said Debra, blanching.

"And then I saw I had an email from Jessica in my spam folder. She'd used her Gmail. I guess she was reaching out to all of us. . . ."

"What did it say?" said Caitlin breathlessly.

Olive paused, upping the tension.

"Come on, spit it out!" said Nikki.

"Shhhh! John is coming, everyone be calm," said Debra. They watched as John walked over, gliding on his tiptoes, one of his many oddities.

"What are you all chatting about?" he said, pushing into the middle of the group, shoulder to shoulder with them. Nikki could see her face reflected in his sunglasses.

"We were saying that not only are you an amazing boss, but you're also an impressive sportsman," said Olive, smiling.

"Yes, that's what we were saying," said Debra.

"Uh-huh," chimed Nikki.

"You're a double threat," added Caitlin.

"Oh, you girls are the best," said John.

Right then, a large iguana skulked by, running into a nearby bush.

"Those things are absolutely disgusting," said Olive, grimacing.

A slight breeze broke through the still, hot air, ruffling Nikki's dress, providing a measure of relief.

Caitlin Levy

———

Caitlin Levy had a thick white rope between her hands and was tugging as hard as she could. She hadn't done this since she was a kid, at sleepaway camp in New Hampshire, and she was enjoying the sensation. There was something satisfying about the push and pull, the challenge of putting her entire body into something physical. She was nestled in front of John and behind Debra and could feel both their bodies pressed against hers.

She and John had been partners in the pickleball game, and had lost badly, but they'd had fun. Caitlin had enjoyed herself more than she had expected. She'd noticed that John kept finding ways to brush against her and speak to her closely. He'd taken her hand last night, and she'd experienced more excitement than she'd felt in years. (She and Mike had sex once or twice a week, and it was fine, but she viewed it more as a job than a perk.) Later, when she'd gone back to her hotel room, after staying out too late, yet again, she'd masturbated—with her hand!—to the thought of sleeping with John. Jessica Radum was dead, and Caitlin was getting off on John Shiller.

Was she having a midlife crisis? Removed from her marriage, was she only realizing now that something was amiss? Sure, she and Mike bickered like everyone else. They had a few pain points (her selfishness, his laziness) that they avoided for everyone's sake. But that was normal, right? She'd wanted this job because she thought she'd needed the professional change, not a personal one. Well, she felt changed on many levels, already.

"One, two, three, go!" said John, and she pulled the rope as hard as she could, closing her eyes and feeling the weight of her torso press into John's as she leaned back. "One, two, three!" Someone let go, and the rope went slack. They all tumbled back, and Caitlin allowed herself to fall freely, landing on a pile of executives, laughing and checking themselves for bruises.

"Ow! Ow! Get off me!" Caitlin heard someone shout, in real distress. She turned to see Debra underneath Chase, his elbow lodged in her stomach at a weird angle. He scrambled up, embarrassed and apologetic, helping Debra to her feet. She bent over in pain.

"I am *so* sorry," said Chase. "Are you all right? I couldn't see where I was landing," he said. His cheeks were red, and Caitlin felt bad for him. He'd been forced to make line calls in pickleball, run a relay race, and now this. Caitlin thought about how ridiculous they must look. Grown-ups in matching shirts, playing tug-of-war. Madison was running around, trying to keep order.

"On to the next game! It's best of three!" she pleaded. But everyone seemed to have lost interest. Debra was sitting on the grass, looking miserable, and Caitlin sank down next to her.

"Are you okay?" Caitlin asked. She watched as Madison brushed dirt from John's orange shorts, John scrolling through his stock portfolio, not even noticing her.

"I'm fine, I think," said Debra. She put her hand gently on her stomach and sighed. Caitlin, who had two sisters, who worked almost exclusively with women, was struck by a thought. She remembered that Debra had gone home early from LIV, and that she hadn't seemed to be drinking at Carbone. She looked at Debra's complexion, tired and drawn since they'd arrived in Miami.

"Debra," Caitlin said, looking down at her own body, stretched and softened by two babies. She lowered her voice. "Debra, are you pregnant?"

Debra, the sensible, strong chief people officer who Caitlin barely knew but who already felt like an old friend, took off her Oakley sunglasses. Her eyes were damp.

"You can't tell anyone," Debra whispered. Caitlin grabbed her hand and squeezed it supportively.

"But why? This is great news," she said. "Babies are amazing. And you can have one and still do your job. You can be a mom *and* a success. It's fine. It's great!" said Caitlin. She meant it, sort of.

The years when Caitlin's children were very young were a total shit-show. She had vague memories of getting absolutely no sleep, and then struggling to get to the office by 8:00 A.M., looking presentable, acting sharp. She'd floated through it in an exhausted, hormonal trance, making it to the end of the day as best as she could. Once, when Caitlin was just back from her second maternity leave, she'd had to give a presentation to over a hundred people about Viacom's up-front strategy. She'd gotten up onstage, sweating heavily in the bright lights. About a minute after she started speaking, she'd felt her breasts tingle, harden, and then begin to leak milk all over her turquoise sheath dress. She'd crossed her arms and continued, nearly crying in pain by the time she'd finished, immediately running off to the tiny pumping closet for relief.

She'd had many moments like that when the kids were small—the month when Joey refused to take a bottle, leaving Caitlin to slink home from the office in the middle of the day to breastfeed rather than have her tiny baby starve (she'd enlisted a few close female colleagues to cover for her, never telling her male boss more than he needed to know). With Lucinda, she'd had massive postpartum anxiety. They were still living in the city then, and Caitlin became unhealthily obsessed with the idea that an air-conditioning unit would fall on Lucinda's stroller, crushing her. In the middle of meetings, at drinks with friends, at business lunches, Caitlin was haunted by the thought of her baby being in danger. But it passed. It all passed. The pumping, the lack of sleep, the endless hours toggling between spit-up and PowerPoints.

Eventually the kids got older, they went to school, everything became less of an emergency, and Caitlin could concentrate on work in a way she'd been able to prechildren. She could barely remember the struggle, barely remember what it felt like to be rocking a baby and worrying about a big meeting the next day.

She wanted to share all this with Debra, to let her know that it would be hard, but she'd get through. And that having a child was the best possible thing. You can do it all, Caitlin wanted to tell Debra. Granted, a few years later you might end up having a midlife crisis on a company retreat, and possibly entering into an affair with your boss. But she didn't have a moment to say any of it. Instead, Zach came over, settling next to them in the grass.

"Girls, lie down with me, look up at the sky," said Zach. Caitlin, feeling drained, took the opportunity to stretch out on the soft, damp ground next to her new coworkers. Debra did, too. The sky was startlingly blue, having cleared quickly after the storm, with a few clouds floating calmly along.

"Debra, you all right?" asked Zach. "I saw Chase elbowed you."

"Yes, I'm fine," she said. "Thanks for asking."

"You seem a little blue," said Zach. "Let me know if I can be of any help. Do you want me to do a tap dance or something? I can juggle some pickleballs? The sale will go through. I mean, it's horrible about Jessica, but she was clearly troubled. That's not your fault. It's all going to be fine. Remember the time I dressed up like an Indian to motivate the sales team?"

"An Indigenous person, Zach. How many times do I have to tell you?" said Debra, sighing.

"Yeah, yeah, whatever, right, an Indigenous person. With my fancy headdress. It was fab, and I still stand by it. That was a great gag! Anyway, we got through that, didn't we? Together?"

"*I* got through it," said Debra, laughing now. "I'm the one who dealt with eight separate HR complaints and made sure no one outside of Aurora heard of your little stunt," she said.

"I heard of it," said Caitlin, giggling. "All of New York did." Zach started whooping, and the three of them broke into hysterics.

Caitlin realized that, like any successful team, they all had separate roles beyond their actual work duties. Zach's was to keep everyone happy. Debra's was to solve problems. Olive made them laugh. Martin was her comic foil. Nikki kept them in line. Dallas made them all cooler. And John, what did John do?

Caitlin sat up and stared at him. He was still on his phone, his brow furrowed. He looked up, caught her gaze, and smiled, a genuine smile, one she hadn't seen before. She wasn't sure what her role here would be, either.

Madison was attempting to motivate the group to do a second round of tug-of-war, but disinterest won out. Marc was now lying next to Debra, their heads close together in conversation.

Caitlin excused herself and walked over to Nikki, who was huddled with Olive off to the side. They certainly made a striking duo, the stylish Black woman and the posh, pale Brit.

"Caitlin, darling, we're going to head back to the hotel and, you know, *strategize*," said Olive. "Would you like to join us?" Caitlin nodded.

"Let's leave without saying goodbye," said Nikki. "Pretend we're walking to the bathroom and then just go. Otherwise, it'll be a whole thing. Madison will probably start crying." They walked away across the field, and Nikki pulled out her phone to call an Uber.

"I know this is all cloak-and-dagger, and I get that in a worst-case scenario the sale of our company could be derailed, and we'd all lose our potential millions . . . but . . ." said Olive, smiling mischievously, "this is fabulous! A mystery! Who would have thought that the Finger Waggers would turn into a detective squad."

"A woman is dead," said Nikki darkly.

"And we're going to find out why!" countered Olive in a singsong voice.

They'd nearly reached the road when Caitlin felt a hand on her shoulder. The three of them turned to see John, his arms crossed over his over-developed chest, a disappointed look on his face.

"Three of my favorite female executives! Where are you off to? The games aren't over. And I've got a special surprise for everyone. You can't leave yet."

"Oh, god, John," said Olive. "Another surprise?"

"You'll like this one, I promise. Come back, please. That's an order." John put his arm around Caitlin—Caitlin caught Nikki and Olive giving each other a look, but what was she supposed to do? Shake him off?— and escorted her and Nikki and Olive back to the others. They were all sitting on the grass, sunbathing. Dallas and Martin had both taken off their shirts, and Caitlin was struck by their competing abdominals. Mike had been steadily adding to his gut for the past few years, and it was nice to see toned men for once. She immediately felt bad about this line of thought. Why was she so down on Mike? He hadn't done anything to her, other than act icily while she was off partying with coworkers and caressing John Shiller's hand.

Madison was fanning John with her clipboard. He cleared his throat.

"My Aurora A-team! What a wonderful morning we've had, filled with healthy competition and impressive athletics. I think joint physical activity is a great way to bring coworkers' relationships to the next level, and I appreciate your participation—some of you more enthusiastically than others."

"Let's hear it for Martin!" chimed in Zach. Martin gave two thumbs-down.

"As a reward for your efforts," said John, "I'm letting everyone off the hook for today's brainstorming session." Caitlin had seen that the afternoon's schedule included something amorphous, from 3:00 to 5:00 P.M. in the hotel's conference room, called "Aurora and Beyond: Thought Starters." She'd been dreading it. Caitlin was very much a "get shit done" kind of employee and hated agenda-less meetings, which generally became a forum for the male team members to hear themselves talk.

"Tonight, we'd had a dinner planned at Stubborn Seed, but I have a treat for you all instead." (Martin booed softly.) "A final-night surprise for your hard work and good attitudes. A pick-me-up for our collective loss. I mean of a person, not a pickleball game." John paused for laughter. No one laughed. "Madison, can you do the reveal?"

Madison pulled a piece of paper out of her clipboard and held it up excitedly.

"The surprise is a spreadsheet? Awesome!" said Zach jokingly. Madison looked down and realized she'd pulled out the wrong sheet.

"God dammit," she muttered as she riffled through the papers, finally finding the right one and holding it up with a big smile. The executives moved closer. It was a printout of a picture of a yacht.

"Yay?" said Dallas tepidly.

"I get seasick," said Martin. "Can't we just go to Stubborn Seed?" This was followed by a chorus of support. Caitlin could see that John was getting more and more annoyed and wanted to diffuse his anger, even at the risk of seeming like a kiss-ass.

"I love a boat ride," she said. "John, tell us about it."

"Why thank you, Caitlin," he said. "I'm glad at least someone is feeling grateful. Think about how lucky we all are. Here, together, working for an amazing company, in an amazing moment in time. For tonight's evening event, we've chartered an eighty-foot yacht to take us around Miami's harbor. Martin, you'll be happy to know that Stubborn Seed is catering, by special request—and a lot of money—and so you won't have to miss out on your fancy dinner. There will be plenty of drinks, sweets, and even a DJ! We shall use this as an opportunity to dance off some stress. Who's excited?"

Chase raised his hand immediately, which seemed to cheer up Martin. In truth, Caitlin *was* excited, and she'd started to think about what she would wear. She'd brought one dress on a whim, red and low-cut, not thinking she'd use it. Mike called it her "Miami dress." Perhaps this would be her Miami dress moment. She wondered if John would like it.

"Can we go back to the hotel now?" said Debra. Caitlin felt for her; she remembered how tiring it was being pregnant at social events. Caitlin was intensely curious about the father, though she knew it wasn't her place to ask. She couldn't imagine going through it all alone, and, for a minute, was racked with guilt at the idea that she was masturbating to thoughts of her boss while her dutiful husband was in Bronxville watching their kids. But she put that to the back of her mind. She'd be home soon.

Madison Bez

———

Madison Bez was spiraling. She'd spent months planning this executive retreat, taking care of every tiny detail, from the dinner reservations to the T-shirts to the handwritten welcome signs. She'd been hoping it would be the most memorable, perfect, productive work trip ever. Instead, someone was dead, items had fallen off the agenda, and John seemed focused on Caitlin Levy, who Madison was starting to hate. But right now she needed to focus on the task at hand: ensuring the yacht party went smoothly.

Madison was back from the Aurora-thon, sitting in the lobby of the 1, checking her hundreds of unread emails. She'd just gotten off the phone with Mac, the guy who ran the boat rental company, to talk through the specifics of the evening, including the drinks menu (specialty tequila cocktails and espresso martinis) and the decor. She'd taken pictures of the executives from their Instagram feeds and had them blown up into life-size cardboard cutouts, which would be placed around the boat. She thought it'd be a nice touch and hoped they all would appreciate it. Stubborn Seed was catering, so she'd also been on the phone with them earlier, organizing the food timing and delivery, and she'd handled little touches, as well, like putting John's favorite brand of hand soap, Space NK, in all the bathrooms.

She'd be on the boat with them all, but in the shadows, working out any issues with the staff, ensuring John was happy and taken care of. She was looking forward to it. That's what "fun" had morphed into for her.

She knew it might seem sad to another twenty-six-year-old, the kind of girl who hung out with John socially.

"Madison!" She looked up from her phone to see Zach approaching, still in his Aurora-thon T-shirt. She liked Zach, maybe the best out of anyone besides John, because he spoke to her like a real person.

"How's it hanging, Bez?" he asked. Madison knew there was something going on between him and Olive. Madison admired Olive; she thought she was glamorous and smart and more than a little bit intimidating. She knew Olive had worked her way up from assistant level, just like Madison was trying to do. It hurt Madison's feelings when Olive treated her like a peasant. She wasn't quite sure what she'd done to make Olive dislike her, and it made her sad.

"I'm fine, how are you?" Madison said as Zach sat down next to her on the white leather couch. Sometimes she felt bad for Zach, which she knew was silly, given he was so much richer and more powerful than she was. But she couldn't help it, especially when John was mean to him, which he had been lately.

"You know, stressed as always," he said. "But going to rally for this yacht party. I know how much work you put into this retreat, and if no one else tells you, we all appreciate it." She felt her face get hot.

"It's just my job!" she said, though she was happy to hear it.

She looked at Zach, his curly hair rumpled, his shirt clinging to his middle-aged body. Madison wondered if Zach was a good dad to his son. She knew he was divorced and shared custody. She hoped Zach saw his son more than Rick had seen her.

"Well done, truly," said Zach. "I'm proud of you." At his kind, fatherly words, Madison felt her eyes water with tears. She quickly wiped them with the back of her hand, embarrassed.

"Aw, it's okay, don't get upset," said Zach, putting his arm around her. "I know that Jessica's death is a shock. I'm sure you're devastated, like we all are."

At that, something broke in Madison, and she began to cry, large tears, heaving sobs, the works. Maybe it was the fact that a man hadn't put his arm around her in so long. Maybe it was the stress of executing the executive retreat and having something so large go so wrong. She tried so hard to make these events fun for everyone, and this time it felt like she couldn't do anything right. So she continued, knowing but not caring that her eyes would be swollen and red.

Zach sat with her and rubbed her back as guests walked by, trying not to look at the weeping girl in a corporate logo T-shirt. After a couple of minutes, Madison felt her breath returning to its normal speed. She sat up and looked at Zach, who appeared slightly terrified. He handed her a crumpled tissue from his shorts. She dabbed her face. That's when John entered the lobby, walking briskly toward them. She was so in tune with his rhythms, so familiar with his movements, speech patterns, and even his smells (he released a foul body odor when he was stressed, just like Madison's cats used to). Sometimes Madison thought she might be in love with John. Is that what love felt like? An all-encompassing urge to please?

A few times, late at night, alone in her tiny, mouse-infested room, Madison had allowed herself to imagine what it would be like to have sex with John. She'd close her eyes and think of a scenario—say, she'd be writing her daily email, the office deserted, and he'd come up behind her and swirl her chair around, picking her up and putting her down on her desk. Then he'd lift her dress and unzip his pants (always orange in her mind), and penetrate her right there, forcefully. Or they'd be walking in a hotel hallway, and John would pull her into his room, pushing her up against a wall and taking her then. The next day, she'd blush when she saw him in his apartment, puttering around in his pajama bottoms and an AURORA-THON 2019 T-shirt.

"Madison Bez, what has Zach done to you?" he said now, standing in front of them, his hands on his narrow hips. His waist wasn't much bigger than hers.

"I haven't done anything!" said Zach, standing up. "Madison and I were just having a heart-to-heart. You know that women always cry when they're with me. It's my thing." With that, he winked at Madison and walked back toward the elevators, leaving her alone with John. He sat down next to her.

"What's the matter with my most favorite assistant?" said John. She shook her head.

"Nothing, I'm okay. I was just having a moment. Zach didn't do anything."

"Of course he didn't, because he knows I'd fire him if he did," he said. She brightened at his words. "Now, I can't have my assistant upset, because that would be bad for *me*." He looked in every direction but at her. The other executives moaned about how John reframed everything in terms of John Shiller (he'd once said to Olive, "You have nice eyes, just like mine!" and Olive and Nikki and Debra laughed about it forever). But it didn't bother Madison. She figured some men were just like that.

"I'm fine, really, it was nothing. I'm just worried about the yacht party tonight. I want everything to go perfectly." She thought about the drugs she'd taken from Jessica's bathroom.

"I know you do," said John. "It's going to be great. You're doing a wonderful job." He looked away again. Something was bothering him, Madison could tell.

"On that note, I want to discuss something," he said. Madison's heart seized. Was she about to be fired? She didn't know what she'd do without this job. It was her entire life.

"Do you know one of my favorite Winston Churchill quotes?"

"'Men occasionally stumble over the truth, but most of them pick themselves up and hurry off as if nothing had happened'?" Madison rattled off. John shook his head. "'Everyone has his day, and some days last longer than others'?" She could do the same for dozens of others.

"No, not those, but those are great! I mean this one: 'Now this is not the end. It is not even the beginning of the end. But it is, perhaps, the end of the beginning.' Madison, this is the end of our beginning. As of today, you're no longer my executive assistant." Madison felt like she might faint. What would she do? How would she pay her rent? Would she ever see John again?

"Instead, you're officially promoted to deputy chief of staff, Aurora!" A buzz zinged through her, right up to her teeth, which started to chatter uncontrollably. "We will bump up your salary to eighty-five thousand,

and I'm gifting you ten thousand shares. You're a real part of the team now. You've proven yourself invaluable, and I'm happy you're at my side, helping me wage war every day."

Ten thousand shares! Madison couldn't believe it. She'd be able to live alone, to be done with the mice forever.

"Thank you so much," she said, trembling. He gave her a hug, patting her back. She wanted it to go on forever.

"I'm off to my room now to shower and change for the yacht," he said. "I hope you're feeling better about whatever was bothering you. Also, would you mind setting up a call with me, Debra, Martin, and Monica Wu from Minimus?"

"For sure," she said, hearing her twang come out. She'd been working on hiding her accent, but occasionally, when she was tired or excited or upset, it came back with a vengeance.

She thought back to the morning of the twenty-third, when the executives were arriving from the airport. Madison had been in the lobby, having a quick coffee while John went off to shower. In walked Jessica, wheeling a large black suitcase, followed closely by Debra and Caitlin, whom Madison was seeing in person for the first time (Caitlin was annoyingly pretty). Debra and Caitlin went directly to the elevators, but Jessica approached Madison with an odd look. Madison had never trusted Jessica. She didn't like either the direct line Jessica had to John, or that their relationship predated Madison's tenure. Jessica spoke to Madison like she was still a sales associate at the Gap, trailing careless customers, folding shirts in their wake. "I need to get in with John," Jessica said sharply. "Like, now."

"I'll do what I can," Madison said with a fake smile.

"Just tell me his room number, I'll go there myself," said Jessica.

"No," said Madison.

Jessica sat down next to her and got right in her face. Madison could feel her breath and smell her vanilla perfume.

"If you don't tell me his room number, I'll have you fired," Jessica spit at her. Madison bit down on her tongue, hard. Something in her snapped. She was sick of being treated like a piece of Alabama dirt. Who did Jessica Radum think she was?

"Absolutely not. You can't tell me what to do. You think he's going to fire *me* because you tell him to? *Ha!* You're not even getting any equity in the sale!" Madison's accent was in full force, and she put her hand over her mouth as soon as she realized what she'd said. But it was too late. Jessica scrunched up her face. She looked like she was going to say something else, but instead she stood and wheeled her suitcase through the beautiful lobby.

Days later, in nearly the same spot, John skipped away from her, leaving her alone with her clipboard and her guilty conscience. She looked at her massive to-do list—

- Finalize menu
- Make sure there's Poo-Pourri in the bathrooms
- Give the DJ all of John's do-not-play songs
- Remind DJ that he'll be fired if he plays "Don't Stop Believin' "
- Make sure there are no baby carrots on board (John's choking fear, etc.)

Her whole life was one long to-do list, and she loved it. Deputy Chief of Staff Madison Bez. It had a nice ring. She got out her phone to text Sandy the news.

Debra Foley

———

Debra Foley was lying on the bed in her suite at the 1, fantasizing about marrying Marc Kerry. After the tug-of-war debacle, he'd joined her in the grass. "We know each other," he'd said softly, breaking the amiable silence. "We can talk about it later. But I'd like to hang out more." Debra's heart swelled with happiness. They'd spent the afternoon together, grabbing lunch at a nearby Mexican restaurant, where Debra had two sips of a margarita.

He was perfect. He was amazing. He'd asked her questions about her life, was interested in her job, and gave her good advice about it, too. He told her that she needed to stand up to John, that she should hold him accountable for his bad decisions instead of letting him blame her. He said that keeping Jessica's death a secret was an outrageously crazy thing to do (but that, as Aurora's lawyer, his job was to protect the company). She knew he was right. It felt so good to hear someone say it. It felt so good to have someone look at her with concern and care. To not, for once, be the one who had to coddle and listen and comfort.

She rubbed her belly, which still only looked bloated. When would she pop, she wondered? She'd told Caitlin the truth, but only because she'd asked (unlike the rest of the executive team, Debra had a hard time lying to people's faces). Caitlin wouldn't tell anyone, she was sure of it, but Debra had limited time to keep the secret to herself. Her body would soon betray her. Then what would she do? How could she ever tell Marc?

On the way back to the hotel, walking on the shady side of the street, the air smelling of car exhaust, Marc had broached the topic of what had happened the night of Lisa's party. Debra had been avoiding it, awkwardly, and was relieved that she hadn't had to bring it up herself. They were strolling in tandem, and every now and then, Marc's hand would brush against hers, causing her stomach to swirl.

"Uh, so, about when we met . . ." Marc had said, his voice cracking somewhat. Debra's throat felt tight. He continued. "I had such a fun time at the party with you, and then back at your place. . . . And I'm so sorry I didn't get in touch after. I don't usually drink that much, and I was embarrassed. And I'd also forgotten to get your number. Though I know that's not an excuse. . . . When I was offered the chance to work on this deal, I took it immediately. I hoped I'd see you here, Debra." He looked at her, his mouth twisted. She'd wanted to kiss him right then.

"It's okay," she said, and she meant it. "I felt the same way." She left it at that. They walked a few more beats in silence, and then he took her hand. She let her fingers relax into his. They stayed that way until a block from the hotel, when Debra slipped hers back into her own pocket.

"I just don't want any of my colleagues to see, is the thing," she'd said as they crossed Twenty-Third Street and continued toward the 1.

Clouds had returned to the sky, lessening the oppressive heat from earlier in the day. They passed a family of four making their way toward the beach—a mom, a dad, a baby in a stroller, and a little girl, running ahead. "Cynthia, wait, not near the cars!" the mother yelled after her daughter, who was wearing a pink bathing suit and cat-eye sunglasses. The dad, young and fit and proud, was pushing the baby, whose legs were kicking in the air. Debra looked at Marc, with his floppy hair and nicely toned arms. Could that be Debra and Marc one day? Heading to the beach with their kids, heading toward a future together?

They'd parted discreetly at the elevators, but not before Marc had said, "I'm really looking forward to seeing you again tonight." Debra felt like she was in a dream. She'd found the father of her baby, and he was lovely, and he liked her! This didn't happen to women like Debra. Debra was plain. Debra was sensible. Debra worked and worked and worked.

But now she just wanted to sleep forever. Jessica, the pickleball, the tug-of-war incident, the emotional drain of spending time with Marc . . . She needed a break. Though at least she didn't have to call the police. Jessica dead was better than Jessica missing. For Debra, at least.

Debra heard a knock on her door. Not now, she thought. Just give me a moment. She remained still, hoping whoever it was would go away. The knock came again. And again. She got up, reluctantly, and opened the door to see Olive, Nikki, and Caitlin, all crowded in, their faces lit up with anticipation. Olive walked in first, sitting on Debra's couch with an operatic "ugh." The other two followed. Let the finger wagging commence.

"Here we are!" said Olive in a high-pitched voice. "And we're going to figure out what happened to Jessica!" So that's why they were all together.

"Jessica overdosed on drugs," said Debra with finality. "That's what happened." She noticed Nikki was holding a laptop.

"Uh, sure, okay," said Nikki. "But according to this"—Nikki waved the computer in the air—"Jessica was researching Aurora's algorithm, and also reading lots of old articles about WeWork, Bird, that sham scooter company, and the financial aid startup Frank, which was based on a total lie. So . . ." She paused, biting her upper lip, then went on. "I'm not *so* sure about the drug thing. It's a pretty big coincidence that she'd OD right when she was poking around the company. Haven't any of you watched *Dateline*?"

"In *Dateline* it's always the husband," added Caitlin gamely. "But Jessica isn't married."

"But Jessica had a work husband! Or hubby, as you people like to call it here," said Olive. "And we know who that is."

"Olive, Olive, Olive, how could you possibly accuse me of murder? I value my generals too much to kill any of them," said Caitlin in her best John Shiller impersonation.

"Guys, this is crazy," said Debra, laughing and shaking her head. "The sensible one" had always been her default role, and to be honest, Debra was getting sick of it. Maybe John *was* capable of murder. People could be surprising. Look at Debra: secretly pregnant, working at a company full of lies. She'd always been such a good girl. Maybe she'd changed, too.

"Also, according to this"—Nikki patted the computer again—"Jessica wasn't necessarily who she said she was. At least when it came to her love life."

Olive squealed. "I knew it! My gaydar is never off."

This was all so beyond what was appropriate from an HR standpoint, but Debra's tired body was cemented to her bed. She was almost positive that Jessica had simply OD'd, but if there was one iota of doubt, it should be discussed. They did have to make sure the sale progressed. Even though Debra hadn't gotten a ton of equity—an additional 40,000 shares—that would be enough to pay for private school or a live-in nanny. She'd need the help.

"Okay, fine, so if we really think there might be foul play, or whatever you want to call it, let's get on the same page and assign tasks," said Debra.

"Yes! The chief people officer has arrived!" said Olive brightly.

"First, everyone has to show their cards and share what they know that others might not," said Debra. The women looked in diverging directions, avoiding Debra's gaze. "Olive, you go first."

She hesitated momentarily, and then spoke slowly. "I saw Jessica and Dallas fighting outside of LIV." Nikki gasped. "But I couldn't hear what they were saying."

"And another thing," Olive went on. "Before she died, Jessica sent me an email that just had the name of a podcast: *Ladies of Tech*. And we were not, like, *send each other podcast*-type friends," said Olive. "But I haven't had time to listen to any of the episodes."

"How is that possible? You haven't had *time*?" Nikki screeched.

"I'm sorry, Nikki, but I was very tired last night when I read the email, and I couldn't stay awake. I'm not sure if you remember, but I was LAUNCHED OFF A JET SKI yesterday." Olive jumped in the air for emphasis.

"Okay, girls, enough. Next," said Debra with the air of a drill sergeant. "Caitlin, what do you know?"

Caitlin shook her head. "I wish I could remember anything from the end of Tuesday night, but I basically blacked out," she said ("Happens to the best of us, dear," said Olive). "However, I do know something about Martin." Debra's chest seized. Martin? Could he somehow be involved?

"I saw Jessica coming out of the bathroom at ZZ's, wiping her nose. I had a feeling Martin had been with her, and so I confronted him about it, and he confessed that they'd done some cocaine together." Nikki yelped.

"But Jessica was alive a lot longer than that, so I don't know . . ." continued Caitlin. "Martin seemed genuinely upset about it."

Debra wasn't liking any of this. At all.

"Okay, Nikki, you're up," she said.

"I already told you guys everything I know," Nikki said. "For the record, though, I don't think Dallas has anything to do with this. His whole Burning Man, radical inclusion, civic responsibility thing doesn't include killing colleagues." Olive snorted. "Though we did see him poking around Jessica's room, and I'm not sure what that was about.

"What about you, Debra?" asked Nikki, raising a perfectly groomed eyebrow.

If Debra revealed what she knew, she was violating the terms of her job, the HR confidentiality she prized above all, her pact with John. She thought back to her conversation with Marc. Her vow to stop saving John from his own bad decisions.

"Jessica was barely going to get any equity," said Debra at last. The line landed in the room with a thud.

"How is that possible? She's John's favorite," said Olive.

"He wouldn't tell me why," said Debra. Her alliance had now shifted from her CEO to her friends, and there was no going back.

"Let's get to marching orders," said Debra.

"I'll try to figure out why Jessica was interested in Aurora's original algorithm," said Nikki.

"I'll look into that podcast," said Olive. "And I won't fall asleep."

"Caitlin, I'm so sorry that this is how you're entering Aurora," said Debra. She was mortified that they'd dragged their newest executive into this situation. It was quite an unusual orientation. But, in fairness, it felt like months had passed since they'd landed in Miami, Jessica in tow, the sale safely progressing.

"Are you kidding?" said Caitlin. "I've been bored at work for years. This is thrilling." Debra smiled at her. Were any of them normal?

"Then you're on John," said Debra, knowing it was a bad idea, but also knowing it would work. Caitlin blushed, embarrassed at what they all had noticed.

"Get all the information you can out of him about Jessica and anything else that might be relevant, including if he's selling Minimus a bunch of BS," Debra said. "I wouldn't put it past him. We all know he idolized Adam Neumann, and look what happened with WeWork." Nikki snickered.

"I'm going to go through my HR files on Jessica and see what I can find," Debra continued, though she knew there was nothing in there worth finding. What she really meant was: She was going to take a nap.

"All right, my lovely Miss Marples, let's get cracking. We have to be downstairs for the Ubers to the yacht party in just a couple of hours. Let's see what we can do before then," said Olive, leading the way toward the door. Debra couldn't wait for them to go. Her eyes had begun to involuntarily close.

"Wait!" said Nikki, stopping short and bumping into Caitlin, sending her directly into the side of the kitchenette counter.

"Ow!" said Caitlin, rubbing her hip.

"Sorry, but we didn't get to the most important thing," said Nikki urgently. She was still in her yellow tennis dress from earlier, and Debra admired Nikki's strong legs and arms. Debra wondered if her baby was going to be a boy or girl.

"What's that?" said Olive. "Something else to dig for?"

"The most pressing issue"—Nikki smiled—"is: How was your afternoon date with Marc?" Debra blushed and looked down.

"Ohhhhhh!!!" said Olive, and they all joined in, even Caitlin, teasing like schoolgirls.

"Come on, tell," Nikki implored.

"It was nice," said Debra, trying not to sound too positive. "We went to Mexican, then walked back. We chatted. I like him," she said, thinking of the reaction she'd get if she added: And he's the father of my unborn child. She couldn't even imagine; they'd all simultaneously die.

"Oh. My. God," said Olive. "I love this for you. That's one amazing thing to happen on this god-awful trip."

"Yes, this is great news," said Caitlin. Though she didn't know Debra as well as the other two, she was the only one who knew her secret. Half of it, at least.

"I can't wait to see you two together tonight," said Nikki. "You deserve happiness, Debra," she said. At that, Debra felt tears spring into her eyes. Why was she getting so emotional? It must be the hormones.

"All right, you three, out of here," Debra said softly, wanting to end the show.

They filed out, leaving her alone to think. She lay down on the bed. It was 4:00 P.M., and she had some pressing work to do on the equity documents, but she couldn't muster the energy. She couldn't look at the numbers one more time, to see that she'd gotten fewer shares than *Martin*. Than *Olive*. Even Nikki, who'd threatened to leave the company, had been set to get more than Debra, loyal Debra, who always did what she was told.

Well, maybe that time was coming to an end. With Marc's encouragement, she was going to stand up for herself. Advocate for Debra! She'd already ratted John out once. She closed her eyes, resolved. And then she heard another knock at the door. Not again. No. But the knocks kept coming. Once more, she lifted herself up, with difficulty, and opened the door.

"Debra," Martin hissed, grabbing her arm and pulling her back into the room.

"Martin, let go of me," said Debra, shaking him off.

He was jumpy, and his pink shirt was sticking to his chest.

"What's wrong with you? You look like garbage," she said. "And you never look like garbage."

He shimmied closer to her, and she backed away.

"What the hell? We're alone in my room. No one can hear or see us," she said, sitting on the bed and shooing him away.

He hovered nearby, going from foot to foot.

"Martin, spit it out," she said. He was making her nervous.

"I—I . . . did something," he said in a loud whisper. She waited for him to continue, but he just stood there. For a moment, Debra felt sorry for herself. Why did people always confess their sins to her? But then she remembered that it was her job to listen. This is what she'd signed up for.

"Just tell me," she said, patting the bed.

Debra had a soft spot for Martin. He reminded her of her brother Don, a macho show-off with a tender side that he hid from public view. (Both Don, a balding medical equipment salesman in Buffalo, and Martin, a stylish gay tech executive in New York City, would have balked at the comparison.) Martin started to cry, tears falling on the comforter. Debra patted his back. She didn't know how she was going to have a baby; she already had so many.

"I hid a data breach," Martin said softly. He took a deep breath and sat back up, wiping his eyes. He was looking off to the side, unable to face Debra with this news. Her heart sank. She would have preferred him to confess his drug use with a dead executive—anything but this.

"A few months ago, we had a major IT fuckup. Bank account info of a couple of hundred clients was stolen by god knows who, probably Russian cyber criminals. I discovered the breach myself one night, late, and plugged the security holes quickly. I never told anyone, I just hoped it would go away," he said weakly. "I know I should have disclosed it, but I was worried about the fallout. And I wanted that raise!" Debra felt herself veering from pity to anger, but she kept her emotions in check.

"You know this could tank the sale, right?" she said, her voice steady, though she felt like hitting him over the head. What a dummy. This could ruin everything. There goes the live-in nanny! There goes private school!

Debra had always been driven more by love of the work than by her compensation, but during this trip, she'd felt a shift. Maybe it was because she'd been slighted on her equity by John. Maybe it was that she was pregnant and needed to provide for a family. Maybe it was that her colleagues had started to show their true colors.

"It wasn't such a big deal," said Martin, sniffing. "It was only like a hundred clients, not into the thousands. And I spotted it almost immediately."

"Martin, Minimus is now looking closely at all of our systems; if they find out that we covered this up, we're toast."

"In my defense," he said, "it's kind of also Dallas's fault. He's the CTO! He should have eyes across everything instead of constantly riding that dumb bike."

"So this is why we're speaking with Monica Wu? She found something in the due diligence we delivered?"

Martin nodded and put his head back in his hands.

"The call is in ten minutes. You have to help me!" He sat up again and took Debra's hand. She could feel his heart beating in his palm. She should fire Martin, without severance, and possibly look into legal action against him. As chief people officer of Aurora, that was her duty. Instead, she said, "I'll figure something out." She thought of her brother Don, up in Buffalo, his life so unappealingly bland. She thought of the baby inside her.

"Yay!" he said, brightening. Debra was relieved to hear the old Martin back in his voice, as much as he irritated her. "What will you say?" he asked.

"You'll see," said Debra.

Martin lay down on the bed and Debra collapsed beside him.

"What happened with the cute lawyer?"

"We had lunch, we talked. I might be in love with him," she said. It was true.

"That's great!" said Martin, perking up. "Why don't you sound happy?"

"Oh, I don't know," said Debra. "It's complicated. I don't have a history of happy endings with men. I barely have any endings at all," she said. Debra had a sudden thought, so she decided to change the topic in case she got emotional again.

"How did you know how much Caitlin was making?" she asked him.

"I heard about Caitlin from Olive," he said after a beat. Debra made a mental note to ask her about it.

"Come on, Debs, let's go to John's room and get this call with Monica Wu over with," said Martin, pulling her up. Debra allowed herself to get dragged out of bed. She looked at her pillows longingly.

"Martin . . . is there anything else you'd like to tell me?" said Debra deliberately. She wanted to give him a chance to tell her about the drugs. He couldn't have had anything to do with Jessica's death, right?

"That wasn't enough? No, nothing more from old Martin," he said, staring at himself in the hallway mirror, fixing his hair so the side part was perfectly neat. Debra glanced at herself next to him. She was still in her AURORA-THON T-shirt and Umbro shorts, and there were bags under her eyes.

"Stop looking at yourself like that, you're gorgeous," said Martin. "And there's a lawyer who has the hots for you."

Debra tried to channel that energy as they left her room. She would put on lipstick for tonight and wear something that wasn't so frumpy. She was excited to see Marc. But first, she had to save Martin's ass.

Zach Wagner

———

Zach Wagner was standing on the deck of the *Sundancer*, the eighty-foot yacht that John had rented for the evening, next to a life-size cardboard cutout of himself. There was still daylight at 7:00 P.M., the sun hanging low in the horizon, and Zach was admiring the Miami skyline, the white buildings popping up from behind the palm trees. He'd worn a striped linen shirt and blousy blue pants (his cutout, meanwhile, was in a suit, as Madison had used a picture from his nephew's bar mitzvah). For shits and giggles, Zach had purchased a sea captain's hat from a novelty store on Collins Avenue, which was perched on his head.

The boat hadn't yet taken off. John and Martin and Debra were arriving a few minutes behind the others, having been on a mysterious call with the team over at Minimus. Zach had taken an Uber from the hotel with Olive and Nikki. Every time Nikki had turned to look out the window, Zach, in the middle seat, slid his hand farther under Olive's bum, to his right. She'd settled on top of it, nicely, and he'd had to keep adjusting himself to hide his hard-on. Good thing the pants were loose.

He'd wanted to see Olive in between the Aurora-thon and now, but she'd claimed she was "busy." Doing what? And what was this phone call with Minimus that he wasn't briefed on? Why did they want to speak to Martin? He'd heard secondhand, from Debra, that Nikki was staying on in her role instead of leaving for Trade Desk. He hated being the last one to know information about the company, and that's how he'd felt this entire trip.

Zach had returned to the hotel earlier today in high spirits, looking forward to an afternoon of hot sex with Olive. He'd been watching her play pickleball, picturing all the dirty things they'd do once they got back to the room. Instead, he'd been greeted by a weepy Madison. Poor kid. Zach couldn't tell if she wanted to be John's mother or his wife. He'd seen it before—the devoted assistant whose identity becomes so entwined with her boss's that she ends up losing her own.

Zach had gone up to his room alone and put his running playlist on the Bose wireless speaker, trying to psych himself up. It was filled with peak Gen X classics by Guns N' Roses and the Beastie Boys, and some Madonna and C+C Music Factory thrown in for good measure. He'd once played it for his son, Brennan, who'd covered his ears during "Paradise City"—"Paradise City"!—and had made him feel about a hundred years old. He was only forty-six, for god's sake. Still in his prime. He had his hair, his face looked good, he was CRO of a thriving $800 million company. (Even if that company wasn't completely kosher; wasn't every startup a house of cards to a certain extent?) And, with his 125,000 shares, he was set to make millions if the sale went through.

He'd pulled up Brennan's contact on his phone.

Hey, just checking in to see that you're okay, Zach texted. Miami is fun, but hot. I've been sweating up a storm. Zach saw the three dots shimmy, meaning Brennan was texting a reply. But then: nothing. Rejected by his own son.

Zach examined himself in the bathroom mirror, leaning in closely to inspect the shadows under his eyes. He needed a pick-me-up. He decided to go for a quick run on the boardwalk—he didn't want to be in a nap-coma for the yacht party. Still in his shorts and his AURORA-THON T-shirt, Zach went out the back of the hotel; the boardwalk ended around Fourteenth Street, so he'd run there and then loop back past the 1. He wanted to last for at least three miles, though he was already feeling winded. He needed to stop drinking so much, he knew—scotch and whiskey when it was cold, tequila when it wasn't. (He didn't think he was an alcoholic, but possibly by some definitions he was a functioning one. Wasn't everyone in sales a functioning alcoholic?) No matter. He was fine for now. Drinking didn't interfere with his life so much as differentiate his days from his nights.

He had so much stress with everything going on at Aurora, particularly lately. John was a good CEO, better than most Zach had worked for. He was great in board meetings, and he came to life in front of a PowerPoint. He could squeeze money out of anyone; Zach had witnessed him extract millions from investors before anyone even realized what was happening. John trusted Zach to run his part of the organization, and Zach acted as John's public foil, the charming, fun guy to John's oddball persona. But for the past few months, John had been picking on Zach, calling him out in meetings for mistakes, riding him hard as they headed into the Minimus deal. It was taking a toll on Zach's sanity. He wasn't sleeping well, he was eating too much candy, and he couldn't stop thinking about work, work, work, work, work, work, revenue, revenue, revenue.

Zach led the biggest team at the company, he got the most shit from John, he lived and breathed his job. And it was literally killing him. At his last annual physical, he'd had borderline high blood pressure, for which his doctor had put him on a low dose of Micardis. He hadn't told Melissa, who was always bugging him to eat better, drink less, and do Pilates with her (not happening).

He ran past an attractive woman, jogging along in a purple spandex onesie. He smiled at her, and she smiled back. Still got it. He could see the beach from the path, the different-colored umbrellas for each hotel, the women in various states of undress, the shimmering, flat sky-blue ocean. Miami beach was the perfect mix of trashy and luxe. He should look at condos to buy while he was here. The market was just going to keep going up, and it'd be nice to lock in a place before he got priced out.

He walked on the sand for his cooldown, drawn by the breeze and the seminaked women. The 1's beach area was dotted with white umbrellas and blue chaise lounges, and Zach grabbed a towel from the attendant and stretched out on a chair in front of the ocean. He closed his eyes, enjoying the warm air and the soothing noise of the water, and tried to relax.

But he couldn't, because he didn't know what to do about Melissa. She'd been bugging him to move in together, but that wasn't about to happen. He loved his bachelor pad in Gramercy, a sleek two-bedroom in a new building on Twenty-Fourth Street, and he loved living alone in it. He'd gotten divorced six years ago, when Brennan was eight, after a miserable ten years of marriage to his ex. He spent the three following years having sex with half the single women in New York. It amazed him how much his currency had gone up since his twenties; as a divorced, successful forty-year-old dad, Zach was a hot commodity. He'd met Melissa on a semi-exclusive dating app, Raya, which screened its male users by net worth and its female members by looks. She was young, twenty-nine to his then forty-three, and hot in a way that in his earlier life would have been unavailable to him. She was in love with him—or, rather, she wanted to marry him (were those two different things?)—though he'd never felt that strongly about her. But by then, he was finally tired of sleeping around and was happy to have someone to try new restaurants with and take to family weddings.

Over the years, he'd tried to break it off, telling her he wasn't going to settle down again, that he was done with the marriage thing. But she kept coming back, kept making it too easy for him to mistreat her. He did feel badly about it. But not badly enough to stop sleeping with her for good.

Olive wasn't like that at all. Olive didn't put up with his shit. He loved that she challenged him, and that she understood his work and how much it meant to him. Her job meant that much to her, too. Melissa was in the marketing department at a hedge fund, trotted out to take clients to dinner and given a script of how to best sell the company's services. She'd told Zach she'd like to stop working after she had kids. Olive looked down on women like Melissa. Zach also loved that about her. Maybe Zach just loved Olive, full stop. He went back to the hotel in a good mood, armed with that realization. Heading into the evening, he'd been excited for everyone to see his funny hat. But now he felt demoralized and out of control.

Zach saw John walk onto the *Sundancer's* deck, wearing a tuxedo with tails, a polka-dot bow tie, and an enormous top hat. Zach, in his sea captain's cap, could only imagine how preposterous the two of them looked together.

"Zach, Zach, Zach—actually two Zachs!" said John, looking at the cardboard cutout before doing a little twirl, his tails fanning out as he did. "What do you think of my suit? It's sharp, right? I like your hat almost as much as I like mine!" A classic John compliment; Zach would have to remember to tell Debra and Olive about this one.

"You look great, John. Does the outfit have any special significance?" Zach knew he was about to get an earful, and so beckoned over Debra, who was standing with that lawyer Marc, as well as with a cutout of Olive, frozen in a wintry black cocktail dress. Debra walked over with a smirk on her face. Zach noticed she looked pretty. She was in a floaty printed dress and had worn lipstick and curled her eyelashes. Good for her, he thought. He saw Marc watching her appreciatively.

"You know that Winston Churchill wore suits made by the great Savile Row tailor Henry Poole," said John, smoothing his hands over his chest with pride.

"I didn't know that, but go on," said Debra, smiling. Debra seemed to be in a better mood tonight than she'd been for the past few days, and Zach was happy to see it. Nothing worse for company morale than a grumpy head of HR.

"Henry Poole reissued some classic Winston Churchill looks in 2017 in honor of *Darkest Hour*, the movie for which Gary Oldman won the Oscar for portraying Churchill. Now, do I think Oldman should have won the Oscar? I'm not so sure," said John, heading off on one of his classic Churchillian tangents. Zach had heard it a million times before.

"He had the voice, yes, and the infamous stance, but he lacked a certain je ne sais quoi that only Churchill possessed."

"I've never seen the movie," said Debra.

"Oh my, Debra," said John, pretend-staggering back and accidentally smashing into the cutout of Caitlin, in jeans and a T-shirt, her arms outstretched over phantom children, who'd been edited out.

"Excuse me, my lady," said John, giving cardboard Caitlin a little bow. The real Caitlin, wearing a sexy red dress, joined the group. Zach saw her taking in John's elaborate getup.

"What was I saying? Oh, yes, Henry Poole," continued John. Zach looked around for Olive but didn't spot her on the deck. Maybe she was in the bathroom. He wondered if there was a place to which they could sneak away to have sex. He'd do a survey of the space if John ever finished talking.

"This suit is a replica of one of Churchill's favorites, reissued by Henry Poole for *Darkest Hour*. It's a fine bit of marketing, as well as a fine-looking garment. Don't you think?" Zach nodded lazily. Something was off about John lately. His bluster was never-ending, like he was always on high alert. And Zach supposed he knew why.

Madison was standing directly behind John, carrying a tote bag that Zach assumed held the clothes that John would change into after showing off his Winston Churchill garb. Zach gently pulled her away from the others, next to the cutout of Martin, Blue Steel–ing in skinny jeans. Zach lowered his voice.

"Are you feeling better?" Madison nodded her head yes. Right then, Olive sauntered over, her hips swishing in a colorful pink-and-orange maxi dress.

"What are you two discussing?" said Olive, staring at Madison suspiciously.

"Just what's on the agenda for tonight," said Zach. He didn't like lying to Olive, but he didn't know if he could trust her fully on anything. Olive's mouth had gotten her in trouble before.

"Yes, that's right," said Madison stiffly. "After we take off, John has a special game planned for you all. And then dinner and dancing." Zach didn't know what was going on between the two of them, but he didn't like it.

"Oh, dear, I don't think I can take another game," said Olive. "The Aurora-thon was enough for the rest of my life."

"This one doesn't have anything to do with sports," said Madison.

Olive put on her large black sunglasses. "Nice touch with the cutouts, Madison," she said sarcastically, then walked away.

"What was that about?" asked Zach. Madison frowned and walked back over to John, who was still monologuing to Caitlin and Debra. Zach spotted Dallas near the bar, set up outside on the deck, behind a few high tables. Dallas was chatting with a pretty bartender in a minidress. She was giggling at something he'd just said.

Zach, frustrated at constantly being in the dark, decided to ask Dallas about what he'd learned from John the other day. He took off his captain's hat, placing it on top of the cutout of Dallas, his cardboard hair now covered. This wasn't the work of a clown. It was the job of a future CEO. Zach stood straighter at the thought.

He sidled up to Dallas, who was sipping a seltzer with lime.

"Hey, man, how's it hanging?" said Dallas. The boat lurched away from the dock, heading out toward the open waters of Biscayne Bay.

"I'm doing fine," said Zach, trying to figure out the best way to broach the tricky topic. He decided to dive in. That's what a real leader would do.

"I have to talk to you. John told me about this 'virtual events strategy' that's the basis of the sale to Minimus. He said you guys came up with it together. Can you please fill me in?"

There, he'd done it. Zach waited for a moment as Dallas gathered his thoughts, his handsome brow flexed, his tongue wetting his lips.

"Dude, there's nothing to explain," said Dallas, annoyed. "We came up with an idea for hosting events in the Metaverse, where people can gather virtually, using Meta's AI headsets. Our clients can sponsor. Minimus is into it." This felt like a plausible explanation to Zach, though he still sensed there were things under the surface that he didn't know.

He wanted to keep digging, but Madison then handed John a flute of champagne and a spoon, and John loudly clanged the glass until everyone finally stopped talking.

"Team, team, TEAM!" John yelled. They all shut up. John's face looked rather shiny, like he'd just gotten done with a round of squash. It was still warm outside, though the sun was swiftly sinking, and Zach wondered when John would change out of his Churchill tux. It was tough to take him seriously as it was.

"Gentlemen and ladies . . ." A waiter came through the group holding a tray of tuna tartare on mini toasts, walking in front of the cutout of

Zach, a silly grin plastered on its face. John, unfortunately, shooed the waiter away. The real Zach was starving. The yacht hit a small wave, and Zach felt himself sway to the side. John took his top hat off and wiped his brow. He handed his hat to Madison, who held it as if she were accepting an Oscar. "I have some good news to share," said John, speaking slowly. "We just had a productive call with Minimus's leadership team, and everything is moving forward as planned. We should be signed imminently." Madison let out a loud "woo-hoo!"

"I need everyone laser focused on getting over the finish line. As my man Churchill said, 'Never surrender.' And we won't! We shall see this sale through if it's the death of me. Or of all of you."

"Can we eat now?" asked Martin. "Sea air makes me hungry."

"Martin, no," said John sharply. "We're going to play a game before dinner."

"Another game?!" said Nikki. "No way, José." She was sipping a glass of pink champagne; Zach wanted to speak to her later about what had happened with Trade Desk. Debra had told him about Nikki's offer in the Uber ride from ZZ's to LIV. It had been the two of them with Jessica in the car. Jessica was on her phone, texting intently, and Debra had spoken softly to Zach about Nikki, figuring Jessica couldn't hear or, more likely, didn't care. Jessica had always minded her own business, unlike the rest of them.

"Yes, *señorita*," replied John in an exaggerated Spanish accent. Nikki shook her head at his typically un-PC response.

"This isn't a physical game, it's more of an emotional-bonding exercise," said John. ("Enough bonding!" said Olive, to no one in particular.)

"John, you know we can't cross personal lines here," said Debra, exasperated.

"Debra, how I love your verve," said John with a snort. "As if we haven't crossed personal lines before. Now, everyone, please come inside the boat's cabin over here, grab a few bites and another drink, and then sit at the table."

At that, Madison marched through the doors, leading to a luxe living room area, including two plush sectional couches, a few side tables, and a large-screen TV, flanked by cardboard cutouts of John, in his siren suit from the other day, and one of Madison, in her signature floral dress. "Ha! She made one of herself!" Olive said loudly as they entered, causing Madison to redden unhappily. Everything was high-touch nautical—shiny, wooden, and blue. There was a food spread on a bar area off to the right, and Zach made a beeline for it, helping himself to a plate of gourmet cheese, cured meats, and mini hot dogs. After taking a hot dog in his mouth, he looked over his shoulder to see Dallas scowling in his direction.

Midbite, he felt someone pull his arm and turned to see John, who motioned for Zach to follow him. They stopped in front of one of the couches, far enough away so that no one could hear what they were saying.

John's green eyes looked red, and there was a puffiness to his face that suggested he hadn't been sleeping well. "Have you heard anything about Jessica?" John's top hat, which he'd put back on for some reason, slipped down his head a bit, and he pushed it back up with an anxious twitch.

"Why would I have heard anything about Jessica?" said Zach. "She's dead. She died of an overdose. It wasn't even her fault, as you said. The cocaine was laced. I did some research about it, and apparently fentanyl overdoses are common in the Miami club scene. People think they're snorting cocaine, but then—boom—they're turning blue and foaming from the mouth." Zach made a little "arrrggeeee" sound to demonstrate, but John didn't seem amused. "But if there's something you want to share with me, I'm all ears. . . ." Zach continued, conveying the seriousness of the request by placing a hand on John's arm. "I'm the CRO of Aurora, and, more importantly"—and here Zach knew he was manipulating, but he wanted to be in the loop, for once in his goddamn life—"I'm your *friend.*"

He grasped John's arm a little tighter and looked at him imploringly. This is what Melissa did to Zach when she wanted him to buy something for her, and it usually worked. It was working here, as well. Zach saw John's face slacken, and he stepped toward Zach, putting his mouth close to Zach's ear. Zach could feel John's sour breath on his skin, and he had to struggle not to gag.

"We are totally fucked," said John, so softly that Zach thought that maybe he'd misheard. "We have to sign this deal in the next day, or Minimus is going to uncover the truth," he said. Zach felt his throat tighten. He swallowed, hard.

"What do you mean, 'the truth'?" Zach said, not turning his head. His body had begun to shake somewhat, and he couldn't tell if it was from shock or from the boat's motor.

Madison walked over, interrupting them. She was in a long green dress, her hair in an intricate updo, like she was headed to senior prom.

"John, it's time to start," she said, checking her clipboard. "Otherwise, we're not going to get to dinner on time. And I know how you feel about that." John was like a child that way. If he missed a meal, he'd be headed toward a tantrum. Madison made sure his blood sugar levels remained high.

"We will continue this chat, Anthony Eden," said John, tipping his hat at Zach casually, as if they'd been speaking about the weather. Zach sighed, his long-held dream of becoming a CEO fading away. He looked over at Olive and admired her shape in the setting sun. Then he took out his phone and sent a text to Kaya Bircham.

"Aurora A-Team!" John shouted. "Gather 'round." The cutout of John preened behind him as he spoke.

Olive Green

———

In another life, Olive Green thought, she'd have been a great reporter. The one digging instead of the one running interference. In the hours before the yacht party, Olive had done some serious investigating, and what she'd found had changed everything.

First, she'd looked through all two hundred episodes of the *Ladies of Tech* podcast, searching for a clue as to why Jessica had sent her there. But it was an impossible task; there were too many women featured, too many interviews to scan in the scant hours she had before the event.

Then it occurred to Olive, based on Jessica's interest in Aurora's original algorithm, to think back to the company's origin story, the one Olive was always regurgitating to the press. Robbie Long. He was the brilliant engineer who'd died before his time, the one whom John and Dallas and even Nikki spoke of with such awe. Olive looked him up, running into some dead ends on Google, including a few dark social media profiles and a short obituary for Robbie in Berkeley's monthly magazine ("Robbie Long, '05, Gone but Not Forgotten"). She'd found Robbie's parents in an online directory for their local church but decided against contacting them—the idea of a child's death was overwhelmingly sad, and she didn't want to bother a grieving mother or father in the name of white-collar intrigue.

Instead, she focused on locating Robbie's fiancée, Meagan Hudson, who was set to receive a large payout in the sale of the company. Meagan proved a little tricky. Olive could see in an outdated LinkedIn profile that

Meagan had been at PayPal, so she called a friend of hers who worked there, Renee, a fellow corporate PR lifer. Renee picked up on the first ring.

"Olive Green, why are you calling me? Has someone died?" said Renee. They'd worked together years ago, as assistants at PMK, right after Olive had moved from London, and had kept in touch, occasionally meeting for a gossipy drink after work.

"Well, yes, but no one you know," said Olive with a chuckle, knowing her dark humor was in poor taste but unable to rein it in. She was on the couch in her hotel room, in her robe. She'd just taken a quick bath. A soak always cleared her mind and did her good. It was one of the few customs she'd retained from her British childhood.

"I have something to ask of you. Can you please look someone up for me? Meagan Hudson. She worked at PayPal around eight years ago, but I'm not sure if she's still there."

"Sure, hold on a sec," said Renee, asking no follow-ups. People in PR knew when to pry and when not to, and Olive had done many favors for Renee over their careers. She owed her one.

"She did work here till a year ago," said Renee, after a minute or so of silence. "According to HR, she left for a startup, a restaurant reservation service called SnaggIt."

"I think I've heard of that," said Olive, remembering an article in *Businessweek* that had mentioned it as a leading competitor to Resy. "Thank you so much for the info! And as always, let's keep it between us," said Olive. "I'll buy you an espresso martini soonest."

Olive had then commenced researching SnaggIt, learning it had just closed its second round of fundraising and, according to a blurb in *TechRadar*, was proud of its all-female engineering team, led by a brilliant woman named Meagan Long.

Meagan Long! So she'd started using Robbie's last name at some point after Robbie died, which Olive found both sweet and depressing. Olive was running out of time; the party started shortly, and she wasn't yet dressed.

Thankfully, she knew exactly where to go. Olive returned to the *Ladies of Tech* page in her podcast app. About six months ago, the podcast's guest was someone named Meagan Long, an engineer who led SnaggIt's all-female team. Olive buzzed with excitement as she hit play, carrying her phone around with her as she put on her dress and makeup.

The beginning of the talk, led by a journalist named Tina Allowith, was a basic introduction of Meagan and her role at SnaggIt, with questions about what it was like to be a woman among so many men. Olive found Meagan to be articulate and likable, able to explain engineering concepts in a way that Olive, a layperson, understood.

Olive loved hearing women speak about their career paths, and it pleased her to learn of glass ceilings being shattered. She knew it was very Gen X of her, but she didn't care; all these girls coming into the workplace had no idea how Olive and her cohort had strived and suffered to get where they were. The young people in their office were so entitled, so sure that they were always right. It killed Olive to hear them speaking about "self-care" and "burnout" and "boundaries." Boundaries! Ha! When Olive was in her twenties, she'd slept at her desk, she'd worked all hours until she'd collapsed, she'd lived for the job. She'd had bosses who'd screamed at her, bosses who'd made passes at her. She had one boss—a woman—who'd thrown a telephone at her head when she'd messed up a press release. A landline!

Toward the middle of the podcast, Meagan began talking about the culture at SnaggIt. Olive was in the bathroom, applying mascara. She had only a few minutes left before the Ubers were arriving to take them to the boat.

"As a team of women, we know how important it is to have time for our families, for babies, for having lives outside of the office," said Meagan, answering a question about work-life balance.

"Do you have children?" Tina asked. Olive was surprised they hadn't covered this earlier in the interview, but she supposed that everyone was so touchy nowadays, you could barely ask basic questions about people's bios without worrying about offending.

"No, I don't," said Meagan, with what Olive thought was a touch of remorse. Olive had been so focused on her mission—figuring out what

Jessica was up to—that she'd lost sight of the fact that this person's fiancé had died before their life together could even start. Tracy, for once, shut up. (What was it with podcast hosts needing to hear themselves speak?) Meagan continued unprompted.

"My fiancé actually passed away before we got married," she said steadily. Olive admired her stoicism. "He was also an engineer. I often think about him when I'm making a career move. I try to channel his ingenuity, creativity, and drive. He had big ideas—industry-revolutionizing ideas, which he unfortunately didn't get to implement—and he wasn't afraid to take risks."

Olive jolted, sending her mascara wand sliding down her cheek, leaving a long line of black across her face.

"That's so lovely," said Tina. She sensed that Meagan was done with the topic and promptly moved on to a question about salary negotiation.

Olive was now on the yacht. She hadn't had time to tell anyone what she'd found. Her instincts told her that Aurora's story was murkier than they'd been led to believe.

"Gather 'round, gather 'round," John demanded, corralling them into the area at the back of the cabin, set up with a long rectangular table. Each seat had a place card in front of it. Olive found hers, the *O* of her name written in Madison's loopy cursive, and sat down in the uncomfortable wooden chair. She checked her phone. Poppy had texted a few minutes ago, a selfie of her and Penelope making funny faces. Olive could see their bedroom at Henry's sterile apartment in the background. He'd gotten (or someone had gotten) pink comforters for the bunk beds, even though neither of her girls particularly liked pink. She missed them; it felt like weeks since she'd arrived in Miami.

Nikki slid in next to her, and Olive got a whiff of her perfume, an aggressive citrus-y scent that suited Nikki perfectly. She was wearing a sparkly top and a chunky beaded necklace and was looking at her phone intently. She felt closer to Nikki than she had in weeks. Nikki must have lied to Debra about the Trade Desk offer, hunting for more comp, and then reneged when it became clear she'd get richer by staying at Aurora.

Olive hoped the entire thing was behind them. She still cringed thinking about her conversation with Ben Hooks.

Zach took the seat on her other side, briefly smashing his leg against hers as he scooted under the table. She smiled at him. Olive had arrived on the trip considering their dalliance to be a fun, distracting work fling, something to concentrate on other than Henry's desertion and her dwindling savings. But, over these few days, her feelings had deepened. Maybe it was the sex—she knew that physical intimacy played with women's emotions. She wasn't that young or naïve. But it felt like more than that.

This morning, after breakfast, they'd slept together in his room. The light was soft, and the bedding was glorious. Instead of the bouncy, laugh-y sex from the previous days, they'd slowed down, their bodies in sync, two middle-aged careerists finding joy again.

"My friends and colleagues," said John, after everyone had been seated. A waiter was taking drink orders, and Olive asked for a supersize G&T.

"We've had a wonderful couple of days together," said John. ("No, we haven't," Olive whispered to Nikki, who elbowed her to shut up.) "In the sun, in the water, on the courts, in restaurants and clubs, and now on a boat in the open sea." John was still in his top hat, and Olive was having a hard time stifling her laughter, a lifelong problem resulting in her getting kicked out of several serious events, including her own grandmother's memorial service.

"To start tonight's festivities," John said, "we're going to participate in a classic team-building exercise: two truths and one lie." They all moaned in unison.

"What are we, interns?" said Zach. Olive wondered again if Zach was hiding anything from her.

"The last time I was forced to play this was in my freshman dorm at Yale," said Nikki.

"Yeah, yeah, we all know you went to Yale," said Zach, who'd graduated from Wisconsin and hated when the other execs bandied about their Ivy League credentials. Olive, for her part, had gone to Leeds University, in England, and was happy that no one in America seemed to know that it was a shit school. Her accent helped, she supposed.

They all began to talk among themselves. Olive took a sip of her drink. She was aching to tell her friends what she'd found out about Meagan and Robbie, and also wanted to know if they'd uncovered anything. When would this end?

"Quiet!" said John, tapping the table with his knuckles, his green eyes flashing in the cabin lights. Caitlin was sitting to his right, her red dress nicely showing off her fit-mom bod. Olive had a thought to pitch Caitlin to the *Times* for a soft profile in the business section, something about her new job and transitioning from media to tech, though she'd have to have a better understanding of Caitlin's role before contacting the editor there. What was this hire-to-fire nonsense John had been talking about?

Olive took in the scene—there was Martin, smiling devilishly at the lawyer Chase, who was wearing a fitted black shirt nearly unbuttoned to his navel. Debra and Marc were next to each other, their bodies angled toward one another. Dallas was at the other end of the table, looking bored.

John cleared his throat unattractively. Olive felt Zach's hand snaking up her thigh, and she gently pushed it away.

"Nikki, since you seemed so keen on the game, you start!" said John, and the room finally quieted down.

"John, this is some bullshit," she said. But he didn't relent, just continued to stare at her until everyone was absurdly uncomfortable. Olive saw Nikki's face light up with mischief. Oh no. What was she about to do?

"Okay, here we go. Number one: I scored sixteen hundred on my SATs. Number two: I'm really into country music. Number three: Martin did drugs with Jessica the night she died. Maybe he killed her."

Chaos erupted at the table, Martin screaming, "I did not kill anyone!" Olive and Nikki speaking loudly to each other across the table, Madison dashing among the group like a Ping-Pong ball, the two lawyers looking stricken, likely thinking about getting disbarred, and poor Debra trying to calm everyone down.

"Enough!" John screamed at the top of his lungs, silencing the group.

"Nikki, I assume you *did* get a sixteen hundred and that you *don't* like Faith Hill."

"I love Faith Evans. Who the fuck is Faith Hill?" said Nikki triumphantly. Olive let out a loud laugh. The balls on her. Olive loved every minute of it.

"Martin! Explain yourself," John said. They all turned to look at Martin, who was biting his nails.

"Fine, yes, I did one little line of cocaine with Jessica at ZZ's," said Martin softly. Chase scooted his chair away from Martin, distancing himself from the alleged criminal. Martin noticed and seemed hurt. "But she was alive and well when we left the bathroom, and I didn't speak to her at all after that. But she *was* arguing with Dallas at LIV!" He must have seen the same thing Olive had witnessed. Dallas sat quietly, his face impassive.

"The cat's out of the bag, I suppose," he eventually said. They all leaned in closer to hear him. "*Somehow,*" he said in an accusatory way, "Jessica had found out she was getting less equity than everyone else. She was mad about it and was yelling. I told her to take it up with John. He's the one who made the decision," said Dallas with a shrug. "Listen, you guys know me: I have a bias for action. But Jessica just wasn't in alignment that night." ("What?" Olive whispered to Debra.)

"This has gone far enough," said John with finality. "We are moving on. Jessica is dead. I saw her body. None of this will change that. As Churchill said, 'It is not enough that we do our best; sometimes we must do what is required.' And what is required of us is to keep all this quiet. Period. End of story." Madison gave a weak cheer.

"It's my turn now," John continued, his hat slipping down his head. Madison rushed over and pushed it back up.

"Number one: I appeared in a Cheerios commercial in 1992. Number two: I've shot and killed three iguanas in my life. And number three: My best friend growing up was my pet rabbit, Roxy." No one said anything; the only sounds heard were the clanking of silverware as the waiters brought dinner supplies out. Zach pinched Olive's leg, hard, and she pinched him right back. John had an eager look on his face, waiting for someone to jump in.

"So?" he asked the blinking crowd. "What's true and what's a lie? Any guesses?"

Debra raised her hand.

"Debra! My finest and only chief people officer. Would you like to hazard a guess? Are we feeling emotionally bonded yet?" John smiled, his lips tight.

"Actually, I'm feeling ill, not bonded," said Debra. Her face had a green tint, and she stood up, clearly wanting to get outside but seemingly paralyzed. Olive, concerned, went to help, but before she could reach her, Debra vomited, violently, all over the table, spraying the place cards as well as the cardboard cutout of Madison.

"No!" Madison gasped.

"Oh my god!" whimpered Martin, who put his hand over his mouth. The boat then tilted to the side and back again, and not a second later, Martin also puked dramatically, his head down, all over his own pants.

For the second time in fifteen minutes, the cabin broke into pandemonium, with the executives running between Martin and Debra, and waitstaff bringing in washcloths and water. Olive reached Debra and gently wiped her face and shirt with a napkin, like she used to do for her daughters when they were sick. Debra was crying. Marc stood next to her, frozen. Martin had disappeared into the bathroom, leaving his mess on his seat, Chase kindly cleaning it up as best he could.

"I'm pregnant," said Debra, tears streaming down her face. "And it's Marc's."

Marc nearly toppled over. He caught himself on the table right before he went down, standing up with a wobble. Olive couldn't believe what she'd heard. Debra was pregnant? With Marc's baby? She thought they'd met only yesterday.

Olive grabbed Debra by the waist and escorted her to the couches in front, gently placing her down and holding her hand. Nikki, who'd also taken a seat, elbowed Olive's ribs. The rest of them, besides Martin, who was still in the restroom, and Marc, who'd disappeared to the outside deck, gathered around. John pushed in. He'd finally taken off his hat, and his hair was sticking up straight, his polka-dot bow tie at a right angle.

"You're *what*?" he said, genuine concern in his voice. "Is that your lie? But what are your two truths?"

Debra looked up at him, her eyes wet. "I'm not lying," she said softly. Olive peered over at Marc, who was now poking his head back in the door. "I'm four months pregnant. I'm due in September."

"And Marc, our lawyer, is the father of this baby?" said John. Debra nodded, looking straight at Marc, who swiftly stepped back out to the deck. John shook his head.

"Debra Foley. Debra, Debra, Debra. I'm sorry, but I can't have my head of HR gone for god knows how long on maternity leave. Particularly not when we're in crisis. Your place is with me, in the office. You can't leave *me*," he said, spit gathering at the corners of his mouth. Debra looked down, embarrassed by it all. No one said anything. Then Caitlin, to Olive's surprise, exploded.

"Don't speak to her that way—this is her unborn child! She has a right to take off to care for a baby! Leave her alone!" Debra looked at Caitlin gratefully, and John's face turned a peculiar shade of rose.

Martin emerged from the restroom, slicking down his hair. He wandered over to them.

"I *told* you I get seasick, particularly if I smell vomit," he said. Then, directed at Madison: "We should have just gone to Stubborn Seed." Madison, in a very un-Madison move, gave him the middle finger. Martin paused for a moment, taking the temperature of the group. "Uh, what did I miss?"

"I'll fill you in, Martin," said Zach, leading him outside to the deck. "Let's get you some air, and let's give the Finger Waggers some space." They all walked out, leaving Debra, Nikki, Olive, and Caitlin inside, sitting in a row.

"Debra, we need to talk about this. Congrats! And with Marc, the lawyer?! How is that even possible? Why didn't you tell us? But first, I have to tell you guys something," said Nikki breathlessly, as soon as all the men were out of earshot. Olive quickly checked her phone—one unread email. It was from Kaya Bircham. Fuck. She opened it, shielding the screen to make sure no one could see.

Hi, Olive, I told you I'd keep you posted on my article. I'm going to put it up in two days, and we'd like a quote from John. The gist is that Shiller has misled Minimus about Aurora's strategy, among other things. Please send me a quote from John, either confirming or denying, ASAP. Olive could feel her blood pressure rise.

"I did a deep dive into our tech, but there was nothing off," said Nikki. "But then I did some poking around on Reddit, accessing threads about Aurora from over a decade ago. I came across a few posts that accused John and Dallas of stealing another engineer's idea for the company. That's got to be Robbie."

Before Olive could add what she'd learned, John came back into the cabin. He'd changed from his Winston Churchill costume into pink shorts and a white polo. He looked marginally less absurd.

"Dinner is served, ladies," he said. No one moved. Olive frowned at him. Nikki crossed her arms over her chest. Debra looked away. Even Caitlin gave him the stink eye. He stood there for a moment, his gaze darting from one to the other. Then he sighed, slouching like a defeated man.

"As Winston Churchill said, 'It is not in our power to anticipate our destiny.' Coming into this trip, I didn't know we'd lose one executive to the great beyond and one executive to motherhood. But life brings us the unexpected," he said. "I know I'll survive these travails and emerge stronger for it."

"Somehow, as always, it's all about John. Even when it comes to Debra's uterus," said Olive in a whisper. They all burst out laughing. No one could stop. Olive felt tears rolling down her cheeks, and her abdominals hurt from the effort of it all. John shook his head and left without saying goodbye, which sent them all into hysterics again.

"Do we really think that he's capable of killing someone?" asked Olive, wiping her face.

"Yep," said Nikki.

"Unfortunately, yes," said Debra.

"I just met him, but from what I can tell, he'd do anything to get his way," said Caitlin with a frown.

Olive felt like she was going insane. The lies were surrounding her on all sides, and she couldn't figure out what was up and what was down.

She took out her phone and pressed reply on Kaya's email.

John's quote is: "You can go fuck yourself." She pressed send.

"Olive, who did you hear about Caitlin's salary from?" Debra asked, seemingly out of the blue. Olive looked at Caitlin, who was blushing.

"I heard from Nikki," said Olive. "Sorry, love, but it's true."

Nikki shrugged. "Madison told me," said Nikki. "In the bathroom in the office, washing our hands. I was complaining about the new hire coming in above me, and she volunteered your comp. I think she reads all John's emails." Madison walked by them at that moment, a scowl on her face, her lipstick smudged.

Olive needed some space. She walked out of the cabin, stopping at the bar outside. The sun had set, and the lights on the harbor were sparkling. There was a bit of a chill in the sea air, and Olive shivered slightly. She grabbed a glass of champagne and downed it in one sip. She thought wistfully of Henry, and how he used to give her his sweater when she was cold. John approached her.

"What's the deal, Joan Bright Astley?" he asked. "Any word from Kaya?"

"Kaya's running an article soon saying that we are lying to Minimus," said Olive.

He averted his eyes.

"Is that true, John? How am I supposed to protect you if you don't tell me anything?"

"Listen, Olive . . ." John paused, out of words, for once.

Olive figured she would just keep going. Fuck it. This might be her only bloody chance.

"Did you steal Aurora's tech from Robbie Long?" She let the question hang in the air.

"No. Dallas invented it," said John, gesturing to Dallas, who was looking out at the water, his back straight and strong.

"I listened to a podcast with Meagan, Robbie Long's fiancée, and she said Robbie had some big, industry-revolutionizing idea before he died." John's forehead scrunched in confusion.

"Meagan said that?"

Olive nodded.

"And Nikki found some old Reddit threads saying you and Dallas stole another engineer's idea." John looked out at the water, deflated.

But Olive could only deal with one thing at a time, and *TechRadar* was more pressing than a potential stolen intellectual property issue. For now. "Anyway, I told Kaya to go fuck herself. But we need to somehow get that story killed. You have to deny it all."

"Dinner is served!" Madison declared, pointing to a table covered in delicious-looking food. Olive went over to eat. Kaya, Jessica, Meagan, Robbie, John, Dallas . . . they could all wait until she was full.

Martin Ito

———

Martin Ito was the luckiest man alive. Or that's how he felt, standing in the salty breeze, next to a handsome man, his career having flashed before his eyes. Sure, he'd just puked all over himself, and his Ami Paris cotton-twill trousers were still damp and smelly. But the air was reviving him, and his appetite was returning, just in time for the Stubborn Seed spread to appear. Plus, Chase had been so sweet to him, checking to make sure he was fine, asking if he could bring Martin water or saltines.

They were enjoying the view of Miami, the wind starting to pick up, and Martin felt Chase's leg touch his. They'd been flirting since the moment they met, and Martin was hoping tonight would be the consummation of it all. Maybe Chase could finally break Martin's streak of toxic men. An upstanding lawyer? It was Martin's mother's dream come true.

Martin had joined Aurora four years ago; Debra had found him on the data team at Google, coasting and bored. She'd seen his potential and given him a title bump and a raise, and he was grateful to her for that. He'd swiftly proven his worth, revamping Aurora's IT systems, organizing the internal dashboards so that they were simple and usable. Martin loved when things were clean. He loved to see rows and rows of numbers that made sense; it calmed his mind and body. He kept his desk immaculate, his meeting notes tidy. Everything about Martin, from his clothes to his haircut to his manicured nails, was just so. Professionally and aesthetically, he hated chaos.

Maybe that's why Martin's personal life had always been disastrous.

He went from man to man, from one tumultuous ending to the next. He thought of his poor mother in California, holding out hope that he'd settle down, maybe give her a grandchild before it was too late. Martin was an only child. His dad had died three years ago of lymphoma, leaving his mom in San Diego, in the house in which Martin had grown up. Martin didn't like to think of her drinking her red wine with dinner alone.

Maybe if he got enough from the sale, he could pay for a weekend house for her to use whenever she wanted. They could spend time together there, and then Martin wouldn't feel so guilty for being so far away, her thirty-six-year-old son whose last real relationship was ten years ago. At least he was a success. She could be proud of that.

"How are you feeling?" asked Chase, his blue eyes shining in the darkness.

"Better!" said Martin, "I'm nearly ready for a drink."

Chase laughed.

"I meant how are you feeling about your friend, Debra, being pregnant. But I'm happy your stomach has settled," said Chase, amused. Martin felt himself flush. He shrugged. How *was* he feeling about Debra? He was both surprised and not. She'd kept it all from him, which he was annoyed about, but he didn't blame her for being secretive, especially around this crowd. Plus, she'd just literally saved his life, so, as repayment, he was prepared to be the best guncle that little fetus had ever seen. Martin saw Marc hovering near the food, alone.

"How do you think Marc is going to handle it?" Martin asked.

"I honestly don't know him that well," Chase said. "We were both put on this deal last month, and it's the first time we're working directly together. He seems cool. Very . . . straight. But we're not like you guys, all chummy. I've never seen an executive team who's so weirdly close."

"I know, it's bizarre," said Martin, thinking of the phone call they'd just had with Monica Wu, and wincing again at how near he'd been to going down.

He and Debra had arrived at John's room together. John was staying in an impressive two-bedroom, ocean-view penthouse, with a full kitchen and private balcony. He was in his robe, lounging on his bed, his laptop open on top of him. His hair was wet, and Martin assumed he'd just had a shower. It was wildly inappropriate, certainly, for a CEO to have his employees in his room while he was half naked, but that was John's way.

"I see you brought your lawyer," said John, nodding at Debra. "Anything I need to be aware of for this call?" John was suddenly dead serious, and Martin prepared himself for the worst. He looked at Debra, who was stone-faced. What was her plan? How could she fix this?

"Should we actually have one of the lawyers here with us?" Martin ventured. His voice felt strained. John stared at the spot above Martin's shoulder.

"Not if you didn't do anything," John said. Martin nodded obediently.

"Okay, let's get on with it, then," John said, taking out his phone. He input a number and put it on speaker. A woman's voice answered.

"Hello, this is Monica Wu." Martin would recognize that nasal tone anywhere. Monica had tortured him at Google, undermining him in front of superiors, turning colleagues against him. She was super smart, maybe even smarter than Martin, and though her work was great, her personality was the pits.

"Hi, Monica, you have John Shiller, Martin Ito, and Debra Foley, our chief people officer, here on the line. What would you like to speak to us about?"

"Hi, all, thanks for calling. Martin, long time no talk. It's good to reconnect," said Monica. Martin mumbled in agreement.

"I wanted to go over something with you all, something odd that I found in the documents that Aurora sent over as part of the latest round of due diligence," she said. Martin knew exactly what she was referring to—the data breach he'd covered up. He thought he'd gotten away with it, that he'd buried the evidence deeply enough. But he hadn't counted on *Monica Wu*, of all people, getting access to his systems and tracking. "I encountered something that looks like a leak," she said, her voice projecting out of the phone. "I noticed it yesterday on the report that was just sent over. Are you aware you'd been infiltrated? Have you alerted your clients? I know the deal is progressing, so I wanted to address this right away." John raised an eyebrow at Martin, who put up his hands to say "no idea."

"Uh, I'm not exactly sure what you're referring to, Monica," said Martin, shakily. "Would you mind emailing me the specific information? So I can go over it with my team and let you know what we find." He was stalling. He felt sweat spontaneously appear on his forehead. Was he a criminal now? Had he committed fraud? He looked pleadingly at Debra, still in her Aurora-thon T-shirt and athletic shorts. Martin glanced at John, lying on the bed. His face looked strange. What was John hiding?

Martin thought back to the first night of the retreat. The night Jessica died. Martin had gone to ZZ's bathroom, inside and toward the back of the dark restaurant, hoping to sneak in a tiny bump of cocaine. He did drugs only on rare occasions—he was practically an old man, and he and his friends now preferred to have dinner parties and smoke weed. Many of them were dads, and so the hard stuff was out. But on their run earlier that day, Dallas had passed along the number of a local Miami drug dealer, a shady guy named TJ whom Dallas had known in another life. Martin was able to get a small amount of coke delivered to his hotel room that afternoon. Martin knew if he wanted to hang till late night, he'd need a jolt.

He bumped into Jessica on the way to the men's room. She was checking her phone, its glow illuminating her face in the dim light. He'd never been close to her. He didn't really care for that kind of woman, all done up, a party girl. He preferred his female friends on the dry, low-key side, like Debra (he liked to have main-character energy in any given situation). But there was something about Jessica's slouch, and the tight, stressed look on her face that had momentarily softened him. Who knew what it was like to be Jessica, thought Martin, with some sympathy. Beautiful but single, friends with important people but not an important person, loved by male colleagues but loathed by all the women. He often saw her aimlessly walking the halls of Aurora's offices, her heels clicking on the floor, her red hair swinging.

He'd approached her, touching her arm, surprising her and interrupting her intense text conversation. Maybe she was dating someone?

"How are you, Jessica?" said Martin. She slipped her phone back into her Chanel baguette.

"I'm starting to fade," she'd said, frowning. "It's already been a long night, and I know John wants everyone to go to LIV after this." Martin admired the shape of her shoulders, her arms toned and long. He'd have to remember to ask her what she did for exercise. He was always searching for the latest workout fad.

"I might have something that will help," he'd said, mentally patting himself on the back for his uncharacteristic generosity. He took the coke baggie out of his pocket and waved it so she could see. Jessica smiled at him. He beckoned her into the empty bathroom, and they headed into a stall that locked. Martin then spread two small lines on the back of his hand. He offered the first to Jessica, who sniffed it like a pro, and took the second for himself, feeling the drugs tickle his throat, his heart beating fast in anticipation of their effects.

They stood there, not saying anything. After knowing Jessica for years, this was the first time Martin had been totally alone with her. Their departments didn't overlap, and Jessica had always been an aloof presence on the executive team.

"What do you think about the sale?" he'd finally asked. He was curious about Jessica's take—she had an inside line to John, and he hoped she'd share some privileged info. He'd just given her some coke, so perhaps she'd repay the gesture.

"I don't know," said Jessica, sliding her eyes away from him. "Seems to me like Minimus might not know *exactly* what they're buying." According to John, Minimus was set to pay $800 million for Aurora, based on its market valuation, plus the fact that Zach was headed toward exceeding his revenue projections for this quarter. "You're the chief information officer—do you think we're worth that purchase price? Is everything on your end aboveboard?" said Jessica leadingly, raising one eyebrow. Martin's breathing quickened. He didn't know if it was Jessica's comments or the drugs, but he was starting to feel very, very anxious.

"We're worth as much as someone is willing to pay for us," said Martin, trying to shrug her off. "I just hope I get some actual equity before the sale," he said. "I think they stiffed me initially when I was hired. But I guess I'll know more soon." Jessica nodded. "I'm sure you'll get tons," said Martin. "John loves you." She didn't reply, just half smirked.

"Thanks for the coke," she'd said, opening the stall door and disappearing out of the bathroom, doing a runway walk in her cheesy bandage dress. Martin went to the sink. He turned on the water and looked at himself in the mirror. He thought about those rows and rows of numbers, numbers that showed how many people were using Aurora's tech, numbers that showed how many customers were clicking on products that Aurora's thousands of clients paid to promote. What would happen if they knew their most privileged information had been stolen on Martin's watch?

And he knew how Monica Wu had spotted it, as she was intimately familiar with his tracking system; she'd basically invented it while they worked together at Google.

"Monica, Debra Foley here, so nice to meet you," Debra chimed in, before Monica could answer Martin.

"Hi, Debra, I've heard all about you, it's nice to finally chat," said Monica.

"And you," said Debra. "Before we get into this data anomaly, I wanted to ask you something," she said, her voice turning more official. Debra's mother was a teacher, and she occasionally channeled that authoritative vibe when giving employees harsh feedback (or, rather, feed-forward, as the company was now referring to it). She'd once reprimanded Martin for using "inappropriate language" around junior employees after he'd referred to their content management system, which Martin hated, as "cunty" in an all-hands meeting. "But I wasn't describing a person," said Martin, after Debra had pulled him into her office with a scowl. "I was talking about an operating system! And our CMS *is* cunty!" Debra wasn't having it, and she'd laid into him with gusto. She was using that same tone now, and Martin was here for it.

"After you worked at Google, you did a small stint at a startup called Oviavood, right?"

"Yes . . ." said Monica, hesitating. "It's a fertility app that tracks your period *and* your mood," she said. "Apparently, you're most fertile when you're confused. All our data pointed to that, at least. I worked there for six months before joining Minimus. Why do you ask?"

"Why did you leave?" asked Debra. Martin didn't know where this was heading, but he was intensely interested. Even John seemed to be paying attention, and he never engaged during meetings or calls.

"I got a better job at Minimus," said Monica tersely. "Why are you asking me, anyway? What does this have to do with Martin's breach?"

"I'm asking because I heard something about your time at Oviavood," said Debra, smiling at Martin now. "You're not the only ones who are doing due diligence." Monica didn't say anything.

"Someone at Oviavood told me that there were some issues with your corporate card spending," Debra continued. "That possibly involved some highly inappropriate charges?" Monica was still silent.

"Monica, I know you can hear me," said Debra, going in for the kill. "My intel is that you had to pay back eleven thousand dollars of bogus company charges, and that you left shortly thereafter, with Minimus none the wiser. So, is that true?"

"They *told* me I could charge anything company related," said Monica, sputtering.

"You thought that a movie theater popcorn machine rental was an appropriate business expense?" said Debra. Martin let out a guffaw before putting his hand over his mouth.

"I worked from home, and I like snacks," said Monica defensively. "It was the same as if I'd expensed my desk chair. It was all a misunderstanding."

"Either way, I'm sure your boss at Minimus would love to hear that excuse," said Debra. Martin gave her a thumbs-up.

"No! You can't!" said Monica, loudly enough to cause them to lean away from the phone.

"We will keep this information to ourselves, so long as you stop hounding Martin about his work, which is *fine*," said Debra. "This all feels minor enough to me not to interfere with the sale. We've never heard a word about it from any of our clients."

They could hear Monica breathing, calculating her next move.

"Okay, whatever," she said. "I'll report that everything looks hunky-dory. But, Martin, if you're listening, know that I *see* you," she said. Martin saw John staring at him. "I look forward to firing you as soon as the sale is completed. Now, talk to you fuckers later." She hung up. Martin's legs felt like jelly.

"What a lovely girl," said John. "So that's taken care of, and now I have to prepare for the evening ahead." He stood up, his robe threatening to open at any moment, and shooed them out the door. Martin gave Debra a big hug as they stood in the hallway.

"I owe you everything. Do you think John is mad at me?" Martin asked. She shrugged.

"You never know with him," she said. "But at least the sale is still going forward." She'd walked toward the elevator, leaving Martin to stew alone.

"You get your hot lawyer!" he'd called after her.

Now he was standing with *his* hot lawyer, feeling free. He was covered in vomit, but at least he wasn't going to get fired or, worse, arrested.

He felt Chase grab his hand, leading him toward the back of the boat.

"I found a little bedroom downstairs near the bathrooms," Chase whispered into Martin's ear, sending heat directly into his groin. He allowed Chase to guide him toward a small staircase, past Zach and Madison, picking at the food, and around the side of the bar. Chase caressed Martin's thigh as they walked, and Martin began to have visions of a life together, Martin and this handsome, smart man. He couldn't wait to see how big his penis was.

But just as they were about to make their way downstairs, John appeared in front of them. He was out of his tuxedo, in pink shorts, and the darkness was somewhat obscuring his face.

"Ah, Chase and Martin, just who I was looking for. If both of you will come with me, I'd appreciate it. Let's head down to that bedroom for some privacy. You never know who is listening in." His voice was tight, and Martin felt uneasy. Why did John want to speak with him and Chase? Was he trying to do some gay thing with them? Martin had always half suspected that John swung both ways or, rather, every which way.

He'd once told Martin about an underground orgy he'd attended at a tech baron's brownstone (he didn't tell Martin who, but Martin had his suspicions). He'd described in detail how he'd "fucked"—John's word— some girl in the ass as the tech baron looked on, and John's eyes had lit up in a way that made Martin think that possibly the tech baron was doing more than watching.

Martin braced himself as they went down the narrow spiral stairs, opening a small door to the right and entering what looked to be a staff cabin, with a built-in bunk bed. Leaning against it was a large cardboard cutout of Jessica, wearing an evening gown, which Madison had made before Jessica was found dead. Had Martin contributed to her death somehow? He still wasn't sure. He wasn't sure of anything.

John shut the door, and the three men stood together awkwardly, fake Jessica looking on. It was hot in the tiny room, and Martin felt his linen shirt sticking to his back. The aroma of throw-up was wafting up from his pants, and he gagged as it hit his nose. Martin was suddenly very, very scared.

"Martin Ito, you've been my trusted chief information officer for four years now, streamlining our IT systems, creating efficiencies, work- ing hard, hard, hard. You've gone into battle with me, making sure your team was the best it could be, firing low performers, generally being a top- notch employee." Martin smiled weakly. Where was this going?

"But, after recent . . . revelations . . . I'm here to deliver some bad news." All the breath went out of Martin's lungs.

"Chase is here to make sure this is all done properly, from a legal stand- point, and he and Debra can walk you through what this means for your equity. You won't be getting what I'd promised you, but that's because I didn't have the full story. Now I do. I can't trust you, Martin, and for that I'm going to have to say goodbye." Chase looked at him in alarm. Martin began to teeter. This couldn't be happening.

"No, John, you can't. You don't understand, I didn't do anything bad, I wasn't lying to you, I just didn't think anyone needed to know. . . ." John stood there, stone-faced, while Martin tried to explain himself, feeling more and more unhinged as he went on, unable to stop.

"I've given Aurora *everything*," he said. "I don't have a life, my job is my life, *you* are my life, John." Martin knew he sounded pathetic, but he couldn't lose his job right on the brink of a life-changing amount of money from a sale. There was a knock on the door and in walked Olive and Debra, surprise on their faces as they took in the frantic group.

"What's happening in here? John just texted me to come down and said there was an emergency," said Debra. "Is everyone okay?" Her dress was crumpled, and her hair was wild, but otherwise she looked radiant. Martin had a quick second of appreciation for his strong, kind, pregnant friend.

"John just fired me. In front of Chase," Martin cried, tears rolling down his cheeks, his chest beginning to heave in hysterics.

"What?!" said Debra, looking at John as if he were a murderer.

"It had to be done, Debra," said John. "He betrayed me. And who knows what else he's keeping from us. As Winston Churchill said, 'A small lie needs a bodyguard of bigger lies to protect it.'" Martin hung his head. He knew John was right.

"But it's fine now, John. I fixed it. Martin didn't betray *you*. He's loyal to you!" said Debra.

"It's too late. You and Chase can go over severance with him. Olive, you make sure no one hears about this in the press." Martin moaned.

He supposed he deserved it. Getting fired in front of a man he'd wanted to impress, losing all his equity so close to the deal closing. John was walking out the door, but Debra grabbed his arm, hard, before he could leave.

"Ow! Debra! It's done, just get over it. You've always been too emotional about our employees. I know Martin is your friend, but you can't save him this time."

"We all think Jessica was murdered," she hissed. John stumbled back, banging into the corner of the bunk bed, sending the cutout of Jessica crashing to the ground.

"I don't think you want to do anything rash right now—including firing one of your top employees—before we can get to the bottom of what happened," said Debra in a threatening tone. Martin yelped in shock.

"Jessica snorted a bad batch of cocaine," John said weakly. He ran his hand through his hair. The boat must have hit some wake, because it began to bob from side to side. Martin held on to a towel rack on the wall for stability.

"Why weren't you giving her any equity?" Debra asked.

"She wasn't getting many shares because she wasn't doing anything important for the company," said John. "You all know that's true." ("It's true, she was useless," Martin said quietly.) John started to hiccup, deep and loud, and put his hand over his mouth.

"I didn't want Minimus digging into her role," said John. "I didn't want them digging into anything!"

Martin believed him.

Then John let out a long, watery burp, walked to the corner of the room, and proceeded to vomit on the floor.

"Oh *no*," shrieked Martin. How could this night get any worse?

PART 4

Friday, April 26

There Are a Terrible Lot of Lies Going About the World,

and the Worst of It Is That Half of Them Are True

Olive Green

———

Olive Green, Zach Wagner, Martin Ito, Debra Foley, Caitlin Levy, and Nikki Lane walked together from the entrance of the beach, right across from the 1 Hotel, to the shoreline of the ocean. Madison Bez, in a complicated neck-tie sarong, pink bikini straps poking out, was waiting for them, clipboard in hand. No one wanted to be there—parasailing? Were they on spring break?—but they knew that, given the circumstances, the final group activity would be impossible to skip.

This morning, John had disappeared with Chase and Marc, working on the Minimus deal in earnest, and giving the team hope that their paydays might arrive shortly. Maybe even by the end of the trip.

Olive had spent the early hours stewing. Her British skin was burned from the previous days in the sun, and so she'd holed up in her hotel room, crafting some early press releases on the chance that the sale would go through in the next couple of days. She'd FaceTimed Poppy and Penelope, finding comfort in her daughters' giggles. In the middle of the conversation, Penelope had delivered an unwelcome surprise.

"Dad told us he's going to introduce us to the lady he's dating soon. How do you feel about that?"

How did she feel about that? She felt wretched and burned. She could sense splotches starting to climb up her chest, and wanted to get off the phone before Penelope, sharp like Olive, spotted them.

"It's up to him. I'm sure she'll be fine, if dull," said Olive, smiling at her lovely child. "I've got to hop off now, work calls. Love you girls! See you tomorrow!" She'd waved and hung up, feeling a cast of depression that hadn't yet lifted.

Now, walking on the beach, she tried to focus on anything other than her pathetic personal life and empty bank account. Zach looked back at her and smiled. She affectionately rolled her eyes at him. They'd had sex last night after they'd gotten back from the yacht—twice—but hadn't spoken much beyond that. This was all getting too complicated, and Olive was considering ending it. Madison knew about them, which meant that eventually John would, and he was acting unpredictably. Olive had her daughters to worry about; she couldn't lose this job. She had feelings for Zach, but she'd have to do her British thing and swallow them. She'd been swallowing her feelings her entire life.

Olive stopped when she reached Madison and took her phone out of her little beach pouch. She glanced over at Martin, standing nearby, still very much employed by Aurora, rubbing lotion on his six-pack.

It was difficult to see in the sun, so she moved under a nearby umbrella, set up over an empty 1 Hotel lounge chair. She sat down, relieved to be off her hot feet. One unread email from Kaya Bircham, whom she hadn't heard from since telling her to fuck off.

> Hi, Olive, I assume John doesn't actually want to be quoted in *TechRadar* as saying, "Go fuck yourself." I don't think Aurora's board would be pleased with that! But luckily for you, the story is off. I can't go into details, but just know that you really caught a break this time. P.S. I'd still like to trade in on that Shiller profile. Can we discuss? Kaya

Olive felt relief. Another story that was posing a threat to Aurora squashed, though this time she wasn't quite sure who'd done the manipulating. It certainly hadn't been her.

Last night, after they'd gotten back from the yacht and before Olive had snuck into Zach's room, she'd received a long text from John.

> Olive, Olive, Olive, my Joan Bright Astley, my trusted
> keeper of secrets. I'd appreciate it if you didn't share what
> you learned about Meagan with the other executives.
> I don't think we need to upset everyone right now. No
> need to rehash the past when we have such a bright future
> together! I'll make it worth your while. 30,000 more shares
> for you. Your CEO and commander in chief, John Shiller.

Olive had considered ignoring him—the Finger Waggers had made a pact to solve this riddle together, and someone was dead—but in the end, she'd decided to keep it to herself. Deep down, she'd known something wasn't quite right. Did she really care if Aurora wasn't profitable? No startups were. Or that it was based on some dead guy's algorithm? She didn't even know what an algorithm was. She'd read all the stories about WeWork and Quibi and Juicero, among many, many other high-profile failures. She'd known they were living on the edge. Caitlin's hire should have sent Olive running for the hills, but instead she'd stayed, seduced by the promise of equity, wanting to send a "fuck you" to Henry, wanting to be close to Zach. But really, it was all about the money. That's always what it came down to, right?

She felt a tug; Zach pulled her up and led her away from the group, toward the hotel. The sun was roasting her bare shoulders, and her feet were burning in the sand.

"I need to tell you something," said Zach, staring at her with purpose. His cheeks looked red, as if he'd applied blush, and he was standing with a slight stoop. Olive could picture what he'd look like in twenty years, and she didn't mind the mental image. Her legs felt weak. Her skin immediately bloomed. A nearby palm tree creaked, and Olive saw an iguana the size of a large cat scurrying down its trunk.

"I broke up with Melissa," he said softly. She didn't know how to respond. For once in her life, she didn't make a joke.

"I love that you don't put up with my shit," Zach went on, the words racing out of him. "I love that you challenge me and understand my career. I love that you love working. I love your ass and your enormous, perfect breasts," he said. Olive started laughing. Then she started to cry.

Caitlin Levy

———

Caitlin Levy had completely screwed up. She'd kissed John Shiller. Her new CEO. *The* John Shiller. The tiny Napoleonic lunatic whom the *Wall Street Journal* once called "the most egocentric man in tech." She'd cheated on Mike with *that* guy. *That* guy, who might be a killer! What had possessed her? This entire trip, this stupid, crazy retreat, had led her to that moment of wildly out-of-character infidelity. And the worst part was, now she was watching him strut across the beach on his tiptoes, in his ridiculous green bathing suit, and it made her want to kiss him again. She loved her husband. She loved her life. This was insane.

Last night, after John, Debra, Olive, Chase, and Martin emerged from some secret meeting downstairs, John theatrically ordered the yacht to "turn the fuck around!" They were back twenty minutes later, John scowling, the rest of them shoveling Stubborn Seed's soon-to-be-wasted feast into their faces, Zach pouring Dom into champagne glasses to chug before they docked.

The poor DJ was just getting started; he'd played "Paradise City" at Zach's request. Zach, who'd put his sea captain's hat back on, head banged alone on the little dance floor. Caitlin quickly downed three drinks, the liquid courage making it easier to get into the Uber with John, shutting the door on Madison's disapproving gaze. It had been her duty to get info for the other Finger Waggers, and she'd been falling down on the job.

Feeling slightly ridiculous in her sexy, possibly age-inappropriate

"Miami dress," Caitlin slid to one side of the car's backseat, leaving the middle seat open. John, on the other side, glanced at it.

"Is that for the Holy Ghost?" he said, moving closer to her, the car speeding in the darkness toward South Beach. They stopped at a red light. Caitlin felt unable to speak, though she had so much to ask him. What had happened with Jessica? Why did Martin look like he'd just been hit by a bus? Most of all, she needed to know: Why was she, Caitlin Levy, there at Aurora at all?

John's leg was connected to hers, and she saw her dress was riding up, exposing the top of her thigh. He turned to face her, and she couldn't escape.

"Caitlin Levy, what are we doing here?" said John, his nose nearly touching hers. She thought about the current scene in Bronxville, Mike tucking in Lucinda, letting Joey read one more book. What *was* she doing here? It was a good question, and one she wasn't ready to answer. She shrugged.

"I don't know," she said. "You still haven't told me. That's why I'm in the Uber with you—to ask that question." John blinked a few times.

"You're my bait for the sale, Caitlin. You know that. I told you the other night, at LIV. Remember? Ha! Events in the Metaverse! Ha! Mark Zuckerberg really is such a moron. Do you know he's learning how to be a pilot? He and Elon and Sam Altman can crash and burn together."

That, of course, was the conversation Caitlin couldn't remember.

She nodded. It all made perfect sense. He couldn't tell her what she was going to do, because she didn't have a real role. She was the perfect front woman for "events," and he must have dangled that in front of Minimus to get the deal done. She felt so stupid. She felt used. He'd known she'd be so blinded by the money that she wouldn't do proper due diligence.

"Is everything okay at home? Is Mike"—he sneered at "Mike"—"not to your satisfaction?"

"Mike is my husband, not a product I've purchased that I can return," snapped Caitlin. She turned toward the window, not looking at him, crossing her arms grumpily. She felt like she was arguing with a boyfriend, not a boss.

"Caitlin, Caitlin, Caitlin," said John, taking her shoulders and turning her to him. "Have you ever heard of Doris Castlerosse?" Caitlin shook her head no.

"Winston Churchill, unlike John Shiller, was not a very sexual man," he went on. "But there was one woman, a socialite named Doris Castlerosse, whom he couldn't resist. It was rumored that Churchill cheated on his wife, Clementine, with Doris, before World War II and then ended up securing her passage home to London from New York during the war," he said. "I'm not going to compare you to Castlerosse," John said. "She was a nut; slept with every rich man and woman she met, ended up killing herself with sleeping pills." He reached out and touched Caitlin's face, running his fingers down her cheek, down her chin, his hand landing on her exposed chest. She could feel her heart beating underneath it. "But there's something about you that's similarly irresistible to me."

Without thinking, Caitlin took John's head in her hands and kissed him, deeply, closing her eyes, thinking of nothing but his mouth, only pulling away when the car lurched to a stop at another red light.

"John," she said, out of breath, tingly. Now was the moment. "Tell me about Robbie Long. And tell me about Jessica."

John looked out the window. For a second, Caitlin thought he might be angry at her. Instead, as they drove through the Miami night, he started to talk.

He told her first about Robbie's death. The five of them—John, Dallas, Jessica, Robbie, and Meagan—had rented a private villa near Cancún, with plans to hang at the pool during the day and party at clubs at night. They'd all been into drugs like ketamine, mushrooms, even cocaine, when the mood struck. But not in any way that seemed dangerous or a cause for concern. Robbie did the least amount of anyone. He'd often end up cutting Meagan off, dragging her home as she complained that he was no fun.

That night, they'd all been out at Mandala, in the heart of Cancún's party district. They'd done shots at the villa beforehand and then snorted a bit of cocaine as they were exiting the car. Jessica had used a promoter connection to make sure they could cut the line, and so they'd strolled right in, smiling and laughing at their good luck in life. That was the last time they all saw Robbie alive.

John lost track of the group early on, dancing alone, then finding a group of college girls to hang with. He was still at the point in his life when any female attention shocked and delighted him. He'd so recently been thought of as a troll and was happily learning that money could solve that pesky problem. He ended up drunkenly sleeping with a pretty brunette and had woken up in her hotel room at 5:00 A.M., groggy and hungover, his phone filled with frantic messages and texts.

> Come back now, Robbie is in the hospital.
> Where are you?
> WHERE ARE YOU
> Robbie isn't good.

And finally, a rambling voicemail from Meagan.

"John, I don't know what happened," she'd said, cracking into a sob. "We got separated in the club—I couldn't find Robbie after I went to the bathroom. I went back to the villa, and he was in our room, lying on the floor, not really breathing. Dallas came and we called the ambulance, and they took him to the hospital. They're saying he might not make it! I don't know what to do. I called his parents. I called my parents." She started to cry. "How could this happen? Robbie wouldn't have done this."

John had stood in the middle of the shitty hotel room, in his underwear. He'd known there was the possibility of *something* going wrong (someone getting too out of it, one of the girls ending up alone with the wrong guy), but he'd never thought that Robbie, of all of them, would be the one to miscalculate that risk. The rest of the trip had been a whirlwind of depressing logistics: figuring out how to get Robbie's body out of the country, dealing with his grieving, confused religious parents. John just wanted to go home, to pretend it hadn't happened, to never see Meagan's face—red and blotchy and changed—again.

She went back to her and Robbie's apartment in New York, and instead of supporting her, checking in to see how she was, John retreated. They all did, for a time. Jessica put her head down at work, and she stopped going out so much. Dallas, for his part, stopped drinking and doing drugs for good. John thought it was an extreme reaction, but Dallas was an extreme person, he supposed.

Slowly, over the course of the next few weeks, he began to see Jessica and Dallas again. They never spoke of Robbie, or about what had happened that night. Meagan was just—poof—out of the picture. That's when John started honing his potential founder schtick in earnest. He lost more weight and began speaking in fully formed paragraphs, like he was reading a composed email aloud. He wore ridiculous clothes, stopped making meaningful eye contact, and became even more focused on starting a company.

"Then we came up with the idea for Aurora," said John, still looking out the window of the car. Caitlin felt herself get goose bumps.

"We gave Meagan a good chunk of equity at the outset," said John. "We felt really bad about everything. I still do. And now Jessica's gone, too. It's unbelievable."

Caitlin realized they'd arrived at the 1, parked in the same spot as the taxi that had dropped her off from the airport three days and a lifetime ago.

"John, I need to ask you something. You can tell me the truth. I think you know you can trust me. You have the power to ruin my life, too."

John nodded.

"Did Jessica really overdose? She was clearly threatening to reveal things about you and Aurora in order to tank the Minimus deal. You had a motive. I can't believe I'm asking my new boss this, but: Did you kill her?"

John chuckled. He stroked Caitlin's hair. She let him.

"No, I didn't kill Jessica. I loved Jessica. Do you think Churchill ever killed one of his own generals? Sure, Jessica could have taken me down.

But at this point, all my executives know enough to ruin everything. Do you think I'd kill Zach? Debra? Do you think I'd kill *you*, Caitlin?" He leaned in and kissed her again, his tongue probing the back of her mouth. She wanted to simultaneously punch him and have sex with him, right there. The thing was, Caitlin believed he was telling the truth. John Shiller was a lot of things. Manipulative. Brilliant. Generous. Insecure. Self-centered. But he wasn't a murderer.

Before she could do anything else she regretted, Caitlin hopped out of the car without saying goodbye. As she entered the hotel, she thought she saw Madison out of the corner of her eye, standing near a potted plant in the lobby. But then she was gone. Was she waiting for John? Caitlin spent the following hours tossing in her hotel bed, poking at what she'd done.

This morning, exhausted and remorseful, she'd called Mike, but he hadn't picked up, instead sending her to voicemail.

In the middle of drop-off, he'd texted coldly, as if he knew what she'd done. Kids fine. See you later. Caitlin's flight was set to take off at 5:00 P.M. There was just one group activity left—parasailing—and Caitlin had been dreading it. At first it all had seemed exciting, this new job, these new, unpredictable people. But Caitlin was missing her old life, where "drama" entailed a broken cold brew machine rather than a mysterious death and corporate lies.

John was now heading straight toward her on the beach. She looked left and right. Could she run away? Jump into the ocean? She saw Dallas, coming up behind John. He cut a male model–esque figure in flowy linen pants, his eyes hidden behind black sunglasses. Caitlin watched as Aurora's CTO stalked its CEO, following him down the beach like a cougar.

John Shiller

———

John Shiller was scared of heights. He always had been. As a kid, at his lowest point, he'd refused to go up in elevators, or even look out second-floor windows. He'd get dizzy just thinking about it, feeling as if he were about to fall to the ground, anxiety gripping his tiny heart. His dad, Erik, helped him through it. He'd stand with John and push him up in a swing, higher and higher, or take him up to the top of a nearby hill, slowly exposing him to the thing that John was most afraid of. They had a special signal—John would scratch his left arm—to let Erik know that John had had enough for the day, that they could try again tomorrow.

Eventually, his fear became manageable, though it still reared its head occasionally, at times on airplanes, often in tall buildings, and also, right now, flying in a parasail, an activity he was cursing himself for including in the itinerary. He'd known it was a bad idea as he began to go up, up, up, but by that point, it was too late to back out. Plus, Dallas had insisted on speaking with him, and, after going through the final draft of the agreement with Minimus, with only the t's left to be crossed, he was ready. Nothing could derail this thing. Nothing.

He looked down toward the ocean and his head began to spin. He thought he might throw up again and swallowed hard, closing his eyes and trying to disappear. He pictured his dad, holding his hand as they went up in an elevator, calming him as each floor passed. He thought about how proud Erik would be to know that John, his John, had surpassed Erik's wildest dreams for himself, becoming one of the tech titans whom Erik worshipped. That made John feel good. It made John feel a little less queasy. He'd done it. All the drama they'd experienced on this trip had flown under Minimus's radar, all the crises miraculously averted. Yesterday, he'd found out his head of HR was secretly pregnant, that his chief information officer had covered up a damaging data breach. His EVP of engineering had gone fishing for another job at their rival. His head of partnerships was dead. Nothing else could go wrong.

"John? John!" John looked at Dallas, sitting in his harness to his left, a life jacket over his shapely chest, his defined arms exposed. The wind was warm. John focused on a spot ahead of them, far in the distance. He couldn't look down. He tried to do the breathing thing that Nikki had taught him, in and out, in and out, but it wasn't coming easily. He scratched his left arm, his sign to his dad that he'd had enough. But, of course, Erik Shiller was far away, in every sense of the word.

He'd started to notice changes in his dad around the time that Aurora was taking off. He'd gone home to visit over Thanksgiving and could tell something was deeply wrong. His dad had always been kind and deferential to his mom, but there was a belligerence to him during that trip that gave John a bad feeling. Erik had yelled at John's mom about the flavor of the turkey and had snapped when John wanted to change the TV channel. He'd gone downhill quickly after, forgetting what had happened the day before, wandering around the house looking for things he'd just been holding in his hands. John's mom had put him in the assisted living facility about a year ago. She couldn't handle him alone.

When John launched Aurora, his dad sent him a handwritten note that read, "As Winston Churchill said, 'No one can guarantee success in war, but only deserve it.' You deserve it, son. I love you. Dad." He'd had it framed and hung in his office.

"John, can you hear me?" Dallas said.

He nodded, though he kept his eyes on the horizon.

"She knew about the algorithm."

John sighed.

"I had my suspicions but wanted to believe you wouldn't do that. That you wouldn't *steal* from a friend," John said.

"Cut the shit, John," said Dallas harshly. "You've always known; you just didn't care, so long as you were going to get rich. And now you are. Because of me." A wooziness came over John.

"Jessica spoke to Meagan," Dallas continued. "She called her when she learned she wasn't getting the equity she'd been promised, and unfortunately for everyone, Meagan was in a sharing mood. Robbie had told her about some big breakthrough he'd made right before we went to Mexico together. He'd said he was about to show you. Meagan has his laptops still, John. Jessica wasn't going to let it go." John's eyes were still closed. Robbie had been his platonic soulmate. He knew Dallas had always resented that.

"This is on you, John," said Dallas. John felt nauseated again. He pictured his dad standing next to him. He thought about the night Robbie died, he and Dallas helpless in the hospital's fluorescent lights as their best friend stopped breathing.

"What did you do, Dallas?" Though they were high in the air, John was transported back to when they'd first met, in New York, at a party in a Brooklyn warehouse to which he'd tagged along with Robbie. He'd been in awe of Dallas then. He was so slick and good-looking, and John had been so insecure. A nobody. Dallas and Jessica had seen something in him. They'd believed in him. People started to pay attention when he spoke. He was able to get investors interested in Aurora. They'd given him the confidence to do that. And he'd repaid them. Why did none of them understand that, without John Shiller, they'd all have nothing?

"Don't worry, nothing can be traced back to me," said Dallas. "It was someone else who actually pulled the trigger."

John felt like crying.

"What do you want from me?" he asked, resigned. He'd give Dallas anything to disappear, to take the knowledge of their misdeeds with him.

"I want even more equity before the deal closes. I also want Caitlin out. If not, I'm giving Kaya Bircham the go-ahead to release the story in *TechRadar*. And not just about the stolen IP, but also about how Aurora is imploding—two executives are secretly fucking, we covered up a data breach, we skewed numbers for Minimus—and that your big virtual events strategy is a sham."

"Well, when you put it that way, it doesn't sound great," said John, deadpan. "You'd be surprised at how much people want to believe a successful narrative. You're forgetting that I'm a very talented salesman," said John. "I've got everyone convinced that events in the Metaverse are the future of the industry. I've nearly even convinced myself! What utter bullshit people will swallow. Though, as Churchill said, 'There are a terrible lot of lies going about the world, and the worst of it is that half of them are true.'" The boat was beginning to slow down, much to John's relief, and it seemed their ride would soon come to an end.

"If this got out, Dallas, you'd be ruined, too," said John.

"I'd blame you. You're the top dog. You'd take the fall," said Dallas. "How's that for blue-sky thinking? Literally." Dallas chuckled to himself. John knew he was right.

"Why do you want to oust Caitlin? I can't fire her until after it's signed. And even then, it will take a few months. That was always the plan."

They were drifting down slowly, the water coming closer, and John pictured himself crashing into the ocean, the waves swallowing him whole.

"Fine, whatever, just do it at some point. Give me my equity, and I'm out. You'll never hear from me again. I protected us when it mattered. I've always protected us," said Dallas darkly. "More than you know." John could see the rest of his team on the beach, looking bored and overheated. He'd have to remember to tell Madison that, from now on, parasailing was a no-go on future Aurora retreats. If there were any.

Debra Foley

———

Debra Foley was shattered. For this entire trip, sleep had been taunting her, calling to her, begging her pregnant, exhausted body to come to bed. She was just now starting to experience second-trimester symptoms. Her breasts were expanding beyond what she'd thought possible, her nose was constantly stuffed up, her belly was rounding and firming. It was time to call her mother and tell her. This was real, and it wasn't going away.

She hadn't spoken to Marc since last night. She'd wanted to tell him before everyone else, coolly throw in a "you're the father of my child" be-tween dinner and drinks and brainstorm sessions. But instead, she'd blurted the truth in front of everyone. The secret had been caught in her throat for weeks, and she'd vomited it out along with her lunch. He'd avoided her for the rest of the evening, taking a car alone after they'd docked early, Debra unable to catch him in the swirl of John and Martin and everything else. And he hadn't answered the text she'd sent from her room later, lying in her bed, so tired but unable to close her eyes, her mind whirring with worry. I'm sorry I didn't tell you. I'd like to talk. Nothing.

She wasn't sure how to handle the situation, which was a very foreign feeling for Debra Foley, chief people officer. She'd dealt with a lot of touchy issues at work—how many family illnesses, divorces, miscarriages, and financial problems had she worked through with employees?—but this was beyond her expertise. It all had seemed so simple when she was sitting in Dr. Benne's office. She hadn't known who the father was, and that was that. And then Marc came strolling into her life, attractive and charming and kind. She was putting him in an impossible situation, she knew. Debra was sick about it all.

Now she was sitting on a lounge chair on the beach, watching John and Dallas glide by on a parasail, way up in the sky, Olive and Zach flying closely behind. She could feel her eyes starting to close, feel her mouth about to go slack with rest. But then Nikki, a gold caftan draped across her shoulders, sat down beside her.

"What a great trip," Nikki said sarcastically. Debra nodded.

"What do you think they're talking about up there?" Nikki said, shielding her face with her hand to get a better view.

"God knows," said Debra. She stared at Nikki. She was so beautiful and so stubborn. Debra couldn't put herself in Nikki's place—a Black female executive in a world of white guys—and so was trying hard not to judge her. But it was tough.

Earlier that morning, Debra had called Ben Hooks, Trade Desk's chief people officer. She'd been surprised by how quickly Nikki had conceded to John and had a suspicion that Trade Desk hadn't offered her as much as she said they had. She was curious about the compensation at their biggest competitor and wanted to know if Aurora was way out of line. If that was the case, she'd have to start adjusting salaries accordingly. She knew Ben professionally; they'd traded employees enough that she felt comfortable doing a little digging. Plus, he was friends with Olive, and she figured he'd do her a favor if she asked.

"Hi, Ben, it's Debra Foley from Aurora. Hope you don't mind the cold call."

Debra was sitting at the desk in her hotel room, the sun pouring in the windows. She'd just gotten back from breakfast and was feeling kind of shaky—she'd been too thrown by last night to finish her eggs.

"Heya, Debbie," said Ben. (Debra hated when men called her Debbie.) "You calling to ask for a job? I heard Aurora's in the shitter."

"Very funny," said Debra. "I was actually calling to ask you for some general information," she said. "Chief people officer to chief people officer."

"Go on," said Ben, clearly intrigued. HR professionals loved dirt more than anyone, which was ironic, given the confidential nature of their work.

"We have an employee, Nikki Lane, who was in the running for a big role over there. She said you offered her double her salary here, and I wanted to check on that."

Ben paused, considering what to reveal. "I'm only telling you this because, honestly, I feel bad for you, having to work with John Shiller and that ragtag crew," he said. Debra had to hold in an annoyed snort.

"We'd spoken to her about the chief product officer role, yes, but she didn't get past the final round. Some info came to light from our friend Olive that made me reconsider Nikki's fitness for the job. I just don't think she's Trade Desk material," he said smugly. "In short: We didn't offer her anything, let alone double what she was making at Aurora." Fuck this guy, thought Debra. And then: Olive?! Nikki?! Debra sucked in her breath.

"Okay, got it. Thanks so much for the info, I owe you one," she said.

She spent the next few hours turning the facts over in her mind. Nikki had lied to Debra's face; Olive had somehow torpedoed Nikki's offer. *What* was going on with everyone?

Martin sauntered up to Debra and Nikki, pulling a chair across the sand, close to where they were sitting. He was in a surfer-style outfit, with colorful board shorts and a neon-green shirt.

"How's it going, guys?" he asked lightly, as if he hadn't almost gotten fired last night. Neither Debra nor Nikki responded.

"I wonder what they're talking about up there," he said.

"Don't we all," said Nikki.

Caitlin dragged a beach chair to the little circle. The group watched as the parasailers descended from their top height, gradually making it down in tandem. They looked so peaceful up there, thought Debra, though she knew better than to believe it. Martin smiled at her gently. She loved Martin, but she needed a break from him.

The boats zoomed back to the shore, and the executives were helped down by identical guys in Ray-Bans, the four of them crunching in the white sand toward their coworkers.

The air was shimmery with heat, and Debra, sweat dripping into her eyes, thought she saw Zach and Olive holding hands as they walked. She must be hallucinating. Was this yet another second-trimester symptom? But no, as they neared, she saw two of her top executives with their fingers interlaced. She stood up, as if in slow motion, ready to explode. She'd had it with everyone. These jokers, violating every code in Aurora's employee handbook. Her possibly murderous boss. Her lying engineer friend. Her other lying engineer friend. Everyone! Even Dallas, who didn't bug her, was bugging her, just by existing and being a man and not having to deal with getting pregnant out of wedlock.

But then, she felt a warm hand on her neck. She turned to see Marc, biting his bottom lip, which she was learning was something he did when he was nervous. He smiled at her and gave her a supportive squeeze. She leaned into him, and he gently kissed the top of her head. Zach and Olive could wait. In fact, let those two loony bins have each other. Debra had Marc. She had Marc!

"Debra!" screeched John. "Come with me," he commanded, wiping moisture from his forehead with the back of his hand. And apparently, John still had Debra. He motioned for her to walk with him. Debra jogged to keep pace as they headed back to the hotel, Marc trailing them. "Tell the lawyers to meet us in the conference room on the third floor," John said hurriedly. "We have some work to do before we sign. I'll explain soon." Debra looked back to see the other executives watching them hustle away. Madison's sarong had come partially undone, and a piece of fabric was hanging around her neck like a limp noose.

Dallas Joy

———

Dallas Joy was thinking about what he was going to do with the rest of his life. For now, he was at lunch, watching his colleagues slurp oysters while he waited for his vegan entrée to emerge from the kitchen at the Surf Club at the Four Seasons Hotel. An hour ago, he and John had put the final signatures on the documents for Minimus, completing the sale. Dallas would soon have $40 million deposited in his bank account. He'd never have to work again. Champagne was being poured, appetizers were arriving, and the mood at their table was ebullient.

This was the culmination of everything they'd worked for, from the moment Dallas and John and Jessica had sat at Pomodoro, discussing the idea for what would eventually become Aurora. Had John really bought it, at the time? Maybe he'd wanted to believe the lie so badly that he'd convinced himself that it was true. Jessica certainly hadn't. But it was too fantastic an opportunity to pass up, for all of them. Robbie was dead, and there was nothing they could do about it. Why waste his genius?

Across the table at the Surf Club, John gave Dallas a wink, his scallop crudo dangling precariously on his fork. John was in a white shirt and khaki pants, the only trace of Winston Churchill on his wrist, an 18k yellow gold Lemania chronograph that he'd bought at auction at Sotheby's a few years ago. His beard was closely clipped, and his eyes were roaming the group, studying the people whose lives he'd just changed forever.

Debra was to his right, glowing, staring at Marc, who was sitting at the opposite end of the table. Zach and Olive were on his other side, focused only on each other. Martin, Chase, Nikki, and Caitlin were sipping drinks but not saying much of anything. Madison, especially, looked pleased to be there, having been given the empty spot at the table, filling in for Jessica's ghost. She was out of place at the swanky restaurant, her girly pink dress clashing with the chic, monotone midcentury decor.

Dallas was relieved that this was the last event of the retreat. Minimus had compelled John to sign a one-year contract to stay on as Aurora's CEO, but Dallas had done no such thing. Within a year, Aurora would be fully absorbed into Minimus; Minimus would keep what it needed (Aurora's tech, possibly parts of its CMS) and discard the rest. The executives would work through the transition—part of the deal was that they'd all be offered plum yearlong gigs—and then either be integrated into the larger Minimus team or find new jobs. Dallas wanted to put as much distance between himself and this process as possible. He was done. Jessica wasn't a problem anymore. John banged a glass with a knife.

"My dear executive team," John began, his voice somewhat hoarse. "We've pulled off a win. A very impressive win. First, we invaded, then we grabbed the land, and finally, we cut off our enemies' heads." ("Is Jessica the enemy he's talking about?" Dallas heard Olive whisper to no one.) "Today, we will celebrate. We've sold Aurora to Minimus! And we will all reap the rewards." John paused for cheers, but no one made a sound.

"We are making the world a better place!" he said, a tad desperately.

Debra stood up abruptly, interrupting John. She looked a little wobbly. Dallas had always liked Debra—she was hard-working and loyal, and though John outwardly treated her like shit, Dallas knew he'd be lost without her. Marc rushed over to Debra, steadying her with care. Debra turned to John, waved goodbye, and stuck her tongue out at him.

She gave a little salute. "General Foley, signing off for now!" she said cheerfully. Martin gasped and put his hand over his heart. Then Debra and Marc walked out of the restaurant together, arms linked.

John was still for a moment. He cleared his throat, one of his longtime nervous tics, and pushed on, ignoring what had just happened.

"I'll end this speech with an apt quote from Churchill: 'My tastes are simple: I am easily satisfied with the best.' You, my friends, are the best executives in tech. Cheers to you all, and cheers to Aurora."

"Hurray!" said Madison. Dallas raised his water glass and took a sip. What he wouldn't give for a Tito's on the rocks right now.

Olive then pulled out her phone and began texting, likely confirming a story on the sale with Kaya Bircham. Madison glared at Caitlin, who'd moved next to John, speaking into his ear. She wouldn't have to put up with Caitlin for much longer. Dallas had taken care of that.

Dallas took another sip of water, wishing he could somehow get out of this awkward lunch. He got up to go to the bathroom, heading out the interior restaurant doors into the hotel, past indoor palm trees and under large white arches, checking to make sure he was alone as he did. He patted his pocket and felt the solid lump of drugs.

He was a few steps from the bathroom when he felt a sharp tap and there was Nikki, hands on her hips. He loved Nikki.

"Where are you heading?" Nikki was gorgeous and spiky, and he'd always been attracted to her (and she him—he could tell by the way she stared while he was coding; he had that effect on certain STEM women).

"Bathroom. Why are you following me?" He said it flirtatiously, but from the puss on her face, it was clear she wasn't in the mood.

"Engineer to engineer: Was it yours? Was the algorithm yours, Dallas?" She looked at him pleadingly, willing him to say yes.

Dallas thought back to that rainy day in New York, before they'd gone to Mexico, before Robbie died, before everything. He'd been in Robbie and Meagan's apartment in Williamsburg, in a new building that overlooked the East River. Meagan was still at her office, and Robbie had invited Dallas over to show him something "big" he'd been working on. Dallas was standing at the floor-to-ceiling windows in the living room, studying the shrouded Manhattan skyline, when Robbie approached, carrying his laptop. Robbie had scruffy brown hair and a slight build, with sharp, narrow shoulders. He looked younger than the rest of them. He handed Dallas his computer.

"Remember how I've been wanting to take on adtech?" Robbie asked shyly, as Dallas scanned the code on Robbie's screen.

"I wanted to get your eyes on it before I showed it to John," Robbie said. "I haven't even let Meagan see it; I told her I need it to be perfect first." Dallas felt like he might vomit.

"Dude, it's already perfect," he said, genuinely in awe of his friend. Robbie's face glowed with happiness. "You're going to disrupt the shit out of this industry," said Dallas, feeling unsettled. "Can you send this to me so I can take a closer look? It'll be easier for me to give thoughts if I can sit with it at home." Robbie had hesitated for a second. But just a second.

"Sure, but just don't send it to anyone else, obviously."

Dallas nodded emphatically.

His mind darted to Tuesday night, when Jessica had closed in on him outside of LIV, her long body coiled, as if about to pounce.

"I'm going to get you, Dallas," Jessica had said. A couple looked at them as they walked by. Dallas edged closer to Jessica, putting his finger to his lips to quiet her. She had to be quiet. "You just wait," she'd said, nearly shouting. "It'll come when you least expect it. When you're floating in an infinity pool in Santorini. When you're riding your stupid Brompton down a dirt road in New Zealand. When you're zooming through space with Elon Musk. You can't get away with this. Meagan has evidence! She has Robbie's computers. I'm going to get it all."

She turned away for a second, hesitated, then faced him again. "That night in Mexico . . ." said Jessica, a flash of revelation crossing her symmetrical face. "You would have already seen the algorithm." Dallas didn't say anything. He felt his mouth go dry. In the weeks before that trip, he'd examined Robbie's code again and again, looking for errors, testing for kinks. But it was flawless. Dallas turned it over so many times that it almost felt like he'd written it himself. He knew that Robbie would take it to John, and they'd start a company together as cofounders. They'd become billionaires while Dallas languished at Facebook, slaving away for Zuckerberg, that little twerp. It was all wrong. Dallas was supposed to be the one.

That's what he'd been thinking when he'd gotten back to the house in Cancún to find Robbie in his room, wasted, barely coherent after their night out, vomit everywhere. Robbie had done coke, taken shots, taken Special K. He could never keep up, though Dallas and John certainly pressured him to. His breathing sounded weird, and his face was starting to look gray. Dallas took out his phone to call Meagan; she needed to come take care of him. But he didn't. Instead, he called a car to go back to the club. He'd partied there for another hour, finally heading back to find Meagan with Robbie, trying to revive him. Had Dallas really thought Robbie would *die*? Had he hoped that? He couldn't even remember at this point.

Back in Miami, the atmosphere warmed by guilt and anger, Jessica ran into the club, giving Dallas just the opportunity he needed. He'd pulled out his phone and texted TJ. I need something special, he typed.

"It was my algorithm," he said to Nikki now. "I promise." He couldn't tell her too much. He didn't want to have to do something to her. She was his work wife. His friend. "You know how it is," he said to her. "Robbie started with something, and I took it and ran." She nodded understandingly. They'd all done it. Coding was like music. There were chords. Progressions. Engineers built upon what was there. Satisfied, Nikki turned to leave, but before she could, Dallas called her back.

She looked at him expectantly.

"I know you didn't get the Trade Desk offer," he said, frowning. "I also know that your so-called friend Olive was the reason why." Nikki staggered back a little at the news. "She panned you to Ben Hooks. I heard from the guy who eventually got the role. Everyone in this industry talks."

Nikki nodded and was off.

Dallas then went into the bathroom's stall, took out the drugs, and did a quick line, feeling it rush up through his nose directly into his beating heart. He'd placed the rest of the laced cocaine in Jessica's toiletry bag in her hotel room but had kept this pure bit for himself. He'd missed it so much. He deserved a treat for a job well done.

Back at Aurora's executive table, John was taking selfies, a small pucker on his lips. Fucking John. Dallas had waited a month after Robbie died to approach John with the idea for the company. He'd done it at a dinner with Jessica—he'd purposefully included her; the more people who witnessed him presenting it as his own, the better. They'd all agreed to the lie, to building an empire with a dead person's code. And then only at the prospect of being stiffed did Jessica go to Meagan. She was as bad as any of them. Dallas patted his pocket again. Everything would be fine. The deal was signed.

Olive Green, Nikki Lane, Debra Foley

———

The original three—Debra, Nikki, and Olive—had one last outing together in hot, hot Miami. After lunch, they'd gone shopping in the Design District, killing time before heading to MIA and then back to New York. They all wanted to purchase something with their newly acquired jackpots, and so had gone in and out of luxury boutiques—Balenciaga, Fendi, Dior, Armani, Gucci, Hermès—Debra trying on ridiculously big designer sunglasses, getting Olive and Nikki to laugh every time.

Nikki bought a Céline bag. Olive bought an Hermès scarf. Debra, on a whim, spent $1,000 on Chanel flats. Though they were having fun, celebrating their big win, there was a slight chill among the women that hadn't been there previously, a foreboding that this was the end of something and the beginning of something else. They didn't discuss Jessica, or their various suspicions about the men who ran their company, or their discoveries about Meagan Hudson and Robbie Long. That could come later. Or not.

For now, they were attempting to enjoy the moment. Debra was pregnant and newly in love. Nikki was about to become CTO, achieving the stunning success she'd dreamed of. Olive was coming into enough money to be able to give the middle finger to her ex. Plus, she was together with Zach. Everything had worked out for them. At what cost wasn't something they wanted to think about.

"Debra, what did you and Marc do when you left lunch?" asked Nikki. They were sitting on a smooth stone bench, surrounded by the poppy

pastels of street art and sculptures, people watching. The scene was out-
rageous; women decked in head-to-toe labels, tight D&G dresses, LV
everything, Gucci, Gucci, Gucci. Long hair, puffy lips, breasts, breasts,
breasts. The friends were taking it all in, giggling with each other, making
duck faces in imitation. They'd gotten cups of ice cream, which were
quickly turning into soup.

"What do you *think* we did?" said Debra, trying to suppress a smile.

"Ohhhhh!" said Olive. Debra blushed.

They sat in amiable silence, finishing their desserts, thinking of their
next moves. "Shall we?" said Olive, motioning for them to go. Nikki
looked at her, hard. She hadn't addressed Olive's betrayal, and she wasn't
sure she ever would. But Nikki didn't forgive and forget. As they walked
back to the road, they passed the entrance to ZZ's.

"It feels like we were there a year ago," said Debra, with a wistful shake
of her head. She wanted to say more—about how nervous she was to
bring a child into this corrupt world, about how strange she felt about
Jessica. But instead she said nothing.

Debra then called an Uber back to the 1, and when it arrived, they all
piled in, a strange finale to what had been a truly bizarre executive retreat.

They slowly inched along 195, the same route to South Beach that
Debra had taken from the airport with Jessica and Caitlin. Debra could
still conjure the feeling of Jessica's legs against hers, the specific smell of
her perfume. She shuddered.

"Where do you think Caitlin is?" asked Nikki.

"I don't want to know," said Olive.

"Can you imagine what it's like to have sex with John?" said Debra.
It was very un-Debra to say something like that. But maybe this was the
new Debra.

"Like an overgrown lizard with a darting tongue," said Olive, laughing.

"An iguana with a whip," added Nikki.

"In a Winston Churchill suit," said Debra.

"I bet his penis is very, very small," said Olive. "Like a little, tiny nub.
A baby-waby penis." They all cackled at the image, clutching their newly
purchased spoils as they did.

Caitlin Levy

———

Caitlin Levy was in bed at the 1 Hotel, naked, next to her boss, wondering how she'd arrived there. Well, she knew how she'd *physically* arrived. Via Uber. Via elevator. Via the hallway. Via the door. And now she'd cheated on Mike and broken her vows. For the past four days, Caitlin had been wearing tight dresses, dancing at clubs, and drinking irresponsibly. Middle-aged men acted like this all the time, trading their hair for girlfriends and Porsches, burying themselves in work instead of heading home to their families. But when a woman had a "moment" there had to be something wrong, something rotten.

Was Caitlin rotten? She didn't feel like it. She provided for her kids, tucked them in at night, took them for annual flu shots. She cooked Mike dinner, made sure the homework was done, that gifts were wrapped on birthdays. On top of that, she excelled at her job, acted as a mentor to younger colleagues, and kept up relations with every event vendor in town. She was responsible. She was good. But was she happy? What did "happy" mean, anyway? She'd checked her phone as they were finishing up lunch at the Surf Club, picking at her lobster thermidor, and had seen a message from John, who was sitting on the other side of the table.

I'm heading to my car, Doris Castlerosse. Please join me.
Now.

They'd gone straight up to his room, not bothering to take different elevators, John's hands already wandering over Caitlin's backside, up through her hair, along her waist. He'd led her through the enormous suite, lifting her dress over her head in one motion, then pushing her down on the bed. He was standing over her, still fully clothed, and she went to pull him down on top of her. Mike popped into her mind, but she batted him away. She hadn't been this turned-on in years. A decade.

"Would you like to try something different?" John asked, a glint of naughtiness in his eyes. Caitlin nodded. He went to the closet and came back with a long black whip. Caitlin nearly moaned with pleasure at the sight of it. This was what she'd been waiting for. She surely wasn't bored anymore.

Later, exhausted, satisfied, Caitlin considered what had just happened. She was set to fly home in a couple of hours and worried that Mike would be able to smell the sex and betrayal. John was napping next to her, breathing heavily, his barrel chest going up and down and up and down, his eyelids fluttering in REM. How could she work for him now? How could she not?

She picked up her phone and looked at her messages, seeing one missed text from Mike.

Hope you're enjoying yourself. Safe trip home. Caitlin winced at the thought of having to explain what she'd been up to.

She opened her camera, scrolling through pictures from over the years, Lucinda as a baby, Joey with no front teeth. She and Mike, all dressed up for a holiday party before they'd had children. They looked so young. He used to be so handsome. She used to be so beautiful.

John stirred, and she flicked over to her empty PowerPoint presentation, the one she'd been working on during the plane ride to Miami, the one that she'd never had to give.

"Events at Aurora—a New World!"

She laughed a little, thinking about how naïve she'd been. John opened his eyes and looked at her.

"What happened with Jessica?" she asked him softly.

"I can't tell you," he said seriously. Then: "My lie was the iguanas." For a moment, Caitlin had no idea what he was talking about, before realizing he was referring to his two truths and one lie.

"I hire someone to kill them. I don't do it myself."

"I'm going back to my room," she said. "I'll see you in New York."

He grabbed her hand and kissed it, and she smiled at him. "Caitlin, Caitlin, Caitlin." He sighed.

Caitlin found her clothes on the floor and slipped them back on, holding her sandals in her hand as she crept out the door, the hallway lights momentarily blinding her. As her eyes adjusted, she saw the outline of a figure standing at the end of the corridor. Then Madison came into view. She briefly walked toward Caitlin before turning and speeding in the other direction.

"Madison!" Caitlin called after her. But she was gone. Caitlin considered going back into John's room and telling him what she'd seen. But what would that accomplish? Instead, she took the elevator down to her own room, collapsing on her bed, knowing she had to pack quickly to make her flight home. She rubbed her backside. No welts yet.

Tech's Golden Boy, John Shiller, Can Do No Wrong

By Kaya Bircham

John Shiller is living it up. The thirty-nine-year-old California native just sold his company, Aurora, to tech giant Minimus, for what's rumored to be close to a billion dollars. He personally made more than $75 million in the sale, and is still operating as Aurora's CEO as the company transitions. We caught up with Shiller in Miami, where he's building his dream home, right on Biscayne Bay. The famously quirky business leader had plenty to say.

This interview has been lightly condensed and edited for clarity.

Kaya Bircham: Firstly, congratulations on the sale. That's quite a purchase price. How are you feeling?

John Shiller: Kaya, Kaya, Kaya. I'm feeling *great*. The market knew our value, and we got what we were worth. I've been telling everyone for years that Aurora had nowhere to go but up, and Minimus got the memo. As Winston Churchill said, "I can answer in one word: It is victory, victory at all costs, victory in spite of all terror, victory, however long and hard the road may be; for without victory, there is no survival." Not only have we survived, we've thrived.

Bircham: There's a rumor going around town that Aurora has a new business strategy that will allow it to break the adtech ceiling. Is there any truth to that?

Shiller: Yes! And I'm finally able to talk publicly about it. We are getting into events! Not in-person events, oh no, the margins on real-life events are terrible, even though I do love a good shindig. I'm talking virtual events. In the Metaverse. They're going to be, as the kids say, lit. Our clients will sponsor them, and they'll be open to the public. Everyone get ready to paaaartaaayy! That side of the business will be led by the genius Caitlin Levy, whom we recently hired away from Viacom.

Bircham: Is the rest of your executive team coming over with you, post-sale?

Shiller: Yes, mostly.

Bircham: What does "mostly" mean?

Shiller: My star PR whiz, Olive Green, will clarify for you after this interview.

Bircham: I'm asking because, as we've all heard, there was a bit of a shake-up right after the deal closed, with Zach Wagner leaving the company.

Shiller: Tragically, in more ways than one, I can't comment on that.

Bircham: What's it like for a CEO when a member of his inner circle dies?

Shiller: As I said, I can't comment.

Bircham: On a lighter note, what do you plan to do with your windfall?

Shiller: First things first, I need to finish my new house in Miami. There will be not one, not two, but three "party decks," all with water views, plus a state-of-the-art indoor gym, complete with a full-size basketball court.

Bircham: You play basketball?

Shiller: Well, no. As we know, I'm vertically challenged. But I'm friendly with some members of the Miami Heat. The part of the house that I'm *most* excited about is the guest home, which I'm converting into a mini Churchill museum, complete with all the artifacts I've collected over the years. It's getting designed by the same architect who just redid the Guggenheim.

Bircham: *TechRadar* would love a tour once it's done! What's behind the decision to stay on as CEO? I know that your cofounder, Dallas Joy, has chosen to leave immediately.

Shiller: We all felt it would be best for the continuity of the company and team—and to make clients feel comfortable—for me to stay on for the time being.

Bircham: What's the one piece of advice you'd give to aspiring entrepreneurs?

Shiller: That's a tough one! I have two. I suppose this one will sound trite, but here goes: Know who you are. Stay true to yourself and your vision, and good things will happen. The second is a quote from my hero, Winston Churchill: "History will be kind to me, for I intend to write it."

Bircham: What do you mean by that?

Shiller: I mean that there is no path to success other than total domination.

Bircham: Fascinating. Thank you for your time, John. I'm so sorry again for your loss.

Shiller: I appreciate it, Kaya. Great to speak to you.

PART 5

Tuesday, December 17

We Must Look Forward

The Finger Waggers Reunion

———

Olive Green, Caitlin Levy, Debra Foley, and Nikki Lane were sitting at a table at Gramercy Tavern, sipping prosecco and perusing the lunch menu. The Finger Waggers, together again. Debra had taken the train in from Greenwich, Connecticut, where she and Marc had bought a stately five-bedroom house. She was still on maternity leave; their son, Jake, was nearly four months old. Debra, in a festive Christmas sweater, had the happy, worn-out look of a new mom.

Nikki and Caitlin had walked over from Aurora's headquarters, just a few blocks away, bundled in their coats against the New York winter. They were set to move into Minimus's new offices in Hudson Yards in February but were still on Park Avenue South for now. The restaurant had a lively vibe, with tables filled with coworkers and friends celebrating the end of the year, and chic red and green and gold decor glinting under the dimmed lighting. The group hadn't been alone together like this in months, since they'd returned from Miami, and it felt both comfortable and strange. They all knew each other so well. Even Caitlin, who'd only started at Aurora seven months ago.

They started off with friendly chatter, catching up on each other's personal lives. Olive gave updates about her new job and shared an amusing anecdote about moving in with Zach. Debra spoke about her breastfeeding woes and told them that Martin and Chase were still together, and were currently en route to meet Martin's mother in California. Nikki gave details about her upcoming wedding to Clive at Amanyara, in Turks and Caicos. Caitlin showed pictures of her new summer home in Quogue. As the main course arrived—brick-pressed chicken, pork shoulder, duck meat loaf—Debra banged her glass lightly with a knife.

"I would like to propose a toast," she began, stifling a yawn. "Sorry, sorry, I'm just up in the middle of the night with Jake, is all," she said. They nodded understandingly. "First, I want to say how nice it is to see the Finger Waggers again. It's been too long, and I've missed you all. And second . . ." She trailed off, having seemingly lost her train of thought.

"Oh, bloody hell, can't we be real for a moment?" interjected Olive. No one said anything.

Olive, Nikki, and Debra had drifted apart since the retreat. In September, Olive had accepted a new role at Trade Desk; Ben Hooks had finally come calling with a chief communications officer title, and she'd readily accepted. It was a tough workplace, but she was rising to the new challenges, and happy, too, not to have to think about Robbie Long or John Shiller or Jessica Radum or Nikki Lane. When Nikki heard about Olive's new job, Dallas's story about what happened with her own offer had been confirmed.

"Come on, someone please speak up. Are we going to the police or not?" Olive said.

"We have no evidence," said Nikki weakly. Debra squinted at Nikki. They'd never addressed Nikki's lies, but it was a permanent wedge between them. When Nikki got back to New York, she'd told Clive about her Trade Desk misfire. She'd needed someone to be on her team. He'd acted suitably sympathetic and didn't once say "I told you so," even though he was thinking it. They'd gotten engaged the next month.

"I don't know, I feel like no one will believe us," said Caitlin. Hours after her afternoon with John, Caitlin had returned to Bronxville, emotionally drained and physically sore. Mike had asked about the trip, and she'd replied lightly, "It was fine." They'd left it at that. They both knew there was more to the story but were too deep into their marriage to rock the boat. Every now and then, Caitlin would catch Mike staring at her, as if he didn't know who she was.

Her role at Aurora had officially started the next week, and she'd spent her time crafting a virtual events strategy, which everyone, including Caitlin, knew to be a high-profile fool's errand. She'd avoided John as best as possible but still thought about him nearly every minute of the day.

"I just feel like there's so much to do with this sale and integrating our teams," said Debra. "Martin officially got the chief information officer title across all of Minimus the other day, and then immediately fired Monica Wu, so I'm dealing with that paperwork. . . ." She trailed off for a moment. "John's hyped up, he's acting seminormal for once, and I'm not sure what going to the police would really accomplish," said Debra. "Jessica's dead. She snorted cocaine. That was a risk she was willing to take," she finished. They all nodded. "And what would we even say? We don't actually know what happened."

"Well, I guess that's that," Olive concluded. "John's jolly lucky to have all us women protecting him." She'd meant it to be funny, but it wasn't.

On Friday, April 26, while the Finger Waggers were flying back to New York, back to their jobs and lives, back to their new pots of Minimus money, details of Jessica Radum's death appeared in a small item in the *Miami Herald*. The reporter had gotten a tipoff from the police and had gone digging at LIV. Apparently, the club's staff hadn't checked the restroom before closing at 2:00 A.M., leaving the gruesome find to the morning cleaning crew. An ambulance was called, but she'd been dead for hours, a clear-cut overdose, a relatively common occurrence in the Miami club scene. She'd snorted a bad batch of cocaine, laced with a strong opioid, fentanyl. No one had heard her suffering in the stall alone, her breathing labored, her lips turning blue. Police checked the camera footage to see if anyone else had been involved, but from what they could tell, Jessica was alone when she did the drugs. They'd seen it hundreds of times. Miami was a dangerous place. They found the remainder of the laced drugs in Jessica's hotel room, ruling out foul play.

Kaya Bircham and the rest of the tech press corps picked up on the piece, but it was only in light follow-ups, nothing involved or re-reported. The news came as a string of Google employees committed suicide, and that story took off, burying the sad accidental death of an Aurora executive.

No one ever found out that Zach had been leaking information about Aurora to Kaya Bircham. He'd done it out of self-preservation. She had had two former Aurora employees willing to go on the record saying that Zach, when he'd found out they were pregnant, had openly joked about wanting to put birth control in Aurora's water supply. If the story came out, Zach's chances of becoming a CEO would have plummeted to zero. So, like Stewart Holden, he'd acted as Kaya's source. But after the yacht party, the night he decided he loved Olive for real, he'd reneged, telling Kaya he'd been making it all up out of spite. Kaya was pissed, sure, but didn't end up running the hit piece on Zach—he promised he'd find something else for her eventually. Maybe he would.

In the wake of it all, Zach rethought his career path. Who needs to be a CEO when you've got millions of Minimus money? With Olive's help, Zach launched a small-batch barbecue sauce company out of his East Hampton home. Citarella had recently placed a large order, and he and Olive had celebrated by drinking wildly expensive champagne and having sex all night long. Zach was finally a king.

The Aurora team moved on. Jessica's office was reappropriated as a common space, a small conference table replacing her desk, her personal items whisked away by anonymous assistants. John renamed the room Iwo Jima, though Debra had strongly counseled him against it.

"Think about our Japanese employees," she'd said to him over a Zoom call from Connecticut. She was burping Jake, patting him on the back as she spoke, John looking at her as if she were holding an alien.

"Oh, Debra, you're always too sensitive. We must not lose our battle against the wokes," he'd said. He was sitting at his enormous desk. Debra could hear Madison puttering around in the background, her heels clicking on John's dark wooden floor.

"Has anyone heard from Dallas?" asked Nikki now. Her engagement ring glittered in Gramercy Tavern's lights; the rumor was that she'd bought it herself after Clive had proposed with something less than impressive. "I haven't," she said. In the wake of Dallas's exit, Nikki had been promoted to chief technology officer, reporting directly to John. Her hope was that Minimus would consider putting her over the entire company-wide department. It would be great PR for Minimus to have a young, woman-of-color CTO, and Nikki knew she could handle it. She'd put her dreams of launching Thrifteez on hold, happy with her new compensation and title. For now.

"Nope," said Debra. "I helped Dallas with his severance package, but nothing since then." Recently, Debra had been waking up in the middle of the night, before Jake even started to cry, her heart pounding, not able to catch her breath. Marc thought it was just postpartum anxiety, but Debra knew better.

"Not me," said Caitlin.

"No, but I heard from a friend who works at Bloomberg that he's bought a large estate in New Zealand, close to Larry Page and Peter Thiel," said Olive. A decadent chocolate pudding arrived at the table, covered in salted whipped cream, for each of them, plus a gorgeous cheesecake to share, decorated in edible foil, shining like gold.

"Let's just enjoy our dessert," said Debra with finality. Debra, the rule follower. Debra, the best of them all. Debra, whose new house had a pool and an outdoor pizza oven.

After Dallas's additional equity was sorted, upping his takeaway by millions, Debra had pulled John aside in the 1's conference room.

"You know I never do this," said Debra, her voice steady. "But you need to give me another two hundred thousand shares, or I'm going to tell everyone everything."

John blinked a few times. "Debra, Debra, Debra," he said, a sly smile on his lips. "You're finally learning how to play the game." He patted her on the shoulder. As she walked back to the group, Marc gave her an encouraging nod. Marc was taking some time off in between jobs, doing the daddy thing, enjoying his new life and his new, rich wife. He was a lucky man.

"John likes this Winston Churchill quote, so I'm going to do the most Aurora thing ever and use it now," said Debra, looking around the table at her former friends and colleagues.

"'We cannot afford—we have no right—to look back. We must look forward.'" They all dug into their golden desserts.

Madison Bez

————

Madison Bez's life was good. She had her new title, and enough money from the sale to comfortably rent a one-bedroom in the Flatiron District, just a quick walk to work. She'd been able to fly her mom, Sandy, to New York for a visit, showing her around SoHo, going to Broadway shows, attending the Friends Experience near Columbus Circle. Sandy ohhh-ed and ahhh-ed at every turn, so proud of her cosmopolitan daughter who'd "made it" in Manhattan.

And most important, Madison had John Shiller at her side. He'd even met her mother. Madison had taken Sandy to the office on the last day she was in town, excited to show her Aurora's fancy headquarters. John had been in that day—Madison managed his schedule, so she knew he would be—and Sandy beamed in the company of such an important, successful man. John had rambled on, praising Madison, praising himself. He'd told Sandy that Madison was "the most important woman" in his life, and Madison thought that if she died that day, at least she'd die happy.

But she wasn't dead. Jessica was. In the months since, John had become even more dependent on Madison, not letting her out of his sight, requesting she accompany him on his personal vacations. They'd recently traveled to Greece, where John had commissioned a superyacht to go island hopping, inviting ten of his closest friends, plus a rotating cast of hot young women. Madison had organized it all, down to the color apron of the kitchen staff (Aurora blue, naturally), and she'd been invited to dinner one night after a few of the girls came down with norovirus.

Sitting among John's tech mogul crew, eating the meticulously prepared food—all the ingredients were local, as per John's zest for sustainability, and had been flown in on various private jets—Madison felt like she was in a dream. If only her friends in Tuscaloosa could see her now.

Today, wrapped tightly in her cashmere throw, shivering in the air-conditioning, Madison watched from her desk as Caitlin and Nikki walked in from the elevator. Madison hadn't seen them together much in the months since the retreat; the group had gone its separate ways, the Finger Waggers disbanded.

John popped out of his office, a bright look on his face, wearing a white shirt and yellow wool pants, his beard clipped neatly. He bounced around on his tiptoes for a moment. Madison saw him eyeing Caitlin, who was still at Aurora, torturing Madison with her existence.

"Ladies! Where have you all been hiding?" They stopped in front of him, mustering fake smiles.

"We just saw Debra and Olive for a Christmas lunch," said Caitlin.

"They're doing very well," added Nikki.

"And how are you, Caitlin?" asked John, focusing his attention on her in a way that made Madison see red. Caitlin was supposed to have been fired by now. Madison didn't know what John was waiting for.

"Fine, just going back to my office. We have that presentation to Minimus next week, so my team has been bogged down with that," she said, her cheeks flushed.

"We were discussing Dallas at lunch," said Nikki, staring at John. "What's he up to? Do you guys talk?"

"Not really," said John, looking sideways. "But I know he's in the Southern Hemisphere somewhere, enjoying the sun, riding his bike."

They stood in silence. John then began to whistle, something he did when he felt supremely awkward. The tune was "Battle Hymn of the Republic," his favorite, and it made Madison feel sick to her stomach. John had sung that song, which had been performed at Churchill's funeral, at Jessica's family's memorial service.

It had taken place in June, at a funeral home in Darien, Connecticut, near Jessica's second cousin's house. It was unseasonably warm that day, in the high eighties, and the tasteful room was stuffy and smelled oppressively of flowers on the verge of rot. When they'd entered, John had cornered Jessica's eighty-two-year-old great-aunt, going on about his "magical experience" with Jessica a few years ago at Burning Man, at which he'd dressed up as a steampunk Winston Churchill, complete with lasers shooting out of his top hat. Jessica's aunt had looked very confused.

Then John had made his way up front, shaking hands with Jessica's distant relatives, patting her cousins on the back, apologizing for not knowing the extent of Jessica's drug problem. Madison, feeling nervous and slightly ill, sat in the back pew, listening to speeches about how much Jessica would be missed. Her mind had wandered, as it often did, to that night in Miami.

After dinner at ZZ's, she'd gone in an Uber to LIV with John and Dallas, at John's request. John had been in the front seat, next to the driver, and she and Dallas had been in the back. She'd had so much fun that evening, hanging with the executives, John in such a wonderful mood after having announced the sale. She was a real part of the gang now, invited to ride along with the CEO and the CTO. Everything she'd ever wanted was finally coming into view.

John and Dallas had entered the club ahead of her, walking with the confidence of good-looking, rich men. Madison had taken a deep breath and followed. Her job that night was to keep tabs on John, bring him whatever he needed, and make sure his car was ready when he wanted to leave. Madison stood a few feet from the Aurora table, shimmying from foot to foot, glancing at John, sitting alone, bored and unhappy. John hated clubs. At one point, he got up and wandered away, and Madison briefly lost him in the crush. He finally returned to the table, bouncing on his tiptoes, seemingly in a better mood. This made Madison nervous. Who had he been speaking to?

About thirty minutes later, John gave her his usual signal—a thumbs-up—and she texted the driver to come to the front of the Fontainebleau for pickup. She escorted him through the crowd, his white polo glowing in the club's lights. She had the urge, as she often did, to grab his hand as they went.

Once he was safely driving away, Madison was free to go home. She was tired. Her feet, bound in tight high-heeled sandals, were aching. Out of the corner of her eye, she saw Jessica, heading past her, back inside. Madison stood in front of the bubbly reflecting pool near the hotel's entrance, staring at the blue-green water. She found a stone bench nearby and sat down. She didn't know how long she stayed there; she'd zoned out, thinking about all that she had to do during the rest of the retreat.

That's when she saw Dallas coming toward her. Dallas rarely spoke to Madison. He was the kind of guy she'd found attractive growing up in Alabama: dreamy features, thick hair. But she felt nothing toward him. She felt nothing toward anyone but John. He took her arm when he reached her, pulling her up and outside the awning of the Fontainebleau, underneath a large palm tree on the left side of the hotel. People were milling about, but no one was paying attention to them.

"I need you to do something for me," Dallas said in a low voice. It was warm outside, the Florida wind swirling. Madison could hear loud rap music coming from a passing car.

"I need you to give this to Jessica," he said. He handed her a small baggie of white powder. Drugs? Why would she give Jessica drugs? Madison didn't want any part of this.

"Absolutely not," she'd said, feeling her accent emerge with strength. She tried to hand the bag back to him, but he turned the other way.

"*No*, Dallas." He didn't answer. "NO," she'd said louder. She went to put the drugs down on the sidewalk, but Dallas grabbed her, hard.

"It's for John, Madison," Dallas said more gently, letting go of her. Madison felt scared.

"Please give it to her. This is for Aurora. John is asking you to. He just couldn't say it himself." She felt her face burn. Was Dallas telling the truth? If so, she'd have to do it. She'd do anything for John. She thought about her dad, Rick, in California, ignoring her. She thought about Sandy, hoping for her to succeed. She thought about John and how much she loved him. He must love her, too. He must.

Madison slipped the drugs into her Coach bag and said a quick prayer to God for forgiveness.

"Say you got it from Martin, but it's not your thing," Dallas instructed. She'd turned and headed back into the club. She saw Nikki sitting on a chaise with Martin. Caitlin was dancing under the laser show. Then there was Jessica, perched on a black leather settee, Aurora's head of partnerships in a black-and-white dress.

"Hey, Jessica!" said Madison, trying to act casual but feeling like she might explode. Jessica looked at her as if she were a stranger. Madison kept on.

"Listen, about today, I'm sorry I spoke to you like that," she said. "I shouldn't have said any of it. It's not my place." Jessica glared at her.

"The intel about my equity was helpful, so thanks for that," said Jessica finally. Madison felt a shiver of fear. What chain of events had she set off? "I managed to get in touch with Meagan Hudson. Your precious boss is hiding a lot more than you know. Same with Dallas." Madison had a sudden nauseating thought. But she had to push on, it was too late to go back.

"You were there from the beginning, and you *should* get your due. Men are the worst, right? They always take all the credit," said Madison. Jessica nodded, her face softening. Madison moved closer to Jessica, who didn't back away.

"I have something you might want," Madison whispered, slipping the baggie out of her purse and putting it in Jessica's accepting hand. "Martin gave it to me." Jessica nodded, as if she already knew. "It's not my thing, so please take it as an apology gift," said Madison. Then she winked at Jessica, who smiled back. She looked so pretty in the lights. "Enjoy!" Madison said, standing up with nowhere to go. She went out onto the dance floor, alone, and started to spin.

John's warbly voice had echoed through the funeral home as he sang in front of his dead employee's friends and family. Glory, glory, hallelujah!

Now, in the office, he'd finally stopped whistling. They'd all gone, leaving John and Madison alone at her desk.

"My favorite deputy," said John, patting her on the back. "I don't know what I'd do without you." She wondered if she'd ever have sex with him. She wondered if she'd ever have sex again. She'd thrown out the pills and powders she'd found in Jessica's room on the final day of the retreat, chucking them into the ocean before leaving for the airport, drowning any shred of evidence. If the police found those drugs, unlaced and pristine, perhaps they'd start raising eyebrows. Better to be rid of them. No taking chances.

That morning, before parasailing, she'd tracked down Dallas on the boardwalk near the beach. He was about to get on his Brompton bike and was wearing blue spandex. Madison could see the exact outline of his penis and had to stop herself from staring at it. She was already in her outfit for the day—a sarong over a pink bikini. She'd once heard John say that women in pink bathing suits were like "squids flashing a color that say they're ready to mate."

"I need something from you," said Madison bravely. He nodded.

"I want to get rid of Caitlin. I want her gone. That's all I'm asking for," she said. Dallas took a deep, audible breath. She waited for him to speak.

"John's never going to be yours. He's your boss. He doesn't love you back."

Madison felt like she'd been punched in the stomach.

"But okay," continued Dallas. "I'll make it part of my demand."

Dallas had kept his word; Madison had seen in John's emails that he was planning on axing the entire events department by the end of the year, due to "a worsening macroeconomic climate," essentially pulling a trump card over Caitlin's one-year contract. But he hadn't yet. Caitlin was still here, and it was making Madison miserable.

"Can you do me two favors?" John asked now, putting his hand on her midback. "First, can you set up a recurring payment from my private Citi account to Manny Morales? Ten thousand dollars a month for the next year."

"Sure, is that a business associate?" asked Madison.

"You can google him. He's a great general," said John. Madison nodded.

"And second, can you please find the address for someone named Meagan Long? Or maybe it's under Meagan Hudson. I'd like to pay her a visit." Madison willed his hand to remain on her body.

"It feels good to win," he said, walking back to his office. He winked at her and shut the door. A few minutes later, Madison pulled up John's email and saw he'd just written one to Debra. She clicked it open. Debra, Debra, Debra, he started. I know we'd planned on firing Caitlin before EOY, but I've had a change of heart. I need her here with me. Cheers, John. Madison stifled a scream. She felt like smashing through the glass of Jessica's old office, the conference room now called Iwo Jima, with her bare hands.

Instead, she took out her phone and found Kaya Bircham's number in her contacts. Then she sent her an interesting text. Kaya, Kaya, Kaya, Madison began.

Epilogue

ARTICLE ON TECHRADAR.COM

10:00 A.M., Tuesday, February 11

Shiller Out of Aurora in a Dramatic Exit

The startup had a spectacular rise, thanks to its charismatic leader, John Shiller. But it was founded on lies.

By Kaya Bircham

In a stunning turn of events, Aurora founder John Shiller has been forced out of his company, sending shock waves through the entire tech world. The move comes after *TechRadar* exclusively uncovered that Aurora's original algorithm was not the work of cofounder Dallas Joy, as Shiller and Joy claimed, but instead that of a deceased engineer named Robbie Long.

The evidence includes records stored on Long's old laptops, provided to *TechRadar* by the late Long's fiancée, Meagan Hudson (who goes by Meagan Long). Hudson is a higher-up at Resy competitor SnaggIt. She declined to comment for this article.

In a legal twist, Minimus, which just acquired Aurora for a hefty $800 million, still retains the rights to Aurora's IP, regardless of who invented it. But a wrong deserves restitution: We're told Minimus has settled on a heavy payout with both Hudson and Long's parents, who live on the West Coast.

How could this happen? Aurora's leadership is not only to blame: the tech world is happy to ignore red flags when a company is on fire. On the way up, businesses are rarely scrutinized by investors, so afraid of missing out on a big return that they willingly overlook a startup's exaggerated claims.

And Shiller was a king of exaggeration. He founded Aurora nearly a decade ago, providing advertisers a faster and scrappier way to get eyeballs online. Shiller publicly channeled Winston Churchill, his hero, and liberally quoted the dead prime minister in interviews. He also positioned himself as a champion of women's rights, hiring a mostly female executive team and giving interviews about the power of women's business intuition.

"There's a cult of John" at the company, says an inside source. "His employees would do anything for him."

But there's more.... To distract from its shortcomings, Aurora crafted a false narrative in which it was pivoting to "events," hosting parties in the Metaverse. Since announcing the initiative, no such events have taken place. The woman hired to front the operation, Caitlin Levy, formerly of Viacom, was let go last month.

Shiller, who declined to be interviewed for this article, relocated to Miami during the pandemic. Joy recently moved out of the country, and *TechRadar* was unable to locate him for a quote. Aurora was also recently hit by tragedy. During its latest executive retreat, the company's head of partnerships, Jessica Radum, was found dead of an overdose in the bathroom of LIV, the nightclub in the Fontainebleau hotel. No foul play was suspected.

With Shiller, Joy, and Levy out of the picture, vulnerable employees at Aurora include Debra Foley, chief people officer, Martin Ito, chief information officer, and Nikki Lane, Aurora's newly appointed CTO. Industry betting says all three will be ousted within the month.

Whether Shiller and his gang will face criminal charges remains to be seen. We are closely following the story and will keep *TechRadar* readers updated daily.

Photo caption: Shiller, pictured here, exiting his private jet just after learning of his ousting. Behind him stands his deputy chief of staff, Madison Bez.

Acknowledgments

———

I would like to extend my deepest thanks to . . .

My children, Monty and Sandy, for being the lights of my life, for delighting me every single day, and for helping me come up with the book's title. Their idea of *Bad Winter People* was pretty close to the end result!

My husband, Charles, for his continued support and love, and for kindly pretending to listen to me ramble about plot holes until his snoring gave away that he'd already fallen asleep. He says he doesn't have to read this one because he "basically wrote it," so I hope one of you will tell him what happens in the end.

My mom and dad, Barbara and Scott, for everything, literally, and Casey, Jared, Jude, Olive, Sully, Ari, Julie, and Kai for being my biggest fans. I love you guys.

Linda, Marcus, Alice, Lee, Daisy, and Olive, all of whom I love, too! Your enthusiasm and good cheer are never-ending, and I'm so grateful for it.

My perfect agent, Alexandra Machinist, for always advocating on my behalf and for making me laugh while doing so.

My brilliant editor, Megan Lynch, for yet again improving upon my mental mush and for continuing to make this process such a pleasure.

The fantastic team at Flatiron Books—Bob Miller, Malati Chavali, Marlena Bittner, Nancy Trypuc, Katherine Turro, Claire McLaughlin, Kukuwa Ashun—and also the geniuses at Macmillan Audio.

My UK editor, Joel Richardson, for your super insightful edits and much needed help landing the plane, and the rest of the talented team at Penguin Michael Joseph, including Gaby Young and Emma Plater.

My lovely UK agent, Cath Summerhayes, for your stellar support from afar. Let's hang again in London soonest!

My book-to-TV agent, Josie Freedman, for keeping it all moving in the face of industry upheaval. Here. We. Go.

My BDG dream team: Trisha Dearborn, Lindsay Leaf, Emily DeSear, Tiffany Reid, Charlotte Owen, Karen Hibbert, Eileen Cain, Wes Bonner, and the dearly departed Jason Wagenheim and Kimberly Bernhardt. I value you all so much and will never, ever leave you out of the loop. . . .

. . . And introducing . . . Bryan Goldberg, the ultimate wartime general and peacetime statesman. Victory belongs to the most persevering!

Emma Rosenblum is the bestselling author of *Bad Summer People*. She is also the chief content officer at Bustle Digital Group, overseeing content and strategy for *Bustle, Elite Daily, Nylon*, the *Zoe Report, Romper, Scary Mommy*, the *Dad*, and *Inverse*.